W9-BTG-226

DATE DUE			

THE ULTIMATE BETRAYAL

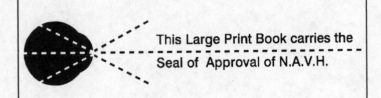

This Large Print Book carries the
Seal of Approval of N.A.V.H.

THE ULTIMATE BETRAYAL

KIMBERLA LAWSON ROBY

THORNDIKE PRESS
A part of Gale, Cengage Learning

GALE
CENGAGE Learning·

Farmington Hills, Mich • San Francisco • New York • Waterville, Maine
Meriden, Conn • Mason, Ohio • Chicago

GALE
CENGAGE Learning·

LIBRARY OF CONGRESS CATALOGING-IN-PUBLICATION DATA

Roby, Kimberla Lawson.
  The ultimate betrayal / Kimberla Lawson Roby.
    pages cm. — (A Reverend Curtis Black novel)
    ISBN 978-1-4104-7984-6 (hardback) — ISBN 1-4104-7984-6 (hardcover)
    1. Triangles (Interpersonal relations)—Fiction. 2. African American
women—Fiction. 3. Mate selection—Fiction. 4. Marriage—Fiction. 5. Large
type books. 6. Urban fiction. I. Title.
PS3568.O3189U47 2015b
813'.54—dc23   2015015208

Published in 2015 by arrangement with Grand Central Publishing, a
division of Hachette Book Group, Inc.

Printed in the United States of America
1 2 3 4 5 6 7 19 18 17 16 15

For my uncle — Clifton Tennin, Jr.
(January 9, 1930–June 15, 2014)
I miss you dearly, and
I will love you always.

CHAPTER 1

Alicia's prayers had been answered. She and Phillip were finally going to be married — again. It had been six years since their first wedding, but in two months, she would walk down the aisle of her father's church and live happily ever after. She was fully committed to Phillip this time around, and unlike before, she wouldn't betray him. She wouldn't sleep with another man behind his back. Just thinking about how selfish she'd been and how terribly she'd treated Phillip still upset her, but thankfully, he finally trusted her again. There had been moments when Alicia hadn't been sure he ever would. Still, she'd gone out of her way doing all she could to show him just how much she loved and adored him and wanted to be his wife. From this point on, they would be together until death do us part, no matter what.

Phillip stood at the bedroom window of

Alicia's condo, looking as handsome as ever, and Alicia smiled at him. He winked at her but continued his phone conversation. He'd driven over last night and was now on the phone with her dad, discussing church business. Phillip had returned to his assistant pastor position at Deliverance Outreach in Mitchell, Illinois, which was the reason he and Alicia had purchased a home there. With all his church responsibilities, it was better for him to reside in the same city as his job so he would have quick access to the church and to any members who needed him. Phillip had moved in a month ago, but it wouldn't be long before Alicia joined him, as she now had a buyer for her Chicago-area condo and would be closing on the sale in six weeks. She'd even begun moving some of her belongings out to the house in Mitchell. She would certainly miss Covington Park, along with much of the culture and excitement that the Chicago area provided, but she also couldn't wait for her and Phillip to live as husband and wife again.

Things were going to be good between them. They would have a great life, and she thanked God for second chances. As a matter of fact, God had blessed her in such a tremendous way that she sometimes shed tears uncontrollably. Here she'd committed adultery against Phillip — hurting him to the core — yet he'd found it in his heart to forgive her. And he'd never once stopped loving her.

Then, there was that awful second marriage she'd entered into with the likes of Pastor JT Valentine. The man had slept around with more women than Alicia could count, and the whole experience had been a nightmare. Still, God had delivered her from JT and his madness and allowed her to move on and forget about him.

And if those blessings hadn't been enough, she was a successful novelist who would be releasing her fourth book in a few months. She had such a wonderfully kind and loyal audience of readers; some of whom read her work because of her father's worldwide status, but the majority seemed to genuinely love her stories and she was grateful for that.

Phillip ended his call. "I'm gonna get ready so I can head back home. Your dad and I and some of the other officers are meeting for lunch today."

"I need to get ready myself. I'm meeting Melanie at noon so we can pick out our jewelry for the wedding." Melanie Richardson was Alicia's best friend, and she and her husband, Brad, who was Phillip's best friend, were going to be their attendants.

Alicia and Phillip had considered having bridesmaids and groomsmen, too, but then decided they wanted to keep their ceremony as intimate and as meaningful as possible. That way their day would be about them and the love they shared, versus some massive, impersonal affair.

"Oh yeah, that's right," he said, strolling over to Alicia and hugging her. "But more important, have I told you how beautiful you are today?"

"As a matter of fact, you have," she said, kissing him. "You're so good to me, and you make me so very happy."

He squeezed her tighter. "Not as happy as you make me."

"My life is finally complete."

"I'm glad to hear that. And although it took a while for me to propose to you again, I hope you know that I never stopped loving you. Not once."

"I know you didn't, and I never stopped loving you, either. And I'm also sorry for . . . well, everything. I destroyed our marriage, and I will always be indebted to you for forgiving me the way you did."

"God forgives us all, and we have to do the same thing with others. Sometimes though, just because you've forgiven someone it doesn't mean you can still be as close with them. You can still love them and be there for them if they need you, but forgiving someone and trusting them again are two different things. So I thank God that in our case, I was able to do both."

"You're a good person with a huge heart, and I love you with everything in me," she said.

"I love you, too," he said, kissing her.

Alicia's yearning for Phillip was strong and intense — it was the kind of yearning she couldn't act on or ask him to satisfy. He talked a lot about how he couldn't wait to make love to her again, except Alicia wasn't handling this celibacy thing nearly as well as he was. She knew Phillip was a minister and that he was serious about his faith, but Alicia had certain needs and desires. For her, kissing and cuddling only meant tons of torture, and she longed for their wedding day. It couldn't come fast enough, and she'd gone without for so many years that it was almost funny. Especially since the sole reason she'd done so was because Phillip had made it clear that he wouldn't have it any other way. He'd insisted that the only way things could work between them was if her love and respect for God were sincere. This, of course, meant living by the Word and not having sex until they were married.

11

Still, she'd be lying if she said she was okay with it, because she wasn't. She was twenty-eight, and she couldn't help the way she felt. Phillip was only ten years older, so she couldn't see how he was able to deal with this either. But he was, and he seemed to do it with ease.

After Phillip left, Alicia finished getting dressed and grabbed her large black leather tote from her bed. She disconnected her phone from its charger and saw that she had new emails. When she opened her mailbox, she scrolled through three department store sale reminders and a couple of other unimportant messages. But she swallowed hard when she saw the next one. The subject line said, "Hey Beautiful," and the sender's name was listed as Levi Cunningham.

She covered her mouth with her hand, whispering out loud, "No, this just can't be."

She took a deep breath and sat down on the leather chaise in shock. Her heart beat faster with every few seconds, and although she was curious about the contents of the email, she was afraid to open it. What could Levi possibly want? She hadn't heard from him in five years, not since he'd called her from prison. She'd wondered then how he was able to contact her and talk for as long as he wanted, until she'd learned that he'd gotten in pretty good with one of the correctional officers. He'd called her twice. Once to let her know how much he still loved her, and the second time to tell her that her husband at the time, JT, was sleeping around on her and committing other unimaginable sins.

Although, now that Alicia thought about it, she had spoken to Levi a third time, and that was when she'd told him she was going to do everything she could to get back with Phillip. Levi had been disappointed, but it wasn't like he could offer her something better, not with him still serving time for drug-related felony charges. Back then, he'd been sure he'd be out within a few months, since his attorney had discovered new evidence to help exonerate him. Levi had also cooperated with the authorities, which likely meant he'd told on the right people. Still, as far as she knew, nothing had ever panned out in terms of his getting a new trial.

Alicia stared at her phone, debating whether she should open the email. Her common sense begged her to delete it, but her heart pleaded for something different. And she knew why: After all these years, she'd never fully gotten over him. She'd buried her feelings and gone on with her life, but she'd never forgotten their genuine chemistry. Their hearts had bonded naturally, and their deep emotional connection had been indescribable. It was the kind that only true soul mates could share — the kind she had never experienced with another man, not even Phillip. Although, what harm could Levi do from a prison cell?

Alicia debated no further. She opened the message and read it.

Hey Beautiful,
I'm sure I'm the last person you ever expected to hear from, right? I'm a little surprised myself, but I'm happy to say I finally got my new trial, and I was released yesterday. I'm a free man, and although it hasn't even been a full 24 hours yet, I've never felt better. I wanted to contact you as soon as my mom and my boy Darrell picked me up, but I decided I would spend some quality time with my mom last night first. She has been my rock through all of this, so I owed her that. But this morning, I woke up thinking about you and how much I missed you. So can you please email me back? I really want to see you. Oh and I'm not sure whether you no-

ticed or not, but after being locked down for all this time, I went back to school and learned a lot about commas and when to include them. ☺Even better, I now have a bachelor's degree in business. Amazing what you can do online these days, and I can't thank God enough for it. I'm a totally different man. Anyway, I hope you respond. I can't wait to hear your voice.

Talk to you soon.

Levi

P.S. I never stopped loving you, sweetheart. Not for a second.

Alicia didn't move. She couldn't have if she'd wanted to. Was it really true? Was Levi out of prison and living back in Mitchell? The same city she was returning to as well — the city where she and Phillip were making their permanent home? This was all too much for Alicia to digest, but as she sat thinking, she realized something. Levi's email wasn't going to change anything. She loved Phillip, she was marrying him in two months, and that was that. This was her reality. This was *all of their* reality. End of story.

CHAPTER 2

"Brad, what is this?" Melanie exclaimed, holding her husband's latest credit union statement.

Brad frowned. "What is what?"

Melanie passed him the document. "Here, see for yourself."

"Where did you get this? Were you rummaging through my desk?"

"No, I was looking for a black marker, and I just so happened to see it."

"Do I search through your things?"

"I wouldn't care if you did. I don't have anything to hide."

"Neither do I, but I also don't like stuff moved around in my office."

"Normally, you lay your mail on top of your desk. But not this, though."

Brad ignored her. "What would make you rummage through my stuff like this?"

"You know what, that's neither here nor there. I just wanna know what you needed ten thousand dollars for."

Brad sighed. "I can't believe you went through my desk and opened my mail."

"We've been married for, what? Three years? So as your wife, I have a right to see everything. And until now, you've never had a problem with that."

"Whatever, Mel."

"Why aren't you answering my question? Are you doing something I need to know about?"

"No, I made a bad investment, and I lost some money."

"How?" she said, folding her arms. "Playing around with the stock market again?"

"I wasn't playing around with it. I read about a couple of hot items, and they didn't pan out."

"But ten thousand dollars? You lost ten thousand dollars, and you're acting like it's no big deal?"

"I never said it wasn't a big deal."

"But you're sounding like you lost ten pennies. Not to mention, it's bad enough that you lost more than thirty thousand a year ago for the same reason."

Brad rolled his eyes. "Oh, here we go. Bringin' up the past again."

"I'm simply making a point. It's not like we're getting any younger."

"Are you serious? Mel, you're only twenty-eight years old."

"But you know how careful I've always been when it comes to money. I was cautious and saving as much as I could before you ever asked me to marry you. And since you'll be forty in a couple of years, I would think you'd start being a lot more cautious, too. Especially when it comes to your savings account."

"Look, baby," he said, calming his voice. "I'm sorry. I hear you, and I promise it won't happen again."

"You said the same thing last year."

"I know, but I mean it this time," he said, leaning against his desk. "I traded some pretty high-risk stocks online, and it was only because I thought I could make a lot of money from it. But I've learned my lesson."

"So this wasn't even done through a broker? You did this on your own?"

"Yeah, but I'm done. I know you don't believe me, but losing all this in a matter of days really opened my eyes."

Melanie spoke in a softer tone. "You can't keep doing this."

Brad's cell phone rang, and he pulled it from his blazer. "Baby, it's the office. Just give me a second, okay?"

Melanie sat down in the supple brown leather wingback chair and waited for him to finish his call. She was trying not to be angry, but she couldn't understand why Brad did this kind of thing. She was just the opposite, so it didn't made sense to her. She could never blow that kind of money unnecessarily, not from her individual savings, checking, retirement, or any other account. They had two joint money market accounts as well, and for the most part, she pretended those didn't exist. She just couldn't see spending money so frivolously like there would be no tomorrow. There were times when she knew she might have gone to a bit of an extreme with her vigilant money-management philosophy, but who knew what the future held? Anything at all could happen. Loss of employment, illness, or even death.

Then, to think how hard they'd worked to get where they were professionally. Brad was the newest senior partner at the firm he'd been practicing at since graduating law school — a firm that was known statewide — and Melanie was a nurse practitioner at the most highly recommended internal medicine office in Mitchell. Also, last year they'd built a six-thousand-square-foot home and furnished every room with all new furniture and accessories. Melanie had thought they were spending way too much money, but once Brad had convinced her that they could afford it and that he wasn't working all his life for nothing, she'd gone along with it. Of course, that had been well before she'd known he was going to throw away thirty thousand dollars only three months after breaking ground. She certainly hadn't known he was going to lose ten thousand more last month. It was common for the stocks and bonds that made up their retirement portfolios to fluctuate, but the idea of buying risky items for no reason was uncalled for.

Brad ended his call and reached out his hand to Melanie. "Baby, come here."

"Why?"

"Just come here. Please."

She got up and walked over to him.

Brad sat back on the top of his desk, drew her closer, and wrapped his arms around her waist. "I'm really sorry. I got a little carried away, and I messed up. Can you forgive me?"

Melanie looked at him but didn't say anything.

He caressed the side of her face. "You know you can't stay mad at me forever, right?"

"I just wish you wouldn't do things like this. I mean, if you're just dying to give away money, I'd rather see you give it to families or organizations in need. Because to me, when you throw away money that God has blessed you with, you're being ungrateful."

"I agree. But do you forgive me?"

"Do I have a choice?"

"Not really," he said, wrapping Melanie's arms around his neck and kissing her.

Melanie hated arguing with him, and it felt good holding him and trying to get past what had happened.

"I was planning to wait to bring this up, but now is just as good a time as any," he said.

Melanie wondered why he looked so serious. "What's wrong?"

"Nothing. But I do want us to think more about starting a family. I want you to stop taking your birth control pills."

"I don't know," she said, and although she wanted a child, too, she wasn't sure this was the right time anymore. Not with Brad's latest financial move. She wanted to believe him when he said this would never happen again, but she needed to see it. Another thing that had started to concern her quite a bit was the fact that he worked a lot of hours. She clearly understood what his job entailed, but for the last few months they'd sometimes barely seen each other except on Sundays. They'd had words about that very thing a couple of weeks ago, and she didn't want to be the kind of mother who raised her child alone.

But then there was her other reason, the one she didn't have the courage to tell Brad about. She was terrified of gaining a huge amount of weight from being pregnant. As it was, she was already struggling to lose the same ten pounds she'd been trying to get rid of for more than a year. She was sure ten pounds didn't seem like a lot to most people, but the last thing she wanted was for her mother to start harassing her again — spewing some of the same hurtful comments she'd dished out for years. Melanie had been a chubby child, and her mother had been repulsed by it.

"Why aren't you saying anything?" he asked.

"No reason. I just wanna make sure we're ready."

"Baby, how much more ready do we need to be? We have more than enough room, and we can definitely afford it. Plus, you know it's still my dream to be able to give our children what my parents weren't able to give me. When they were alive, they took care of me the best they could, but they barely made ends meet, and I went without a lot. Even in college."

"I know. Why don't we talk about it more tonight?"

"Fine. And hey — are you losing weight?"

"I wish."

"Why? Because it's not like you need to. You look perfect."

"I'm glad you feel that way," she said, wondering how he could possibly think she'd lost even a few ounces, let alone enough weight that was noticeable enough to see. Especially since she weighed herself every single day, and not much had changed. Although maybe working out six days a week without fail was helping her lose inches.

Brad kissed her again, this time with more passion. "Make love to me."

Melanie gently pressed both her hands against his chest. "Baby, I can't. I have to get dressed so I can drive over to Schaumburg. I'm meeting Alicia, remember?"

"Oh yeah. Well, I guess I'll let you off the hook this one time. I expect you to make this up to me tonight, though," he said, smiling.

Melanie was relieved, because her plans to drive over and meet Alicia weren't the only reason she was putting him off. Truth was, she had long stopped wanting to make love to him in broad daylight because of how pathetic she looked when she was naked. At five foot nine and 165 pounds, she wore a size ten and looked like Miss Piggy, which was one of the many names her father had called her when she was a child. She wasn't nearly as heavy now as she'd been back then, but she was still a size ten for heaven's sake. Just the thought of it made her want to burst into tears. Brad deserved so much better. A wife he could be proud to have on his arm — just like her mother regularly told her. And if it was the last thing she did, she would make that happen. She would do whatever was necessary to drop those ten horrible pounds she was parading around with. That way, she could fit back into her size eights the way she was supposed to. She wouldn't be happy — and neither would her mother — until she did.

CHAPTER 3

"Hey, Mel," Alicia said, hugging her best friend when she walked inside Nordstrom. "Thank you so much for coming. Thank you for everything you've done to help with all of this."

"Please. You know I'm here for you all the way to the end. I'm really happy for you and Phillip. I'm glad you're *finally* getting back together for good."

"Thank you, girl. There were times when I wasn't so sure it would happen. I mean, who could blame Phillip if he'd decided to move on?"

"Well, he didn't, and that's all that matters. He loves you, you love him, and that made all the difference."

"Very true, and I'm so excited."

They walked through the department store and went into the mall area.

"Wow, Woodfield is packed today," Alicia said.

"Not surprised. Not with it being Saturday."

"I remember a time when I would have been either here or at Oakbrook right when they opened."

Melanie laughed. "Yeah, I remember that, too. You used to shop your natural behind off."

"It caused me way too many problems, though, so I had to make some changes. I had to realize I had issues."

"I'm glad you did. Some people never admit that they have a shopping addiction, and they go on for the rest of their lives spending beyond their means."

They walked a little farther, looking inside various stores and chatting along the way. When they arrived at Swarovski they walked in. It was pretty crowded as well.

"So have you thought more about what you want to wear?" Melanie asked.

"Something noticeable but elegant. For example," Alicia said, pointing to a pair of rhinestone earrings in the glass case, "I really like those, but they're a bit on the small side."

Melanie strolled farther down the counter. "What about these?"

Alicia moved closer. "The second ones from the right?"

"Yep."

"I really like those."

"I do, too. They're beautiful."

Alicia turned around, checking to see if one of the salesclerks was free. None were available at the moment, so she said to Melanie, "Since they're all busy, let's just see what we can find for you. Then we can try them on at the same time."

They searched the next case and the one after.

"Oh, what about those?" Alicia said.

Melanie leaned forward. "I like them a lot. Actually, I love them."

They browsed a few minutes longer, until a twentysomething woman walked over.

"Can I help you ladies find something?"

"Yes," Alicia said. "We'd like to see a couple of pairs of your earrings."

"Of course," she said.

Alicia showed her which two, and once she and Melanie tried them on they loved their selections even more. Then they found necklaces and bracelets that were perfect, too.

"Can I help you find anything else?" the young woman asked.

"No, I think that'll be it," Alicia, said opening her tote and pulling out her wallet. She also looked at her phone when she saw a flashing blue light. She had either a text message, an email, or some sort of social media notification, and she couldn't help checking to see which. She hoped Levi wasn't trying to contact her again. But he was. This time, he'd sent her a private message on Facebook. A part of her wanted to read it right then, but she didn't want to do that in front of Melanie, or, more important, she didn't want Melanie to somehow see who the message was from. On top of that, it just didn't seem right to read anything from Levi right now when here she was shopping for her and Phillip's wedding.

After paying for the jewelry, Alicia and Melanie left and browsed in a couple of other stores. When they walked out of Lord & Taylor, Alicia said, "I'm hungry. You?"

"Not really."

"Well, I'm starving. Let's go over to The Cheesecake Factory."

"I don't know about that one. Everything is good, but they give you so much food."

"Just order a salad."

"I guess."

After waiting twenty minutes, the electronic gadget the hostess had given Alicia buzzed, and they were seated in a booth.

"Are you okay?" Alicia asked.

"I'm fine," Melanie said.

"You don't seem fine. I sort of noticed it when we were looking for jewelry."

Melanie sighed. "I'm just a little worried about me and Brad."

"Why?"

"He lost a bunch of money in the stock market."

"How much?"

"Ten thousand."

"Oh my goodness. How?"

"Playing around with some stocks he had no business messing with."

"I remember when he did that last year."

"That's why I'm worried. One time was already enough, but again?"

"Did you talk to him about it?"

"I did, and he swears it won't happen again. But it's like I told him: He said the same thing last time."

"I'm sure things are gonna be okay."

"I hope so, because you know I can't live like that. Then, to add more problems, he's still working a lot of hours. It's one case after another, and if he's not working into the wee hours of the morning, he's sleeping so he can work a ton more hours the next day."

"Maybe that'll get better, too. Maybe he's just trying to prove that he's worthy of his new promotion."

"I'm sure he is, but no marriage can survive when you don't spend time together. Or if it does survive, it's only because two people have made it up in their minds to be together just because it's convenient. Either that or they haven't found someone else who makes them happier."

A young male waiter set a basket of bread and butter on the table. "I'm Antonio, and I'll be your server today. Can I start you ladies with something to drink and maybe an appetizer?"

"No appetizer for me," Melanie said.

Alicia scanned her menu. "I think I'll pass on the appetizer, too."

"Do you need a few more minutes to decide on your entrée?"

"No," Alicia said. "I'll have raspberry lemonade and your stuffed chicken tortillas."

"Excellent. And you?" he asked Melanie.

"I'm not really hungry, so I'll just have a glass of water."

"Are you sure?" he said.

"Yes."

"Okay, then I'll be right back with your drinks."

Alicia raised her eyebrows. "You're not ordering anything?"

"No, I'm good."

"Are you on a diet?"

"Sort of."

Alicia looked at Melanie. She hadn't noticed it or thought about it until now, but Melanie's face looked narrower.

"Actually, you do look like you've lost a little weight."

"Well, the scale says just the opposite."

"But it's not like you need to lose anything. Otherwise, you'll look way too thin. You don't look to be more than a hundred fifty pounds."

"Try one-sixty-five."

"That's just a number, plus look how tall you are."

"That's easy for you to say because you've worn eights since high school. Nothing more, nothing less."

"But that's always been normal for me. It's just the way my metabolism is set up."

"Well, I'll be a whole lot happier when I lose these final ten pounds."

Alicia hoped Melanie's mother hadn't been razzing her about her weight again. She'd done that for years, even though Melanie looked fine. When Alicia and Melanie had been in high school, she had weighed just a little too much, but by the time they'd entered college, she'd lost down to a healthy size and toned up her body with daily workouts.

"You really do look great, Mel," Alicia said, trying to encourage her.

"This is one of those times where you and I have to do what we do best: agree to disagree."

Alicia shook her head and smiled. "It never fails, does it? We're best friends forever, yet sometimes we couldn't be more different."

They both laughed.

"We do agree on one thing for sure, though," Melanie added.

"What's that?"

"Phillip, and how perfect he is for you."

"That he is," Alicia said, but then she wondered . . . if that was so true, why was she still thinking about that email Levi had sent her and dying to read his Facebook message? Why couldn't she leave well enough alone and just be happy?

CHAPTER 4

Alicia grabbed Phillip's hand and looked farther down the front row. Her dad and her stepmom, Charlotte, sat to the left of them. Then, she turned and smiled at her two-year-old nephew, little MJ, who sat to her right. On the other side of him was his dad, Matthew, who was home on summer break from Harvard, and Matthew's girlfriend, Stacey. Alicia's seven-year-old baby sister, Curtina, was over in the other building attending children's church, and Alicia couldn't wait to see her later when they went to dinner. Behind her, of course, were Melanie and Brad. Life was good, and Alicia finally had everything she could possibly want . . . but for some reason, she couldn't stop thinking about Levi.

It had been one thing for him to email her, but when she'd gotten in the car to leave the mall yesterday, she'd read his Facebook message and had found herself almost wishing Levi would call her. She'd had the same cell number for years, and she knew Levi hadn't forgotten it. For some reason, he was waiting for her to respond to his messages first, and knowing him, he wanted her to willingly ask him for his number or ask him to call her. She'd actually thought about doing just that, but thankfully, she'd talked herself out of it.

When the choir took their seats, her father walked up to the pulpit and stood in front of the glass podium.

"This is the day the Lord hath made, so let us rejoice and be glad in it," Curtis said. "It is a blessing just to be alive. A blessing to have woken up in our right minds and in good health. It's a joy and a blessing to be here and have yet one more opportunity to worship our Father, His Son, and the Holy Spirit."

*Amen*s filled the entire sanctuary.

"My plan was to deliver the message this morning the same as usual, but after traveling to three different speaking engagements last week, I'm still a bit tired. I arrived home late Friday evening and met with some of the officers for a lunch on Saturday, but I was sure that relaxing at home last night and getting a good night's sleep would energize me. Unfortunately, it hasn't, and so I've asked Pastor Sullivan to bless you with today's message. And if I could, I just want to say how proud I am to have this young man in my life. I am, of course, proud of all my associate ministers, deacons, other officers here at the church, and my administrative staff, but having my future son-in-law as the assistant pastor is a blessing in more ways than one. He loves God, and he loves my daughter, and I just can't ask for anything more than that. I've watched him for a number of years, and no matter what happens, he always tries his very best to honor God's Word. He tries to do the right thing, and what a great example that is for all of us. I know that none of us is perfect, and that we can never say never, but Phillip, I really do believe with all my heart that you love my daughter and that you will always honor her as your wife. And I love you for that."

The congregation applauded. Phillip leaned over and kissed Alicia on the cheek and then walked into the pulpit. He and Curtis hugged, and Curtis returned to his seat.

"Thank you so much, everyone," Phillip began. "Thank you for continuing to show such love and respect for me, and for all your support. Not just for my position here in the church, but also as our pastor's future son-in-law. When Pastor Black says that he believes I love his daughter and that I will always honor her as my wife, I'm here to tell you that every word of that is true. I simply couldn't be happier about marrying her again, and I thank God for giving us a second chance. I love and adore her. And when we divorced, my biggest worry was that I would surely have to spend the rest of my life alone, because I couldn't imagine loving another woman the way I loved her."

Tears streamed down Alicia's cheeks, and she could hear others sniffling as well. Charlotte reached across Phillip's empty seat and rubbed her arm. She was teary-eyed also. Phillip was absolutely the best, and Alicia silently thanked God for giving him back to her. She loved him, he made her happy, and he was her soul mate. It was the reason she had to push Levi completely out of her mind. She had to ignore any future messages he might send her. Maybe then he'd take a hint and leave her alone.

Phillip pulled a white handkerchief from inside his suit jacket and wiped his eyes. "Well, now that I've made everyone cry a river of tears in here, I think I'd better get started with my sermon."

Everyone laughed and wiped their own

tears away.

Phillip touched the screen of his electronic tablet until he found his sermon notes. "Today, I want to talk about temptation. And to begin, I'd like to read to you the meaning of temptation, as defined by the *Merriam-Webster Dictionary.* 'Temptation is a strong urge or desire to have or to do something; something that causes a strong urge or desire to have or do something and especially something that is bad, wrong, or unwise.' It then goes on to give three examples of temptation which are, one: 'Money is always a temptation'; two: 'The dessert menu has a lot of temptations.' " Members of the church laughed at that one. Phillip chuckled as well. "I knew that one would get everyone's attention, because we all struggle with trying to fight off our desire to eat sweets and all kinds of foods. And then there's number three: 'the temptations of the city.' "

Phillip looked out at the congregation, and Alicia felt uncomfortable. Not because he was saying anything wrong, but because she knew that when she'd had that affair with Levi, she'd allowed temptation to get the best of her. She felt guilty and ashamed, because it wasn't like their church members didn't know what she'd done. They knew the whole story, as did many people nation-wide because of who her father was. There were times when being Curtis Black's daughter was beneficial, but there were other times when it felt like a curse. Being the daughter of a well-known pastor meant you had to take the good with the bad when it came to the media and gossip, and even more so, when infidelity was involved.

This was also the reason Alicia now knew for sure that this thing with Levi had to be squashed. She hadn't spoken to him, she hadn't responded to his messages, and she certainly wasn't planning to see him, but she had to stop thinking about him. Since first reading his email yesterday morning, she hadn't thought about much else, but this was the end. She wouldn't make the same mistake twice. She was older, wiser, and well aware of what happened to people when they made bad choices. There were dire consequences to pay. People were hurt in the process, and in some cases, they were scarred permanently. Phillip was a good example of that, and Alicia wouldn't harm him like that again. She would marry him and be the best wife imaginable. She would be faithful until death.

CHAPTER 5

Melanie walked into the bedroom, set the white plastic grocery bag onto the leather chair, and dropped her red handbag next to it. She and Brad had just gotten home from having dinner with Alicia, Phillip, and Alicia's parents, and Brad was downstairs watching television. Melanie was happy he hadn't followed her. That way, he wouldn't have to see her taking off her dress and become disgusted. Her being appalled was enough, so she made sure to never dress or undress when he was around. At first, he hadn't understood that and had sort of complained about it, but once he'd begun putting in all those hours at work he'd rarely noticed anymore.

She tried not to feel so self-conscious or let her weight issues consume her, but she was to the point where she thought about it all the time. Like now, when she should have been changing clothes the way she'd planned, she walked over to her nightstand and pulled a family photo album from the bottom drawer. She sat on the bed, turned to some of her childhood photos, and cringed. She could barely stand to look at them, as she'd been terribly ugly and fat back then. She'd looked wretched to say the least, and it was no wonder other children had taunted her. They'd bullied and teased her all the time, and her parents had been utterly ashamed of their only child. Truth be told, her mother was still ashamed of her today, and Melanie understood why. She didn't like most of the things her mother said about her, but she didn't blame her for feeling that way.

Melanie flipped through pages of photos. If it weren't for the fact that she needed to be reminded of the way she never wanted to look again, she would destroy every last one of them. Maybe then she wouldn't keep punishing herself this way. She wouldn't scan through this album 365 days a year, reminiscing and regretting her childhood and sometimes bawling like a toddler.

She placed the photos back in her drawer, walked over to the full-length oval mirror in the corner, and slipped off her sleeveless sheath. How disgusting. Here she'd eaten as little as possible all week long, yet she still saw a huge bulge in the middle of her abdomen. She also saw puffy obliques, and her face looked bloated. But she knew what the problem was, and she would fix it. Instead of going every other day without eating the way she had over the last seven days, she would stick to all liquids. She would start tomorrow. That way, she'd be well on her way to losing those ten pounds once and for all. Wearing a size ten just wasn't bearable, and she wasn't sure how she'd allowed herself to believe she could accept looking like this. She also wouldn't tolerate being outright fat again. It was sad to say, but she'd rather be dead than walk around with fifty extra pounds the way she had during her teen years.

For most of her twenties, she'd easily been able to maintain wearing a size eight, but as of a year ago when she'd had no choice but to get a cortisone shot for constant shoulder pain — which had resulted from a boot-camp-style workout class she'd taken — she'd seemed to stay hungry all the time and had quickly picked up weight. Experts swore it usually took much more than one shot to change a person's appetite, but Melanie knew different. Even working out hadn't helped her control the pounds she'd begun gaining. Earlier this year, however, she'd finally slashed her daily calories in half and had lost down to a size eight very quickly. But then, she'd gained it back. She'd yo-yoed up and down and up and down again. Finally, last week, she'd decided to eat only every other day, which was working but not nearly as fast as she needed it to.

So she knew what she had to do: rid her diet of all solid foods whatsoever, except for maybe a small meatless salad each day for lunch. She would drink two protein shakes, one for breakfast and one for dinner, with water in between. She would take a multivitamin to help make up for any nutrients she would lose — she would start first thing in the morning and stick to it religiously. She'd decided this during church service, and while she'd only eaten part of a chicken Caesar salad at dinner this afternoon, she was glad she'd asked Brad to stop by the grocery store on their way home so she could pick up a few items. Since she'd told him she wouldn't be very long, he'd waited for her in the car the way he always did. She'd been counting on this, but if for some reason he'd wanted to go inside with her, she would have purchased something for the general household and gone back to the grocery store later this evening.

42

But again, he hadn't joined her, and she was glad because right before crashing on any new diet, Melanie always ate whatever she wanted. That way she could make herself physically and mentally sick of all high-calorie, high-fat, high-carb foods, and she wouldn't crave them as much. She'd be disgusted just by the mere thought of eating any junk food again.

She was looking forward to devouring and enjoying every item she'd snatched up at the store — items Brad hadn't noticed her carrying upstairs to their bedroom in the plastic bag because as soon as they'd arrived home, he'd shed his suit jacket, loosened and removed his tie, and flipped on the television. ESPN had been showing highlights from game one of the NBA Finals, which Brad had missed last Thursday because of the important trial he'd been preparing for well into the night. Although, as it had turned out, his client and the opposing side had agreed early Friday morning to settle out of court. Needless to say, Brad was ready and waiting for game two, which was airing this evening. That is, if he could stay awake. Melanie knew it wouldn't be long before he dropped off to sleep on the sofa in the family room, taking at least a two-hour nap. This was his Sunday-after-church-after-dinner ritual, especially when he worked on tough cases for more than a couple of weeks straight; which suited Melanie just fine, because it meant he wouldn't be coming upstairs anytime soon — it meant she could gorge herself one last time in peace. She could eat and drink every delicious item of junk food she loved: a family-size bag of Ole Salty's potato chips, a large package of Chips Ahoy! cookies, a ten-pack box of Little Debbie Zebra Cakes, and a two-liter bottle of Nehi peach soda. She would definitely feel stuffed and ill when she finished, but she was still planning to eat all of it. She knew going nearly straight liquid might be tough for the first two or three days, because that's how it had been when she'd done this a couple of times before, but after that, she'd be good. She'd feel fine, and it wouldn't be long before she was ten pounds lighter. She would reach her goal and be happy.

CHAPTER 6

It was a gorgeous Monday, and Alicia couldn't have felt better. The copyedited version of her manuscript had arrived an hour ago, and she was planning to start reading it this afternoon. It was only ten thirty, and she was glad her publisher had shipped it overnight on Friday for early-morning delivery today. Her fourth novel was being published in January, seven months from now, and she'd already written the synopsis and outline for her fifth. She was trying her best to stay on a one-book-a-year schedule, and so far she'd been able to do it. The production process was long, though. First, she submitted her manuscript to her editor, and when she heard back from her, she did rewrites and more rewrites, and then once a copyeditor reviewed it, checking for grammar, punctuation, and other minor issues, Alicia read it again. She made more changes and edits during this stage also. After that, her publisher sent her the proof pages to read one last time. They also gave it to professional proofreaders, making sure that as many typos as possible were found and corrected, but there was always at least something that was missed. There was just no getting around that when you were dealing with nearly a hundred thousand words, but Alicia always hoped for no more than one or two errors.

Alicia was also excited about the national tour she'd be embarking on, because there was nothing like meeting and talking with her readers — the amazing people she never would have had the opportunity to connect with had she not become a writer. Her publisher was sending her to ten cities, some of which she'd been to in the past for signing events and some she hadn't: Chicago, Cleveland, Atlanta, Memphis, Birmingham, Dallas, Houston, Washington, DC, New York, and Sacramento. She was looking forward to spending two full weeks out on the road, especially since Phillip would be accompanying her this time.

Alicia set her manuscript to the side when she heard her phone ringing. It was her mother.

"Hey, Mom."

"Hey, sweetie. How are you?"

"I'm good. You?"

"Can't complain. One of my clients canceled her session, so I thought I'd give you a call. I also wanted to see if there's anything we need to do this week for the wedding."

Tanya was a counselor for battered women, and Alicia couldn't think of a more understanding or compassionate person for them to talk to than her mother.

"No, not really. Now that Melanie and I have our jewelry, I think that's it. Teresa has a lot left to do," Alicia said, referring to her wedding planner, "but you and I can relax a little now. I'm actually glad because I received my copyedits this morning, and when I'm reading through those, I don't like to be distracted."

"I can imagine."

"Phillip had a dental appointment today in Mitchell, so that's another reason I'll be able to get a lot done."

"I'm so happy the two of you worked things out. I know I keep saying that, but sweetheart, I really am. You were very young when you married Phillip the first time, and you made some mistakes. But now God has given you an opportunity to marry the man of your dreams all over again. You've matured a lot over the last six years, and I'm very proud of you."

"Thanks, Mom. It's been a journey, that's for sure. But it's all been worth it."

"Very much so. You could search high and low for years, and I don't think you'd ever find a man who's as loving, caring, and honest as Phillip. Well, maybe your stepfather, but that's about it."

"I know. You were really blessed to find someone like Dad James. Of course, it's every child's dream to have their parents together, but since Dad wasn't the man he needed to be when he was married to you, I'm glad you found someone who was. Someone who loves you so genuinely."

"So am I. Your father has changed a lot, though, and I'm really happy about that. Things didn't work out between us, but he's grown on so many levels. Mentally, spiritually, and emotionally."

"He has, Mom. He's nothing like he used to be. He's the best father, husband, and pastor in the world right now, and he's been that way for a while."

"It's too bad your brother Dillon couldn't see that. I realize your dad denied him when he was born, but if Dillon had been a little more patient, I think he and your dad would have gotten close."

"I think they would have, too. But Dillon

was different. He was all about himself, and to be honest, he wanted nothing to do with Matthew, Curtina, or me. You would think because his mom died when he was only a few weeks old that he would have wanted to be close to all of us. Not to mention, he didn't meet Daddy until he was twenty-seven."

"I hope he gets some help, and that maybe down the road, he'll apologize and make things right with all of you."

"Maybe, but I wouldn't hold my breath. Dillon did some dirty stuff, and if you wanna know the truth, I'm glad he's gone."

"That's understandable. Oh well, I guess I'd better get going. Need to review a few notes before my next appointment."

"Okay, Mom. I'll talk to you later. Love you."

"Love you, too, dear."

Alicia smiled when she hung up the phone. Her mother was everything and then some. Such a kind spirit who loved everyone. The good, the bad, and sometimes the awful. After all the terrible things Dillon had done to Alicia's father and her brother Matthew, Alicia could tell that her mom still felt sorry for him. Alicia didn't feel as much sympathy for Dillon, but she had to admit that one of the things she loved most about her mom was how forgiving she was. She forgave everyone for everything with no strings attached. To her, no one's sin was worse than anyone else's, even if most people thought so. She wasn't naïve about folks who had betrayed her or deceived her at one time or another — she knew who they were and how they were — but she also didn't hate them or talk badly about them.

Alicia answered a few email messages from some of her readers and responded to two more from online bloggers who were requesting a feature interview for her new book. Then she called Phillip.

"Hi, baby," she said when he answered.

"Hey, you. What's up?"

"Just finishing up a few things so I can start reading my copyedits."

"Wow, when did those arrive?"

"Early this morning."

"Then I guess it's a good thing I didn't follow you back to Chicago yesterday after all."

"I guess it is," she said.

Phillip was always off on Mondays, the same as everyone else who was employed by the church, so on Sundays, he usually spent the night with her and then drove back to Mitchell on Monday evenings. Alicia was getting to the point where she no longer wanted him to do that, however, because it was just too hard spending late nights together and not being able to make love to him.

"So how long do you think it'll take you?"

"The rest of today and most of tomorrow. After that, I have to type in any additional changes I have. Which means I won't be completely finished until sometime on Wednesday or Thursday."

"Then you probably won't make it over for Bible study this week, will you?"

"Not sure. I'll be able to tell by Wednesday afternoon."

"I have a pretty busy schedule this week myself. I also have a few business errands to run today."

"Well, I won't hold you," she said, all while looking at her email inbox and seeing a new message from Levi. She could barely contain her anxiety.

"Baby, did you hear me?" he said.

"What?"

"You didn't hear anything I said?"

"Um, no. I was reading something . . . I'm sorry."

"I was just telling you to call me later when you take a break from reading."

"I will. I love you."

"I love you, too, baby. Have a good day."

Alicia ended the call and set her phone on her desk. Why was Levi doing this? During church service, she'd made her decision about not responding to him. She'd come to her senses and had decided that her love and place in life were with Phillip, and nothing was going to change that. She wouldn't do anything to ruin what God had blessed her to have all over again. But now it seemed that if she didn't respond to Levi, he wasn't planning to leave her alone. She wished he would just go away, but since it was obvious that he wasn't going to, she took a deep breath and opened the email.

Hey Beautiful,
At this point, I'm not sure what else to do. I've emailed you, sent you a note on Facebook, and now I'm emailing you again. Most men would assume that you don't want to be bothered, but sweetheart, I think you and I both know that this isn't the case. I'm still in love with you, and you're still in love with me. Even without hearing your voice for all these years or seeing you, I'd be willing to bet my life on it. What you and I have, some people never experience in their lifetime, so I know you haven't gotten over me. And sweetheart, believe me

when I tell you this: You can't have two soul mates. And since I'm your only soul mate, I really hope you're not serious about marrying your ex-husband again. If you do, you'll be making the biggest mistake of your life. You'll marry him and think about me . . . every . . . single. . . . day. So, sweetheart, please don't. Also, unless you've changed your number (which I doubt), I still have it. I was hoping you would email me back and then we could go from there, but if I have to call you I will. I'm not trying to be pushy, but I love you too much to give up without a fight. And you know my motto: I never lie, I don't play child-ish games, and if I say something I always mean it.

With all my love,
Levi

Alicia read the email again and leaned back in her chair. She was speechless. Nervous. Confused. Why was this happening? Why wouldn't he find someone else to harass? He knew she was with Phillip, and he knew they were getting remarried, so why was he making things hard for her? What she and Levi had once had together was in the past. It was over. It had been for six years, and they hadn't seen each other in all that time. Surely he didn't think she still loved him. And as far as she was concerned, there was no possible way he could still love her the same, either. He might still be infatuated with a few lingering memories, but too much time had passed for his feelings to mean anything else.

Alicia sat at her desk with her eyes closed for more than a half hour, thinking and worrying. But when her phone rang and she saw the word *Private* display on the screen, her heart pounded. She knew it was Levi. Part of her was afraid to answer, but she knew she needed to talk to him and get this over with so they could go their separate ways.

"Hello?"

"Hey, beautiful."

"I really wish you wouldn't call me that."

Levi laughed, and for a second, she pictured his mesmerizing smile. The one she'd never been able to resist, no matter how hard she'd tried.

"So after all this time," he said, "that's all you have to say?"

"Levi, why are you calling me?"

"Because you wouldn't respond. I tried to handle things the right way. Tried to give your fiancé his respect. I didn't wanna call if he was around."

Alicia thought about how in the past, Levi had never spoken Phillip's name. He'd always referred to him as "he," "him," or "your husband." She'd decided then that the reason Levi did that was because it made Phillip seem less real. "And you think calling me behind his back is any better?" she said.

"No, but it's like I told you when I emailed you earlier, I'm not giving up without a fight."

"But you know I'm getting married."

"Yeah, and when I heard about that, it broke my heart. My boy Darrell told me last year."

"Then I'm sure you also know that our wedding is set for August."

"The date doesn't matter. The question is: Why are you marrying someone else when it's me you really wanna be with?"

Now, Alicia laughed. "You're really funny, you know that?"

"I'm dead serious. Girl, this is me you're talking to. From the moment you read my email on Saturday morning, you haven't thought about much else. Debating whether you should respond to me or not. Trying to convince yourself that it's your ex-husband you want. I'm sure you've told yourself a hundred times that you and I can never be together."

Alicia hated that he knew her so well, but she would never admit he was right. Not when she knew she had to cut him off for good.

"Look, Levi. I'm glad you're out of prison, but I've moved on. And you should, too."

"Is that what bothers you? That I just got out of prison? Because when I told you that I was a different man, I meant it. I'm done with dealing drugs for good. I read my Bible regularly, and I'm not one of those men who find Jesus while they're serving time and then forget about Him as soon as they're set free. My love for God is real, and my faith in Him is unshakable."

"I'm really happy for you, but that still doesn't change anything. I'm marrying Phillip, Levi."

"Look, I know this is bad timing and that you don't want to hurt anyone, but you can't stop destiny. And I know you haven't forgotten how strong our chemistry was from day one. We were two peas in a pod, and when we were together we could barely keep our hands off each other. You and I shared the kind of love every man and woman prays for. That very rare kind of love that lasts forever. So the bottom line is this:

You can marry your ex, or someone else for that matter, but you'll always be in love with me."

Alicia rested her elbows on her desk, holding her phone in one hand and the side of her face with the other. She closed her eyes, trying to settle her nerves. She wanted to say something, but she couldn't. She wanted to tell him how wrong he was and how he wasn't dealing with reality, but she couldn't force the words from her lips.

"Baby, I know this isn't what you were expecting to happen, especially not right now," he said, "but it is what it is. So please let me see you. Let me hold you and show you that nothing's changed between us. Let me show you how much I still love you."

"Levi, no! Please stop all this nonsense. What we had is over. It's done, and I can't talk to you anymore. I can never see you again."

"You don't mean that. I know you think you do, but you really don't. Your mind is telling you one thing, but deep down, you know where your heart is. You wanna be with me as badly as I wanna be with you."

"Did you hear what I just said?"

"I heard you loudly and clearly. But before we hang up, just answer one question. Does your ex make love to you the way I did?

When the two of you are together, do you wish time would stop so that you never have to spend a single minute without him? Because that's how it always was with you and me. It was never just about our physical attraction. We were good together in every way imaginable. Remember?"

"Levi, I can't do this with you. I'm hanging up, and if you care anything about me you'll never call me again. You won't send me messages, you won't send me anything. You'll just leave me alone."

"Sweetheart, you can't pretend I don't exist and that you're not in love with me."

"Good-bye, Levi."

Alicia pressed the End button on her phone, threw it on her desk, and covered her face with her hands.

She held back her tears for as long as she could, then wept uncontrollably.

CHAPTER 7

Being a nurse practitioner was a dream come true for Melanie, and she thanked God for giving her a gift and purpose that allowed her to help people. For as long as she could remember she'd wanted to be a registered nurse, but as a child, she'd never heard of a nurse who could see patients on her own and write prescriptions. There was a time right after her first four years of college when she'd considered becoming an anesthesiologist, but once she'd discovered that she could move up a lot higher in the nursing field, she'd been thrilled. She'd wanted to be hands-on with patients, where she could offer genuine compassion and more personal attention, and being an internal medicine NP gave her that opportunity. She also loved the two physicians she worked with, as they were extremely knowledgeable, were thorough with their examinations and diagnoses, and they never talked down to her or to the patients who came to see them. Melanie remembered how back when she'd been interviewing for various positions, this had been very important to her. She'd wanted to make sure she had a pleasant rapport with both doctors and other staff members, and this particular group of folks gave her that.

Melanie thumbed through a few charts, and while she hadn't thought much about it, she still wasn't hungry. It was midmorning, and if she could make it to noon without feeling famished, she would have it made. Before leaving home, she'd drunk her dark-chocolate protein shake as planned, and then she'd downed a couple of bottles of water there at work. She wasn't picky when it came to specific shake flavors, but the reason she loved and stuck with dark chocolate was because it was rich in taste, and it seemed thicker. This was likely the reason it sometimes gave her a full feeling for four to six hours.

Although, maybe another reason she wasn't as hungry was because of how sick she'd made herself last night from eating that torturous array of junk food. She'd been so uncomfortable that she'd had to take not just one or two but three laxative pills, and by four a.m., she'd found herself in the bathroom three separate times. The good news, however, was that she'd felt relieved, and she definitely hadn't felt as sick as she had before going to bed. Not that it would matter whether she felt sick or hungry anyway, because this time, she was determined to lose the weight she needed to. She was only two years shy of her thirtieth birthday, and there was no way she was turning the big 3-0 looking disgraceful.

Melanie read through a few more documents, and for some reason, Brad and his savings account crossed her mind. She'd tried her best not to think about it because what was done was done, but it was hard to let it go. Especially since, in the back of her mind, she wondered if he would risk losing thousands again. He'd sworn he was finished for good, but Melanie wasn't so sure. She also hoped there wasn't anything else going on, because something didn't feel right. She couldn't put her finger on it, but this kind of behavior was completely out of the ordinary for Brad. She'd thought the same thing last year, but she'd told herself that while she didn't understand it, everyone made mistakes from time to time. However, now that he'd lost more money, it worried her.

She tossed a few thoughts through her

mind and refocused on her work. She had a 10:45 appointment, and she was sure that by now, Amber, her medical assistant, had brought Mrs. Weston into the examination room, taken her blood pressure and pulse, and reviewed her current medication listing.

Melanie grabbed her starched pure-white lab coat from the back of her office door and slipped it on. Under it, she wore a white long-sleeve button-down shirt with a pair of navy dress pants, and all she could think of was how proud her mother would be. When Melanie had first started in her position, she'd mostly worn khakis under her lab coat, but when her mother had found out, she'd had a fit. She'd complained about it not being professional enough for someone who had earned the right to wear dress pants and dresses to work, so Melanie had finally stopped wearing anything that she knew her mother wouldn't like. In all honesty, Melanie couldn't have cared less about such pettiness, because it was her patients and their health that she cared about more.

She was also ashamed of the fact that she still allowed her mother to dictate so much of what she did or didn't do, and she just wished she hadn't always wanted her mother's approval so badly. Melanie knew she was an adult and that no one should live his or her life based on what others said or thought, but it had always been like this for her when it came to her mother. She feared that it always would be, and now she wished she didn't have to see her today. Her mom had called bright and early this morning, insisting they meet for lunch, and while Melanie loved her mother, she wasn't looking forward to hearing her usual questions. "When are you and Brad going to give me a grandchild? Are you eating the right foods? Are you working out at least six days per week?" It was always such a chore, and Melanie could barely wait for their visit to be over.

She walked down the corridor and saw Amber exiting and closing an examination room door.

"She's in rare form today," Amber whispered, "so I hope you're ready."

Melanie shook her head and smiled. She wasn't surprised to hear this at all, since this had been the norm for Mrs. Weston for a while.

Now that everything was electronic, Melanie no longer had to read through a patient's physical chart beforehand. So she walked into the examination room.

"Good morning, Mrs. Weston," Melanie said, sitting down in front of the small desk and slightly adjacent to the woman.

"I don't see what's all that good about it, but maybe it's a great day for you," her patient said. "So good morning."

Melanie smiled at Mrs. Weston and signed on to the computer system. She read a few lines of disturbing information but kept a straight face. Mrs. Weston had never been small, but as of today, she weighed 322 pounds. And she was only five feet, five inches tall.

"So what seems to be the problem?" Melanie asked.

"I woke up with a terrible headache and called to see if I could get an appointment with Dr. Lambert. They told me he was booked solid and that he wanted me to come see you."

"Well, I'm glad he did. It looks like your blood pressure is quite on the high side. One-seventy over a hundred. And your resting pulse isn't as low as I'd like to see it, either."

"I'm sure all I need is some different medication."

"I'd like to take your blood pressure again," Melanie said, pulling the blood pressure cuff away from the wall and wrapping it around Mrs. Weston's arm. "Sometimes your pressure can be a little high just from having to come to our office."

Mrs. Weston didn't say anything, but Melanie could tell from the slight frown on her face that she didn't think another blood pressure check was necessary.

Melanie placed her stethoscope in her ears and pumped the blood pressure cuff. She soon heard the first beat and then finally the last. "It's still about the same. One-seventy-two over ninety-eight."

"So which medication are you going to change?" Mrs. Weston asked matter-of-factly.

"I first want to do a more thorough examination, and then we'll go from there."

Melanie asked Mrs. Weston to sit on the examination table, and while she would have liked to ask her to remove her clothing and put on a patient gown, she knew Mrs. Weston would complain. So Melanie went ahead and checked her heart, breathing pattern, thyroid area, and circulation.

"Everything seems to be okay overall, and I believe part of the reason your blood pressure has escalated is because you've gained about twenty pounds since the last time we saw you. I know losing weight isn't easy — believe me, I know — but it really is important for you to think more about it. Especially since you have both hypertension and diabetes."

"You know it isn't easy? How could you know *anything* about that?" Her tone was curt.

"I was severely overweight as a child, and I've struggled with weight my entire life. The key is to eat better and to get more exercise. I also think it would help if we refer you to a nutritionist."

Mrs. Weston sighed in a huff. "Look, I'm sure you mean well, but I'm too tired and too old to make all these changes. It's too late for all that. Which is why I told you from the beginning that what I need is some different medication. Something stronger and better than what Dr. Lambert has me on now."

Mrs. Weston was only sixty-five, so she was far from being too old to start a healthy diet or take a walk on the bike path. Still, Melanie knew her suggestions were a lost cause, so she didn't push the idea any further. Had she not said anything, though, she wouldn't have been doing her job, not to mention that she truly wanted Mrs. Weston to feel better.

"For now, I'm going to increase the dosage of your water pill and have you take it twice a day. You'll continue taking your other two blood pressure pills as usual, and then I'd like you to come back a week from today for another check."

"Sounds good to me," Mrs. Weston said with a softer tone. Melanie was glad she'd calmed down, but she hated that it was only because she was getting more medication. She just wished Mrs. Weston and some of her other patients would realize how much medication they would no longer have to take if they took better care of themselves.

After Melanie typed the prescription into the computer and transmitted it over to Mrs. Weston's pharmacy, Mrs. Weston thanked her and left. Melanie now felt a little hungry, but after seeing how miserable one of her own patients was because of weight issues, she almost didn't want to have a salad. Nonetheless, since she'd promised her mom she would meet her for lunch, she didn't have much choice. It wasn't like Gladys Johnson would take no for an answer, anyway.

CHAPTER 8

"So what time do you think you'll be home?" Melanie asked Brad while driving her BMW SUV into the restaurant's parking lot.

"Hopefully, not past eight. But you know how it is when the partners get together for dinner. Plus, we really need to spend some time discussing this case we're going after. It's worth millions."

Melanie turned off the ignition. "Well, I'm here, so I guess I'll see you tonight."

"Enjoy your lunch."

"I'll try."

"Love you, baby."

"Love you, too."

Melanie dropped her phone in her handbag and checked her lipstick. Normally, she wasn't all that happy when Brad had dinner meetings, because he was already spending a lot of hours at the office. Today, however, she was relieved, because with Brad eating out, she'd be able to drink her protein shake for dinner as planned.

Melanie got out of her car and walked toward the building. She loved Gino's, which had the best Italian food ever. It was too bad she wouldn't be able to eat some of her favorite dishes.

When she walked inside, her mother smiled and Melanie couldn't help noticing what looked like a new pantsuit she was wearing. Her mom had never worked much and had mostly been a housewife, but she bought whatever she wanted as if she were rich. Melanie's father earned a good living as a distribution center supervisor, but they certainly weren't wealthy. Her mother had always made it clear, though, that a wife deserved to have some of the things she wanted — whether her husband could afford them or not.

Gladys scanned Melanie's body from head to toe.

"You look tired. How many hours are you working?"

"Wow, thanks a lot, Mom. It's good to see you, too."

"Girl, give your mother a hug."

Melanie embraced her, and soon after, the young hostess escorted them to their booth.

"Trisha will be your waitress today, and

69

she'll be here shortly."

Gladys smiled. "Thank you."

Melanie pushed her purse closer to the wall and rested her elbows on the table.

Gladys leaned back and relaxed. "You look a lot more professional today. So much better than you normally do."

Melanie kept silent, her face stoic.

"I'm glad you finally went out and bought some proper attire," her mother continued.

"Well, it's not like I got rid of my khakis, Mom. And if I wake up some morning wanting to wear them, it won't change the way I do my job."

Gladys waved her off. "Whatever, Mel. I'm only trying to tell you what I think is best. Specifically for your career. You could also stand to color your hair."

"Why? I don't have any gray strands."

"Yeah, but a softer brown would look so much better on you."

"Black is the color God gave me."

Gladys shook her head. "There's just no talking to you, is there?"

Their waitress walked up to the table. She was a petite woman with a pleasant smile. "Hi, I'm Trisha. And how are you ladies this afternoon?"

"Doing wonderfully," Gladys said.

"Fine, thank you," Melanie added.

"Glad to hear it. Can I get you something to drink?"

"We'll both have water," Gladys said.

There were times when Melanie's mother made her want to scream. It was bad enough that she tried to control everything, but deciding for Melanie what she would be drinking? It was so uncalled for. Melanie had planned to order water anyway, but it was simply the principle of the whole thing.

"Great. Also, just so you know, we have two specials today. The first is a rib-eye steak with garlic mashed potatoes. The other is our mushroom ravioli with white sauce. You also get a choice of salad with either of those."

Gladys scanned the menu. "Hmmm. I think I'll have the mushroom ravioli with a house salad. And if you would, please replace your house dressing with a low-fat vinaigrette."

"Will do. And you?" the waitress asked Melanie.

"I'll have your house salad as well."

"Will that be it?"

"Yes, I think so."

"Sounds good. I'll get this ordered for you," she said, walking away.

"So," Gladys said, "when are you and Brad going to give me my grandbaby?"

71

Melanie sighed. There it was.

"Mom, why do you always ask me that?"

"Because you're not getting any younger. Neither am I, for that matter."

"Well, it won't be in the near future."

"Why not?"

"We want to make sure we're ready."

"How much more ready do you need to be?"

"Can we talk about something else?"

"Fine. How about your workouts? Are you still getting one in at least six days a week?"

"Yes."

"And eating healthy for breakfast, lunch, and dinner?"

"Yes, but why do you ask me these same questions all the time?"

"Because they're important. I know this is a tough subject for you, but I also don't want you forgetting how heavy you used to be. Brad is a top attorney in this city, and the last thing you need is to go losing him. Appearances mean everything; I've always taught you that. You have a responsibility to keep yourself up."

The waitress set two glasses of water on the table and walked away.

Melanie drank some of hers and looked over at a few of the other customers.

"I'm sorry that you don't like hearing this,

but if you want to know the truth, the reason I asked you about your workouts today is because you're looking like a size ten again."

Melanie stared at her mother, wondering why she hadn't taken a rain check on lunch after all. Her mother did this kind of thing all the time, and Melanie wished that for once, Gladys would realize how bad she always made Melanie feel, particularly about herself and the way she looked. Her mother and her father had both been guilty of this when she was younger, but her mother's comments had always been the harshest and the most frequent. For whatever reason, during Melanie's teen years, her father had just up and stopped teasing her about her weight, but all that had seemed to do was make her mother worse. She'd said some downright hurtful things to Melanie, and Melanie would never forget them. Her mom, of course, had always eaten very little, and though she wasn't much shorter than Melanie, she'd never weighed more than 150 pounds. She was fifty-two but worked out more intensely than most thirty-year-olds. She also ate healthily seven days a week without fail. That was, with the exception of days like today when she went out to a restaurant, enjoying and eating something "special" like the ravioli she'd ordered. Even with that, however, Melanie could guarantee that her mom would only be eating half of it. And Melanie saw nothing wrong with that. Actually, she was glad her mom took such good care of herself, but she still didn't want her nitpicking about everything she could think of, judging and condemning Melanie every time she saw her.

"I guess you don't have anything to say," her mother said.

"Not really."

"Well, I hope you hear me, because it also doesn't look good for a nurse practitioner, of all people, to be overweight. That's no different than being a hairstylist who walks around with her hair looking a mess. Or being a dentist with crooked teeth. It sends the wrong message to clients, and in your case, to your patients."

"Mom, not everyone can be as perfect as you. I wish I could be, but I can't."

"I'm *not* perfect. But I try to get as close to being perfect as I can. For example, when I asked our waitress to bring me low-fat dressing, you never said a word. Even though you should have asked for the same thing."

Melanie raised her eyebrows. "That's

because I focus more on watching my carbs than I do on fat content. It's sugar that's keeping most people overweight."

"I agree. But for salad dressing, I prefer fat-free."

Melanie didn't bother arguing with her, and for the rest of their time together, she went along with whatever her mother said just to keep the peace. As of late, this was usually how things went during their visits.

Thankfully, time passed more quickly than Melanie had anticipated, and soon they were outside the restaurant, walking to their respective vehicles. But as Melanie prepared to head back to her office, she couldn't help replaying her mom's words: ". . . you're looking like a size ten again." This, of course, wasn't news to Melanie, and it was the reason she'd resorted to her latest diet. But after hearing her mother sound so disappointed in her, she felt like eliminating all solid food, including salads, and having only three shakes a day. She wasn't sure her body could withstand something so restrictive, but one way or the other, she was going to lose all this extra weight she was carrying around. Period.

CHAPTER 9

Alicia read the last paragraph of the second page of her manuscript for what seemed like the tenth time and sighed. She'd tried and tried, but she just couldn't concentrate on her edits the way she needed to. She was surprised she'd been able to read beyond the first page, given how nervous and stressed out she was. And it was all because she couldn't take her mind off Levi. Levi, Levi, Levi. If only he hadn't called her, she wouldn't feel so out of sorts.

She grabbed the top of her head with both hands, stroked her hair back, and took a deep breath. What was wrong with her? Why couldn't she just be happy with Phillip? Why couldn't she just be grateful for the way God had blessed her life for so many years? She'd prayed daily for Phillip to trust her again and to ask her to remarry him, and he had. So why couldn't marrying a man who loved her so genuinely and perfectly be enough? Especially since she'd already gone down this road before, sleeping around on Phillip with Levi, and then ultimately losing both of them. Phillip had divorced her, Levi had gone to prison, and she didn't want to think about the national scandal she'd caused her whole family.

But the more Alicia thought about Levi's words, she couldn't help slipping into the past. She had so many happy memories of him, and more important, vivid recollections of what it was like to *be* with him. She loved Phillip, Lord knows she did, but he had never made her feel as special as Levi had in bed. She was ashamed to even have these kinds of thoughts, but it was true. In fact, not even JT, her second husband, had been able to compare to Levi, because Levi was just plain different. She'd connected with him from the very beginning, and she'd never forgotten it. Over the years, she'd worked hard to bury any feelings she might have for him, but now that she'd heard his voice, every one of those feelings had resurfaced. And she couldn't seem to stop them.

Alicia read the same paragraph she'd been trying to edit for a while, but her thinking trailed off again. If only she could confide what she was going through to her mother or Melanie, maybe they could help her get beyond this. But she knew they would never understand. They'd think she was crazy for even bringing up Levi.

"Dear God, please." Alicia said out loud. "Please help me. Help me to forget about this man and move on. Please, God."

Alicia sat quietly for a few minutes, trying to settle her thoughts so she could get back to work. But when her phone rang, she looked at the screen and shook her head. It was Levi, and though she told herself to ignore him, her heart beat faster and faster, and before she knew it she'd picked it up.

"Levi, why are you doing this?"

"Because, baby, I really need to see you. Not tomorrow or next week but today."

"What? Have you lost your mind?"

"No, I've never been more serious in my life."

"Levi, you know what my situation is, so why are you trying to cause all these problems? You and I can never be. I already told you that."

"Look, just meet me somewhere between Mitchell and Chicago. That's all I'm asking."

"Why? What good will that do?"

"We need closure."

"What kind of closure?"

78

"The last time you and I saw each other was the night I was arrested. We never got to say a proper good-bye or anything. They took me away, and that was the end of it."

"Well, it wasn't like I could come see you. Not after the media broadcasted everything."

"I understand that, and I didn't expect you to. But just let me see you. Then, if you honestly want nothing to do with me, I'll say good-bye, and I'll never bother you again."

"I can't."

"Sweetheart, do you know how many people go through life marrying someone they're not in love with?"

"But I *do* love Phillip."

"You love him, but you're not *in* love with him. And there's a difference."

Alicia replayed his words in her mind. "I am in love with him."

"You don't sound very convincing."

"What is it you want me to say?"

"Nothing. All I'm asking is that you meet me. Just let me see you."

"No."

"Okay, then let me ask you this. If you don't wanna see me or talk to me, then why do you keep answering my calls?"

Alicia didn't respond.

"No comment?"

"I have to go," she said.

"You can hang up if you want, but I'm not giving up. Not until I see you face-to-face. If you really don't love me anymore, I want you to tell me in person."

"I'm telling you now. I don't love you, Levi. I love Phillip, and that's all there is to it."

"I don't believe that."

"Maybe you don't, but that's your problem."

Levi chuckled.

"What's so funny?"

"You. Not in my wildest imagination did I expect you to be in such denial. Not after the way we made each other feel."

"You're caught up in the past, but today things are different."

"Say whatever you want, but the fact still remains. I'm not giving up on being with the only woman I've ever loved. Right or wrong, I'd be a fool to do that."

"Levi, please don't make me hang up on you again. Let's just agree to go on with our lives with no animosity."

"I'm not angry. Frustrated maybe, but I'm not mad at you."

"But you know I'm not going to change my mind, right? You know I'm not going to see you."

"That's fine, just as long as you know I'm not giving up. Not until you tell me in person that you don't want me."

"Good-bye, Levi."

Alicia set the phone down and knew what she had to do: get dressed, pack a bag, and drive over to Mitchell to spend the rest of the day and night with Phillip. She needed to see her fiancé, the man she loved. He would be pleasantly surprised, and she could easily get back to reading her manuscript tomorrow or the next day. Yes, this was exactly what she was going to do, and she was sorry she hadn't thought of it sooner. She was also going to block Levi's phone number, email address, and Facebook account so he wouldn't be able to contact her. It was the only way to prove to him that she didn't want him, and that Phillip was the love of her life. There was a part of her that did feel sorry for Levi because she could tell he honestly believed they could pick up where they'd left off. But Alicia had to worry about herself. She had to focus on Phillip, her commitment to him, and the vows they were preparing to take again. Whether Levi could accept it or not, she had to do the right thing. And she would.

CHAPTER 10

Levi kissed Alicia with such intensity, she thought she was going to die. Her body was on fire, and she hadn't felt this sort of unyielding passion in years — not since the last time she and Levi had been together. He was driving her mad, and while she knew she should beg him to stop — to let her leave — she couldn't. Not when he was giving her what she'd wanted and needed for far too long.

Levi pushed her against the front door, the one she'd tried to escape through just minutes ago, and they kissed and caressed each other as though they would never see each other again. They were tucked away at the home of one of Levi's closest friends, Mark, who lived in one of the Western suburbs. Alicia had never made it to Mitchell. Mark was out of town for a few months and had left a key with his sister just in case Levi ended up being released before he returned. He'd also given Levi full and indefinite access to his home, until Levi found his own place. The interior was exquisite, and Alicia couldn't help wondering if Mark was wealthy because of selling drugs or because he had a legitimate career or business. Nonetheless, here Alicia was, and it was all because she hadn't blocked Levi's number the way she'd planned. She'd actually gotten in her car and had been preparing to drive over to Mitchell for her surprise visit with Phillip when Levi had called her again. He'd pleaded with her to come see him just this once and promised her that after today, he would never bother her again. He'd told her how she owed him at least that much, and this was when Alicia had thought about the way he'd protected her from the police the night he'd been arrested. Hence, she'd finally given in and told him she would meet him "just this once," so they could say good-bye for good. Levi had driven from Mitchell, and since Alicia had traveled from Covington Park, she'd actually arrived about ten minutes before him. At first, all he'd done was hug her, and then he'd asked her to sit down on the sofa so they could talk, but when she'd gotten up to leave, he'd followed her and pulled her into his arms. She'd tried fighting him off, but she'd failed at it.

"Baby, let me make love to you," he said between breaths.

"No," she said, pushing him away with little force.

"You know you want to," he said, kissing her.

She pushed him again. "Levi, no. You said that once we talked, you'd let me leave."

"Why are you fighting what's real? Something that feels so right."

Alicia gazed into his eyes. She remembered how gorgeous, tall, and lean he had been before, but now he had a few more muscles to go along with his perfect build, and his skin seemed more flawless than ever. His jeans and sweater fit him to a T, and the man smelled so good. He was the kind of guy most women secretly dreamed about. A bad boy who was as fine as could be. She tried not to stare at him, but she found herself eyeing every inch of his body.

"You said all we would do is talk, and I trusted you."

"Okay, you're right," he said. "I know I got a little carried away, but I was just so glad to see you, girl. Can't you understand that?"

"I have to go."

"Can we talk one last time? Please."

"Fine," she said.

Levi grabbed her hand and led her back to the living room, and they sat on the sofa again.

Alicia had left her tote in her car, but she set her key fob on the glass table. "I'm not sure what else there is to talk about."

"Us," he said, smiling.

"You're really killing me," she said, resting her arm on the back of the couch.

"Mmm, mmm, mmm," he said.

"What?"

"You're as beautiful as ever. Skin, hair, body. Total perfection."

"I wish you wouldn't say things like that."

"It's the truth."

"Is that what you wanted to talk to me about?"

"No, but can't a man give a woman a compliment?"

"Yeah, except it's the way you say things and the way you look at me. It's not right. And we've done way too much already."

"All we did was kiss."

"Yeah, but we never should have."

"Are you saying you didn't enjoy it? Because it didn't seem like that to me."

Alicia looked away, and he turned her chin back toward him.

"Hey. I can't help the way I feel. I'm

thirty-eight, and still, I've never been more in love with a woman in my life. You're my world."

"How can that be true after all these years, Levi?"

"It just is, and I can tell you feel the same way. There's too much passion between us, too much chemistry, to pretend like you don't."

Alicia turned away from him again.

"You have no idea what it was like being locked up. Someone telling you when to go to bed, when to get up, when to eat, when to do everything. But you know what brought a smile to my face every single day?"

"Levi, please —"

"No, let me finish. What brought a smile to my face was the thought of you. The photos I printed of you from your web site and a few other places online. I held on to the hope that one day I would get out of there, and you and I would finally become man and wife the way we were supposed to."

Alicia looked back at him. "But you know that's not possible. You know I'm marrying Phillip. We've been over this a thousand times."

"So are you saying you don't love me?"

"I have to go now," she said, scooting toward the edge of the sofa.

"Look at me and tell me you don't love me. Tell me that the feelings you had for me are gone, and I'll let you go."

Alicia grabbed her key fob and stood up. "I'm sorry, but what we had is over."

Levi got to his feet and folded his arms. "That's not what I asked you. What I want is for you to tell me you don't love me."

Alicia ignored him and went down the hallway toward the front entryway.

Levi followed her. "So you're not going to answer me?"

"I already did," she said, reaching for the doorknob and holding it.

Levi turned her body around and held her close. "Look at me. You can't answer because you know you still love me."

Tears filled Alicia's eyes. "Why won't you just leave me alone?"

"Because I can't. I wish I could, but I didn't struggle through all I've been through just to lose you again. I'm not doin' that, sweetheart."

Alicia pushed him hard, but Levi kissed her. She beat his chest with both her fists, sobbing . . . still he kissed her on her neck and on her lips again. He devoured her in a rough and powerful manner, and she loved it.

She no longer fought back.

Not even when he led her up to his friend's master bedroom.

Chapter 11

Alicia backed her white Mercedes out of the driveway, and though she knew Levi was standing in the doorway of the house staring at her, she never looked at him. She drove away speechless and ashamed. It was as if she'd had some out-of-body experience and was in shock.

She continued down the street, turned left, rolled to the stop sign, and broke into tears. "Oh my God, what have I done? What . . . have . . . I . . . done?"

She sniffled and wiped her face with a tissue she pulled from her glove box and drove onto the main street. When she heard a loud honk, she noticed her car veering to the left and swerved it back into the center of the lane. She was so distraught, all she could do was pray she got home safely. How could she have betrayed Phillip with Levi again? She didn't want to be this kind of person, a woman who allowed temptation to consume her, but there was something about Levi she couldn't resist. For one, she never should have agreed to meet with him. She never should have taken any of his calls. But deep down, she'd wanted to hear his voice. Truthfully? She'd *needed* to hear it. Needed to see him. Touch him. Be held by him oh so gently, yet firmly. And yes, as wrong as it was, she'd desperately wanted to make love to him.

She'd told herself that she wouldn't, but from the moment she'd laid eyes on him, she'd known it was going to happen. Her heart had begun racing, her body had heated up, and her nerves had whirled out of control. She'd missed him just as much as he'd missed her, and as soon as he'd kissed her, she'd known she was in trouble. It had been obvious that things were going to escalate and that there was a chance she wouldn't be able to leave without sleeping with him. If only she'd followed her first mind and not answered her phone when he'd called her again. By now, she'd be in Mitchell with Phillip, and life would be good. She certainly wouldn't have made the biggest mistake of her life. It was as if she hadn't learned a thing from the last affair she'd had with Levi. This time she wasn't married to Phillip, she was only engaged to him, but knowing that fact still wasn't making her feel any better about what she'd done. She'd fornicated, committed another sin, and gone behind Phillip's back with another man.

Alicia continued down the street and onto the highway that would take her back to her condo. She'd debated whether she should still go to Mitchell after all, but she just couldn't face Phillip. Not now. So she drove along in silence, weeping profusely at times and wondering how she was going to get beyond this.

When she was a little less than ten miles from her home, her phone rang. Phillip's name and number displayed across the dashboard of her car, and her nerves crept up a notch. She wasn't sure what to do, so she held the steering wheel tight and swallowed hard. Thankfully, the ringing stopped. But then he called right back, and she knew she'd better answer.

She sniffled a couple of times, trying to regain her composure. "Hello?"

"Hey baby, how's it going?" he said, and his words broke her heart. His tone was as upbeat and loving as always.

"Fine."

"I hope I didn't disturb you. The only reason I called back was because my phone

dropped the call before I could leave a message."

"No, I was taking a little break, and you
don't ever have to worry about disturbing
me because when I'm reading or writing, I
keep my phone on silent and in another
room."

"You sound like you're in the car."

"I am. Headed down to the convenience
store to pick up some snacks. I was actually
going to call you on my way back home."

"I wish I was there to do that for you. That
way you wouldn't have to go out."

"I know, but if you were here I wouldn't
get any reading done at all," she said as
silent tears seeped from her eyes. She
worked hard not to sniffle or sound nasal.
"Plus, I really needed some fresh air."

"I can imagine. Have you gotten quite a
bit read?"

"Not as much as I want, but maybe almost
half," she said, lying.

"That's a lot. Do you think you'll finish
tonight?"

"I doubt it. Probably tomorrow sometime."

"I really missed you today," he said. "I'm
getting to the point where I don't even like
to go a few hours without seeing you."

"I feel the same way."

"I didn't think it was possible, but I love you more now than I did before."

"I love you, too, baby."

"I hope you mean that, because this is my last marriage. This time, when I say until death do us part, I'll mean it literally."

"So will I," she said, swallowing more tears. "This is it for me, too."

"Oh, and hey, my mom said she tried to call you earlier. Something about two more of our relatives she wants to add to the guest list. She knows the invitations have gone out, but I told her you wouldn't mind sending them one."

Alicia hadn't bothered checking her phone for missed calls or messages, and now she wondered who else had called while she was with Levi.

"Of course. I'll give her a call later today or tomorrow."

"Just think," he said, genuinely excited. "In two months, we'll be heading to sunny Jamaica for ten whole days."

"Yeah, I know. I'm really looking forward to it," she said, wishing she could find an easy way to end their call. She wasn't sure how much longer she could go without crying out loud.

"We'll be all alone and able to catch up on all the lovemaking we've missed. Being celibate hasn't been easy, but I'm glad we did the right thing."

Alicia stopped at a red light and closed her eyes, replaying what she'd just done with Levi. She'd never felt more guilty in her life.

"Are you there, baby?" he asked.

"Yeah . . . um, I was just thinking about my manuscript and all the other stuff I need to get done this week."

"I hear you. I have a lot on my plate, too. Are you almost home?"

"Yes, only a couple of blocks away."

"Well, I'll let you go, then. But call me tonight before you turn in."

"I will," she said.

"I love you, baby. With all my heart."

"I love you, too."

When the light turned green, Alicia proceeded through the intersection and sobbed massive tears. She couldn't change what she'd done, but one thing was for sure. She would never see Levi again, and this time she meant it.

CHAPTER 12

Melanie flipped on the master bedroom television and turned it to one of the news channels. She stretched her arms toward the ceiling and went into the bathroom. She'd drunk a lot of water yesterday, so she'd been going in there a lot. This was a good thing, though, because water always helped flush out toxins and excess fat.

She removed her pajamas, stepped on the digital scale, and waited for it to register. After only one day of being on her new diet regimen, she'd already lost two pounds. She knew it was water weight, but she was still thrilled about it because it meant she was making progress.

Melanie slipped on her above-the-knee terry-cloth robe and walked back into the bedroom. Brad had just come back up from running on the treadmill.

"Good morning," he said, pulling the

towel from around his neck and wiping his face.

"Good morning. You were up early."

"Yep, since five o'clock. After you gave me all that good lovin' last night, I slept like a baby and now I'm wide awake."

Melanie shook her head, laughing. "Whatever."

"I'm surprised you're not downstairs working out yourself."

"I think I'll make some coffee first."

"And you're gonna drink it before you get on the treadmill?"

"Yeah, I read an article that said drinking coffee enhances your endurance, and it also maximizes your fat- and calorie-burning ability."

"I guess. Oh, and hey, when I leave the office this evening, why don't you meet me for dinner? A new steak restaurant opened a couple of weeks ago, and I heard it's excellent."

"I don't know, maybe tomorrow."

"Well, as much as I hate to tell you this, after today, I'll be knee-deep in this new case."

"Another big one so soon? And does this mean you won't be home until late every night again?"

"Baby, I'm sorry, but you know I don't

have a choice."

Melanie frowned. "I'm really tired of spending all these nights and weekends alone."

"I understand that, but what can I do? Quit?"

"If that's what it takes."

"Baby, be serious. You know I can't do that."

Melanie moved toward the doorway. "Sometimes I feel like I don't even have a husband."

"So you're just going to walk out right in the middle of our conversation?"

"What else is there to say?"

"Well, for one thing, it won't always be this way."

"It's already been this way for a while, and if anything it's getting worse."

"I'm sorry, but as a senior-level partner I have certain responsibilities that I have to live up to. You know that."

"I'm glad you've moved higher at the firm, but it's not doing much good for either of us if we can't spend any quality time together."

"That's why I at least want us to go out tonight and have a nice dinner."

Melanie wanted more than anything to be with Brad, but she also thought about her pledge to drink a shake for her last meal of the day. "If you don't mind, I'd rather not. I'm trying to cut back as much as I can."

"You can order something healthy. Baked fish, veggies. I'm sure they have much more than steaks on the menu."

"Yeah, but I don't want to be tempted by food I don't need."

"You're not obsessing over your weight again, are you?"

"No, I just don't wanna eat badly this week."

"Okay, fine. We can just have dinner here. I can pick up something on the way home."

Melanie hadn't planned on telling him yet, but she figured now was as good a time as any. "Until I lose all this weight, all I'm having is a salad for lunch and protein shakes for breakfast and dinner."

Brad raised his eyebrows. "Protein shakes? And that's all?"

"That's the plan."

"Well, what weight is it that you need to lose exactly?"

"Brad, please. Don't pretend you don't see all these bulges."

"I don't."

"You must be blind, then."

"Wait a minute. Didn't you say you had lunch with your mom yesterday? Was she trippin' about your weight again?"

"It's not about her. I decided to make these changes over the weekend."

"Have you looked in the mirror lately? Because if you get any smaller, you'll be skin and bones."

"I only have eight more pounds to go."

Brad dropped down on the bed. "Baby, why have you always been so unhappy with the way you look? Especially when you look fine. I mean, so what if you have a few bulges. I don't see any, but if you do, you can fix that with toning."

"I have to lose the weight first."

"Is that why you still won't change clothes in front of me? Why we never make love unless the room is dark?"

Melanie no longer wanted to talk about this. "Let's just leave well enough alone, okay?"

"Baby, I'm not trying to upset you, but not wanting to be naked in front of your own husband isn't normal. Especially when you don't have a thing to be ashamed of. Plus, I wouldn't care if you were thirty pounds overweight, I would still love you just the same."

"I don't expect you to understand."

"I really don't."

"And you probably never will, but this is

something I have to do for me."

Brad raised his hands in defeat.

Melanie turned toward the doorway. "I'm heading downstairs. You want any breakfast?"

"Thought you were having a shake?"

"I am, but I can still make you something."

"Don't worry about it. I'll get something on my way to the office."

Melanie knew he was angry, but she left the room anyway. There was no sense arguing about something Brad couldn't comprehend. He'd never had a weight problem and could eat whatever he wanted, so how could he possibly understand how she felt?

When she walked through the kitchen, she filled the coffeepot with enough water to make six cups and pushed the Start button. She was glad she'd already inserted the paper filter and poured in the coffee grounds the night before.

She took her multivitamin and then drank her pre-mixed protein shake, which tasted delicious. So far so good. Yesterday, she'd stuck to her plan and she'd lost two pounds, and now she felt energized. She knew that once she finished her workout, she'd feel even better.

But suddenly, out of nowhere, her mother's words struck her again and she didn't feel so great. *"You're looking like a size ten again."* Melanie sat down at the granite island and thought back to her childhood. Her parents had argued all the time, and while she'd hated listening to them, it hadn't compared to hearing the names her dad used to call her. Miss Tubby, Miss Butterball, and Mellie Melon. He would laugh out loud about it and hadn't seen a thing wrong with what he was saying, and as Melanie had gotten older, her self-esteem had diminished little by little. Her mother had never thought those nicknames were all that funny, however, and almost daily, she'd been furious with Melanie for being so heavy. So much so, her mother by-passed nicknames altogether and had flat-out told her she was fat. It was a wonder she'd still had enough confidence and courage to get her bachelor's degree in nursing and then two master's degrees. First, she'd completed a master's in nursing, and then she'd gone back to get a second master's with nurse practitioner specialization. She'd been practicing for two years, and the blessing, too, was that even though she hadn't had the best childhood, God had given her a wonderful husband and a career she loved.

Although, she had to admit, she was starting to worry about her marriage. It was bad enough that she and Brad rarely spent any special time together, but she also couldn't totally get beyond his terrible investment decisions. Or maybe this was all her fault. Maybe he was taking on monstrous cases and spending more and more time away from home because he no longer found her attractive. As recently as Saturday, he'd told her she looked "perfect," but she knew he'd only done so to make her feel good. Especially since she clearly *didn't* look perfect and needed to lose weight. He also still hadn't lost the desire to make love to her, but what man didn't want sex? A man certainly didn't have to love a woman or think she was beautiful in order to feel satisfied.

Melanie glanced over at the coffee, waiting for it to finish brewing. She tried thinking about the positive things going on in her life, but soon, she heard her mother's "size ten" words again. She couldn't stop replaying them, and she also remembered her mother's warning, something she hadn't focused on much until now: ". . . the last thing you need is to go losing him . . . appearances mean everything . . . you have a responsibility to keep yourself up." Her mother's voice was deafening, and Melanie's mind was made up. Today, she wouldn't even have a salad for lunch. She would go straight liquid for the next five days. She'd be down ten pounds — or more — in no time.

CHAPTER 13

It was seven a.m., but Alicia hadn't slept a
wink. She'd cried so much, her eyes were
nearly swollen shut. She'd tossed and
turned, gotten up and paced the bedroom
floor, and tossed and turned in bed again.
For the life of her, she *still* couldn't understand how she'd let something like this happen. Especially since she knew full well that
sleeping with Levi had been the very reason
she'd lost Phillip the first time. She wouldn't
lose Phillip again, though. She just wouldn't.
Not when she knew how much he loved her,
how much she loved him, and how good he
was for her. She'd spent four lengthy years
doing everything she could to regain his
trust, and finally, last year, he'd proposed.
At that moment, he'd made her the happi-
est woman in the world, and she'd shed
tears of joy before God. So there was no
way she was going to ruin things between
them. She'd made yet another grave mis-

take, but she was putting it all behind her. She would forget that yesterday ever happened. As it was, Levi had already called her twice last night and once this morning, but she'd ignored him. Interestingly enough, he hadn't left any voice messages, but she was sure it was because he was dead set on talking to her. When he called again, though, she would answer and explain things to him, letting him know that what they'd done should never have happened. She would tell him how much she loved Phillip and how she was going to marry him two months from now as planned. There was no doubt Levi would try to make his case, attempting to convince her otherwise, but this was the life she was choosing and he would have to accept it.

After Alicia went into the bathroom and washed her face with cold water, she walked downstairs to the kitchen. She turned on the television, pulled a bottle of sugar-free Cran-Apple juice from the refrigerator, and dropped down on one of the barstools. Hours had passed, yet she still couldn't get over the fact that she'd actually slept with Levi. She'd driven to a stranger's home to see him and slept with him like it was nothing. She'd allowed her flesh to manipulate her common sense, and she was ashamed of herself. Phillip deserved so much better than this, and if he ever found out about it, it would kill him.

But this, at least, was the one thing she wasn't worried about, because Levi wasn't the kind of man who played childish games. He'd reminded her of that when he'd emailed her two days ago. He would never tell Phillip or anyone else about the two of them sleeping together, and Alicia, of course, wouldn't tell anyone, either.

Alicia watched a few segments of CNN but found herself feeling more depressed. A few moments ago, she'd even gone as far as deciding that she hadn't slept with Levi after all and that this whole fiasco was nothing more than some horrible delusion. But she knew she was kidding herself and that not only had she made love with Levi, she'd done so willingly. This was the part that troubled her the most. Had Levi forced her to have sex with him or she'd just so happened to run into him by accident and one thing had led to another, she could place more of the blame on him. But, sadly, this wasn't the case. Alicia had done exactly what she'd wanted to do and hadn't done much at all to prevent it.

When she heard her phone ring, she rushed upstairs. She knew it was Levi, and she couldn't wait to end whatever he thought they had and be done with him for good. But when she picked up her phone and saw that it was Phillip, her stomach churned. She wasn't in the best shape to talk to him right now, but since she hadn't called him before bedtime last night the way he'd asked, she figured she'd better answer.

"Hello?"

"Hey, baby. Good morning."

"Hey. How are you?"

"Couldn't be better. But you on the other hand sound like you just woke up."

"No, I've been up for a while."

"Are you okay?"

"I'm fine."

"You also didn't sound like yourself when I talked to you yesterday."

Alicia had been sure she'd sounded normal, but apparently not normal enough.

"I'm good. Really."

"You must have read well into the middle of the night," he said.

"Close to it, but why do you say that?"

"Because you never called me back."

Alicia hated all the lying she was having to do to Phillip. "I know, baby, but it got late, and I was so exhausted."

"How much more do you have to do?"

"Maybe a little less than half," she said,

then quickly remembered that yesterday she'd told him a similar amount. "I added a whole new chapter and did a ton of rewrites, so that slowed my reading down quite a bit."

"The life of a writer. I'm sure you're drained."

"I am. I really hope to be finished reading by this evening, though."

"Are you sure you're okay?" he said.

"Please don't worry about me. I'm a little tired, but other than that I'm fine."

"Okay, well if there's something I can do for you just tell me."

"I really don't need anything, but thank you for asking."

"Of course. Well . . . I guess I'd better get dressed. We have two different staff meetings at the church today, and then I need to go visit two of our members at the hospital. But you call me when you take a break."

"I will, and you have good day, okay?"

"I love you, baby," he said.

"I love you more."

"Bye."

Alicia removed the phone from her ear and held it close to her chest. She rocked back and forth as tears flowed down her face. "Oh my God, baby, I am so, so sorry. I am so, so sorry I did this to you again."

She wiped her eyes, stood up, and went

back down to the kitchen. This time she took her phone with her, and it was less than ten minutes before Levi called her. Her hands trembled and her body tightened, but she knew she had to get this over with.

"Hello?"

"Hey, beautiful, how are you?"

"Not good."

"I'm sorry to hear that."

"Are you?"

"Of course I am. Why would I want you to be unhappy?"

"What we did never should have happened. Which is why I begged you to leave me alone. I told you I didn't want to see you."

"I hate that you're feeling so torn. You're caught in the middle of two men. One you feel obligated to be with and one you love from the bottom of your soul."

"Why do you keep saying that? How many times do I have to tell you that it's Phillip who I love?"

"Sweetheart, have you forgotten the way we made each other feel yesterday? We were so in sync that not even the best writer alive could properly describe it. What we shared was beautiful and very much meant to be."

Alicia held the phone in silence.

"You have to tell him," he said.

"Tell who what?"

"You have to tell your ex the truth. Otherwise, you're going to feel more miserable by the day. Maybe before you saw me again, it was easy to pretend you didn't love me, but now you can't deny anything."

"Love isn't everything."

Levi chuckled. "Are you listening to yourself? I mean, do you really believe what you're saying?"

"Why won't you just find someone else to be with?"

"Because there is no one else for me. All I want is to love and take care of you for the rest of my life."

"Not that any of this even matters, but how will you do that? What job are you gonna get?"

"I'm opening a restaurant. Mom still has hers there in Mitchell, but I'm opening an upscale one, the kind no other restaurant in town will be able to compare to."

"And what bank do you think is going to give an ex-drug-dealer a business loan?"

"I don't need one. Remember years ago, when I talked to you a couple of times on the phone?"

"And?"

"You said something about all my money being confiscated, even my offshore accounts, but what did I say?"

"I don't know."

"I told you that you obviously didn't know me very well."

"That's beside the point."

"I don't see how it is. Especially if you're worried about how we'll be able to pay bills and live the kind of life you've always been used to."

"Why won't you just accept that what we had was great, but it's over?"

"There's a chance that maybe I could have. But not after yesterday. When you and I were making love, you were exactly where you wanted to be. I knew you'd been thinking about me and wanting to be with me again for a long time. Way before I even emailed you on Saturday."

"That's not true," she said, although she knew she'd never fully gotten Levi out of her system. She wasn't sure she ever would, but she had also made up her mind to love, honor, and cherish Phillip. He was the man she wanted to spend the rest of her life with.

"It *is* true, and when are you going to come see me again?" he asked.

"I'm not. Once we hang up, you and I are finished. No more phone calls, no more visits, no anything."

"Remember before I was arrested, how

you and I would lay up for hours after making love, laughing, talking, and holding each other? Remember how you hated when it was time for you to go home?"

Alicia couldn't take this anymore. "Just stop. What we did yesterday was wrong, and I take full responsibility for it. All I can do now is ask God to forgive me, and move on. If you call me again, I won't be answering. If you send me messages, I'm going to delete them."

"We'll see."

"I mean it, Levi."

"So do I."

"You take care."

"You too."

Alicia ended the call and felt relieved. Maybe now Levi was finally taking her seriously. If for some reason he wasn't, that was his problem. It was something he'd have to deal with and get over on his own. She was marrying Phillip, and that was all that mattered.

CHAPTER 14

"Have you lost your mind?" Melanie shouted. "Really, Brad? Another ten thousand dollars?"

Brad had just gotten home and walked into the kitchen, but he was speechless.

From the time Melanie had entered the house two hours ago and gone through the mail, she'd been livid. In all the years they'd been together, she'd never been in the habit of opening any of Brad's letters, even if she did read through them after the fact. But ever since Brad had lost money last year, she'd sort of been on the lookout for his credit union statements. More so once she'd found out this past weekend that he'd lost another large sum of money. However, not for one moment had she expected to learn that Brad had squandered another ten grand. Normally, his statements arrived the first week of the month, but interestingly enough, this one was a few days late. Actually, she'd been so upset when she'd discovered the one on Saturday, she hadn't noticed that it didn't include the most recent figures.

"So when I asked you about the statement on Saturday, you knew all along that you'd lost more money and the one I was looking at was from last month."

"You never asked me one way or the other."

"But when you did all that apologizing, you knew full well that you'd already lost twenty thousand dollars."

Brad pursed his lips and removed his suit blazer. "I didn't tell you any different because you were already screaming and yelling at me like you were crazy."

"What did you expect? A kiss on the cheek?"

"Well, I meant what I said."

"About what?"

"That I was sorry, and I'm done buying stocks."

"And just like that you expect me to believe you? After you lied to me."

"I never lied about anything. I told you I was finished with it, and that was the truth."

"But you also conveniently left out the fact that you'd lost much more than the ten thousand I first asked you about."

"I made a mistake."

"How many times are you going to say that? I mean, how much more money will you lose a month from now?"

"None. I already told you this is over. It won't happen again."

"You need professional help."

"Excuse me?" he said, frowning.

"You need to see a psychologist. You've got a problem."

"Woman, please. I lost some money, and now I've got mental issues?"

"You really do."

"Yeah, right," he said, opening the refrigerator and pulling out a bottle of water.

"I'm serious. We need to find someone for you to see."

"I'm not doing that."

"Why?"

"Because I don't have a problem."

"You do have one. You might not be willing to admit it, but anytime someone loses twenty thousand dollars in two months, it's time to deal with it."

Brad scooted back a chair at the island and sat down. He turned up his water bottle and looked at her. "And what about you? When are *you* gonna deal with your problems?"

"First of all, this isn't about me. And

regardless of what you think, I don't have any."

Brad laughed out loud. "Yeah, okay, Mel. Whatever you say."

"I don't."

"Uh-huh."

"Why are you trying to turn this whole thing on me?"

"I'm not. Just pointing out the fact that you've got issues, too."

"I'm fine."

"Oh, really? Are you fine when you hide your body from your own husband?"

"This isn't about me."

"Are you fine when you walk around here dieting? Losing a few pounds and then gaining them right back? It's a vicious cycle. I never say much about it, but I'm definitely aware of it."

"What's wrong with being healthy and wanting to look good?"

"Nothing, if it's within reason. You're trying to lose weight you barely have, and it's all because of your parents. They really messed you up, Mel."

Melanie glared at him. "Why are you bringing my parents into this?"

"Because it's time you owned up to it. You're so quick to tell me to get help, but you're not even woman enough to handle your own drama."

"I don't believe you."

"I'm just tired of you harping on me about these couple of mistakes I made. And it's not like this is *your* money, anyway. This came from my individual account."

Melanie's laugh was sarcastic. "Oh, so now what's yours is yours, and what's mine is mine? All because you don't wanna hear what I have to say?"

Brad thumbed through some magazines on the island as though he couldn't care less about what she was saying. She'd never seen him so angry and defensive about anything, not since they'd begun dating and certainly not since they'd been married.

"I just think you're taking this judging and criticizing thing too far," he said. "I lost some money, and there's not a thing we can do to get it back. So to me, it's pointless to keep talking about it."

"Are you saying you can do whatever you want, and I don't have the right to say anything?"

"No, but I also don't wanna talk about this anymore. I have a lot of work to do."

Melanie didn't bother saying anything else. She turned and walked out of the kitchen and up to their bedroom. Something wasn't right. Just last night, they'd enjoyed a great evening together, and Brad's attitude had also been good this morning. Now he was talking to her like he couldn't stand her. She understood that he wasn't proud of what he'd done and that he wasn't happy about the way she'd been questioning him. But his tone was curt, and he'd brought her parents into the scheme of things. He'd never done that before, and Melanie wasn't sure how she felt about it. She knew he'd made his comments during the heat of an argument, but he acted as though he was purposely trying to hurt her. Then, there'd been his statement about her barely having any weight to lose. He couldn't have been more wrong about that, and she had to wonder if maybe he didn't care whether she looked her best or not. Melanie had never considered it before, but for all she knew, his late nights at the office had actually become late nights with another woman. She didn't want to think the worst, but Brad was doing and saying things that weren't familiar to Melanie, and she wasn't sure what it meant.

Melanie changed out of her work clothes and threw on some shorts and a T-shirt. She slipped on her socks and gym shoes and went downstairs. She'd already worked out on the treadmill this morning before leaving for work, but she'd decided this afternoon that it was time to double up on exercising. She'd get in at least an hour in the mornings and also in the evenings. She was proud, too, that she'd made it through the entire day with only three shakes. About an hour ago, she'd started to feel a bit hungry, but she'd drunk a bottle of water with Crystal Light, and it had done the trick. She knew tomorrow and the next day might not be easy, but if she could make it past those, she'd be good. If she kept losing at the rate she was expecting, she'd be down to 155 pounds in less than ten days. Maybe sooner. Either way, she'd be back into her size eights and would be happy again. Her mother would be happy, too, and maybe things would be better between her and Brad. Maybe he'd realize that he truly did need help and would get it.

CHAPTER 15

Alicia still wasn't finished reading her manuscript, but she'd driven over to Mitchell for Wednesday night Bible study anyway. After the torturous time she'd spent yesterday and all of today trying to block out her sexcapade with Levi, she was more shrouded with guilt than before. She'd worried herself into a frenzy, and all she could hope was that through prayer, studying scripture, and listening to her father's words, she'd feel better. So far, she hadn't been able to think about anything else, and now sitting next to her beloved fiancé made her feel worse. She had betrayed him in the most malicious way, and she wanted to scream at the top of her lungs, begging God to forgive her. She knew she would eventually get past this, but she just wanted that to be sooner rather than later.

Phillip held her hand, smiling, and more guilt slithered its way into her psyche. Then, sitting on the other side of her was Melanie, and Alicia couldn't look her straight in her face either, fearing Melanie might notice something was wrong. They'd been best friends for a long time, and it wouldn't take much for Melanie to realize there was a problem. Thank goodness her father was getting ready to begin, so Alicia could switch her full attention to whatever he'd be teaching.

Curtis stood at the front of the church in a pair of jeans and a powder-blue dress shirt.

"Good evening."

"Good evening," everyone said in unison.

"I'm glad you could make it out, because no matter who you are, I think you'll be able to relate to tonight's lesson. The topic is Temptation and the Tricks of the Devil."

Alicia was stunned. It was as if her father had chosen this subject on purpose and would be speaking to her directly. But there was no way he knew about what she'd done. It was true that her father was well connected and that he could find out just about anything he wanted, but not this. Not about her indiscretion with Levi. Plus, when she'd first arrived at the church an hour ago and had gone to her dad's study, he'd hugged her and welcomed her with open arms the same as always. He'd been happy to see her, and everything had felt normal.

"You know," Curtis continued, "there are so many times when we've done things that could have been prevented . . . if only we'd kept our faith in God. If only we had seriously kept Him first in our lives the way we proclaim to others. Maybe if we kept our minds fixed on Jesus and we made a conscious habit of praying without ceasing, the devil wouldn't be able to trick us so often. And let's be clear about something else. Temptation will continue to rear its ugly head until the end of time, but if we trust, believe, and stand on God's Word, we won't struggle with it as much. If we focus on doing what we know God wants us to do versus what *we* want to do, temptation won't have a fighting chance in our lives."

"Amen," many of the members said.

"So, if you would, please turn with me to Matthew twenty-six, forty-one," Curtis said, flipping through his standard print version of the Bible — unlike Phillip, Alicia's dad still preferred paper. He was technologically savvy on all accounts and even owned an Android tablet, but he never used it for Bible study.

"Are you all there?" he asked.

Everyone said, "Yes."

"And it reads like this: 'Watch and pray

that you may not enter into temptation. The spirit indeed is willing, but the flesh is weak,' " Curtis said. "Now, to me, this scripture tells you very clearly that we'll always be tempted by something because our flesh is weak. With food, sex, money, alcohol, drugs, you name it. But just knowing that if you have a faithful spirit . . . if you truly want to uplift God, then the only way to accomplish that is by watching and praying. You have to be mindful of your thoughts and desires, particularly if those thoughts and desires are sinful."

Alicia's eyes filled with tears, but she stopped them from falling. If only she'd thought long and hard before going to meet Levi, and she had prayed a little more than she had, asking God to give her strength. If only . . . but she hadn't.

"I'd also like you to turn to First Peter, five and eight," he said, waiting a few seconds for the members to locate the scripture. "Here, the Bible says, 'Be sober-minded; be watchful. Your adversary the devil prowls around like a roaring lion, seeking someone to devour.' In other words, the enemy ain't no punk. And yes, I said 'ain't' and not 'isn't,' " he said, laughing, and so did the congregation. "But in all seriousness, the enemy is cunning and he's always on the lookout for his next victim. Take me, for example; you all know my history and that for many years, I was nothing nice. I stood in the pulpit on Sundays and did whatever I pleased as soon as I walked out of it. But thank God, today, I'm no longer allowing the devil to devour *me.* He still prowls around, trying to destroy me and my family, but I'm always aware of it. Sometimes I can feel his presence, and when I do, I remember Ephesians six and eleven. You don't have to turn to it, but it says, 'Put on the whole armor of God, that you may be able to stand against the schemes of the devil.' "

A middle-aged woman raised her hand.

"Yes, Sister Marshall," Curtis said.

The woman stood up. "First, I just want to say how happy I am that you're talking about temptation tonight. As you know, I've been clean and sober for five years, but lately it's really been a struggle. I don't want to use again, but sometimes I can hear a voice in my head, swearing that if I take just one hit, I'll be able to walk away and never do it again. I'm still going to my meetings, but my thoughts have really started to scare me."

"That's understandable, and the reason the enemy is speaking to you and trying to trick you is because he knows what your weakness is. He's feeding you every lie he can conjure up, waiting for you to fall prey to his deception. And all this means is that you're going to have to pray even more diligently and frequently than you have been. In addition to that, I, along with Pastor Sullivan, will also pray with you before you leave here this evening."

"I really appreciate that, Pastor."

"That's what we're here for, and thank you for standing up and being honest. I realize that's not always easy to do, but being transparent is the only way any of us can get the help we need. The other thing, too, is that you can best believe you're not the only person in here struggling with temptation. Wondering what to do and how to fight it. But the God we serve is true to His Word, and that's what we're going to stand on."

Sister Marshall took her seat, and Alicia tuned her father out altogether. She could barely sit still because during her drive over to Mitchell, she'd heard a voice telling her that maybe Levi was right. Maybe being with the man she was most attracted to was the right thing to do — being with the man who drove her wild with the kind of pleasure and excitement she couldn't seem to get enough of. She'd dismissed that voice and continued on her way, but now, as she sat between Phillip and Melanie and looked toward her father, she heard the voice again. *Everyone deserves to be happy. Follow your heart. Do what makes you feel good. Call Levi and tell him you want to see him.*

Alicia wished she could run out of there. Wished she hadn't bothered to come to Bible study period. She'd thought her dad would make her feel better, but if anything, all he'd done was convince her that the devil was after her and he wasn't going to let up. She wasn't sure how to deal with something like that because the scripture he'd just read, Matthew 26:41, described her far too well. Her spirit was indeed willing, but her flesh was weak. And she couldn't help the way she felt. She didn't want to care about Levi, or actually be with him for that matter, but she was drawn to everything about him. The way he treated her, the way he talked to her, and how good he looked. She'd been trying to deny her real feelings for him, but somehow sitting here in the Lord's house, of all places, she'd discovered what the truth was.

Alicia snapped out of her trance and heard her father reading out loud, " 'Do not be conformed to this world, but be transformed by the renewal of your mind, that by testing you may discern what is the will of God, what is good and acceptable and perfect.' " Alicia recognized Romans 12:2 right away, as her father had recited that scripture on many occasions. He'd always loved the entire book of Romans — his favorite was chapter 7 — because of the way he identified with Paul.

Alicia watched her father and everyone else studying scripture and discussing the topic of the devil and temptation, but all she wanted was to head back to Covington Park. She knew Phillip would want her to spend the night there in Mitchell, but she couldn't take the chance of his seeing how bewildered she was. There was a part of her that wanted nothing more than to listen to that relentless voice in her head, but there was also the part of her that loved Phillip — the part that was indebted to him for forgiving her, loving her, and trusting her again.

So what was she going to do? How was she going to get herself out of this mess of a situation? She had no answers, and she guessed only time would tell.

CHAPTER 16

Melanie opened her long plush robe and let it drop to the floor. She even removed the silver chain-link bracelet that she'd left on by accident before going to bed. She never wanted anything, not even jewelry or underwear, adding to her final body weight. At the office, some people never so much as took off heavy athletic shoes when the nurse asked them to step onto the scale, but Melanie had learned a long time ago that certain shoes or jeans could add as much as three pounds that weren't yours.

She stood on the scale and waited for the digital readout. She'd lost another two pounds, and she was ecstatic. This made a total of four pounds in just three days, so she could tell that doubling up her workouts had helped make a difference. What she'd also noticed is how now that she'd made it past her third day, she didn't feel hungry during most hours, which meant eating no food and only drinking shakes would be a breeze.

She strolled down the hallway and entered their spacious walk-in closet. Melanie's clothing, both dress and casual, lined top and bottom racks on one wall, and Brad's was on the opposite one. The back wall held their shoes, and a large island-like wooden square in the center housed a number of dresser drawers. Melanie opened one of them and pulled out a T-shirt, a sports bra, and a pair of workout pants. After she slipped everything on, she walked out to the bedroom and sat on the edge of the bed, putting on her socks and gym shoes. Brad had worked out and showered much earlier than normal and was already getting dressed for work, but since they still weren't speaking, she didn't question him. After their big blow-up on Tuesday evening, they'd gone to bed angry and had turned their backs to each other like enemies. Then, yesterday morning, they'd said barely ten words. Melanie hated when they were fighting, but she also wanted Brad to know how serious this was and that she wouldn't tolerate the way he was throwing away his life's savings. She'd actually wanted to make up with him last night, but by the time she'd gotten home from Bible study he'd still been working in his office on the first floor, and she'd gone to bed. She wasn't even sure what time he'd come upstairs, although the fact that they'd gone to sleep a second night without talking did bother her.

Melanie remembered a number of things from the premarital counseling sessions they'd had with Pastor Black, but one of his suggestions had stood out the most: "No matter how angry you get or how heated your argument is, never, ever go to bed mad and not speaking." Both Melanie and Brad had taken that piece of advice to heart, and they'd always honored it until this week.

When Melanie finished tying her shoe-laces, she saw Brad inserting a cuff link into the left sleeve of his shirt. He could certainly do that on his own, but normally he asked her to do it for him just because. It was sort of their ritual whenever he wore French-cuff dress shirts. Melanie stood up and Brad looked at her through the mirror.

"So how long is this going to go on?" he asked.

"I don't know. You tell me."

"Whether you believe me or not, I meant what I said. I won't let this kind of thing happen again."

"I hope that's true," she said, moving closer to the door.

Brad grabbed her arm and pulled her toward him, holding her. "I'm sorry. I'm embarrassed, and I'm sorry I upset you."

Melanie hugged him back. "I'm really worried about us. We're still not spending quality time together, and lately, we've argued about everything. We're so disconnected."

"We're gonna be fine, and as soon as this case is settled or the trial is over, we're taking a vacation somewhere. No less than seven days."

"I would love that."

"Then you should start looking. Wherever you wanna go will be great."

"Any tropical island will do."

"Sounds good to me, baby," he said, pecking her on the lips and releasing her. "And as much as I hate to run, I really need to get to the office to prepare for an eight o'clock meeting."

They kissed again, Brad grabbed his black leather briefcase, and they walked down to the kitchen. Melanie felt so much more relaxed and was glad they'd made up. But then their home phone rang, and her parents' name and number displayed on the caller ID screen.

"Gosh, not this early in the morning," Melanie said out loud, debating whether to answer. If it were her father calling she wouldn't feel so hesitant, but since her father rarely called anybody, she knew it had to be her mother. It was better to get this over with now, however, rather than later, because she knew her mother would keep calling until she spoke with her.

"Hello?" Melanie said.

"What took you so long? One more ring, and it would have gone to voice mail."

"I was getting ready to work out."

"Good. Because ever since I saw you at lunch the other day, I haven't been able to stop thinking about it. Overeating and not controlling your appetite goes against God's Word. Proverbs twenty-three, verse two, says, 'And put a knife to your throat if you are given to appetite.' As a matter of fact, overdoing anything is a sin."

Was she serious? Melanie knew she needed to lose weight and that she had to do a better job of watching what she ate, but now she was breaking God's law?

"Mom, I really don't think that applies to me. I'm not some glutton. I'm not obsessed with food. I just have a hard time staying a certain size."

"Then you're not praying about it enough. You're not focused on it the way you should be."

"Mom, I have to go."

"Wait. The reason I called you is to see what you and Brad are planning for your dad. You know this Sunday is Father's Day. To be honest, I've been a little mad at him, so I wasn't planning to celebrate anything. I'm over it now, though."

"Brad's working a lot of hours, but we'll definitely get by there to bring Dad his gift."

"And that's it? What about dinner?"

"Does Dad even wanna go to dinner? You know how laid-back he is."

"Of course he wants to go. What, you don't want to take him?"

"I never said that."

"Well, that's what it sounds like to me. You only have one father, Melanie. And only one mother, for that matter. We hardly ever see you as it is. Maybe for a few minutes after church on Sundays, and then at Bible study you always sit with Alicia and Phillip."

Melanie didn't respond, because she knew what her mother was saying was true. She did keep her distance. And who wouldn't? What child in her right mind would purposely spend lots of time with a mother who treated her like she wasn't good enough and never would be? Then, as far as Melanie's father, he'd stopped criticizing her a long time ago, but because he'd ridiculed her for so many years, their relationship was still pretty strained, too. As a child, Melanie had learned to guard her feelings as best as she could, and this had meant blocking the special kind of love most children had for their parents. She'd figured out at an early age that if you stopped yourself from loving and caring about someone, that same someone wouldn't be able to hurt you as badly. You would still be hurt, but not to nearly the same extent.

"Are you still there, Melanie?"

"I'm here, Mom, and yes, we'll meet you and Dad for dinner on Sunday. I'll make reservations somewhere today."

"No need. I already made them yesterday."

Melanie shook her head. "Where?"

"At The Tuxson, of course. I know it's the most expensive restaurant in town, but it's not like you and Brad can't afford it."

"Is that all?"

"Since you're rushing me off the phone, I guess it is. Oh, and it might be nice if you wore that new suit of yours. The fuchsia one."

"So now the clothes I wear to church aren't good enough, either?"

"No, they're fine. For whatever reason, you always buy nice dress suits. I'm just letting you know which color looks good on you. But never mind, you wear what you want. I'll talk to you later."

When they hung up, Melanie had to take a deep breath. Her mother always wore her out, whether on the phone or in person, and she was already dreading this dinner date on Father's Day. Melanie didn't mind going out with her dad, but her mother was a different story. She also wasn't sure what she was going to do when it came time to order something from the menu. Although, if she lost at least another two pounds by Sunday and worked out both before church and before going to bed that evening, she was sure she could have a salad and not ruin her progress. Yes, a salad, a glass of water, and nothing else would be fine.

CHAPTER 17

Alicia's phone rang, and she looked over at the clock. It was already noon, and Phillip was calling from the church.

"Hey," she said.

"Hey, you. Were you sleeping?"

"No, just tired, so I decided to lie down for a while."

"Nothing wrong with that. I'm sure your eyes need a break from all that reading, anyway. How much more do you have?"

"I'm almost finished."

"Good. Well, it's not like I was calling for anything in particular. Just wanted to tell you I love you."

"I love you, too."

"I'm so glad tomorrow is Friday, so we can spend the next three days together. This sleeping-in-separate-cities thing is starting to get old."

"I know," she said. "I feel the same way."

"I'm actually planning to work only half a

day tomorrow; that way I can drive over early afternoon instead of tomorrow evening."

"That'll be great."

"If you finish up with your manuscript, maybe we can get some dinner and catch a movie."

"Sounds good to me."

"Okay, then, I guess I'll let you go. Especially since somebody needs to get back to work," he said, laughing.

"Yeah, I really do, and I'm going to as soon as we hang up."

"Call me tonight. And again, baby, I love you."

"I love you, too."

Alicia ended the call and set her phone on the nightstand. She laid her head back on the pillow and covered her face with both hands.

Levi turned toward her, propping his elbow on the bed. "Sweetheart, you're going to have to tell him the truth."

"I'll never be able to do that. I just can't."

"Baby, we can't go on like this forever."

"Levi, I shouldn't even be here. You know that, and so do I."

"But you are here. And you came because you wanted to."

Sadly, Levi was right. Because last night,

when Alicia had left Bible study to drive back to her condo, it had taken everything in her not to call Levi to ask him to meet her at his friend's house. But thankfully, after praying, she'd made it home without contacting him. She still hadn't been able to keep her mind off him, though, and this morning Levi had texted her, telling her he wanted to see her. She'd told herself once again that she would go meet him but only so she could break things off with him forever. She'd been sure she'd be strong enough to do it, especially after hearing her dad teach on the subject he'd chosen for Bible study, but her desire for Levi had been more fierce than she'd realized.

Now the two of them had been in bed for the last two hours.

Levi stroked her hair. "The only way out of this is to tell him the wedding is off. You need to be honest with him about everything."

Alicia finally removed her hands from her face and looked at Levi. "How many times do I have to tell you that I can't hurt Phillip like that? I could never put him through that kind of pain again."

"Don't you think you're hurting him worse by being with me behind his back?"

"Yeah, but the difference is he doesn't

know about it. He would never guess in ten lifetimes that I would betray him like this again. Especially with the same man I slept with before."

"If you and I weren't supposed to be together, you would have already married him. I also wouldn't be out of prison. I told you the other day that you can't stop destiny. This is ours, and you can't change that."

"I disagree. Because just last night, my dad was talking about temptation and how even if you want to do the right thing, sometimes the flesh won't allow you."

"Matthew twenty-six, forty-one, right?"

"I guess you really have been reading the Bible."

"Did you think I was lying when I told you that?"

"No, but not everyone can remember the exact chapter and verse of a certain scripture. Plus, it wasn't like I actually quoted what my dad said word for word."

"Doesn't matter. I recognize lots of scriptures, and if you wanna know the truth, I've had to study and recite that one a lot."

"Why?"

"So I won't be drawn back into the life. I promised God that if He got me out of prison, I wouldn't sell drugs or do anything illegal."

"It must be hard giving up the kind of money you were used to making."

"Yeah, but I wanna do the right thing. I want to live a plain ol' normal life like most people."

"I know you mentioned starting a business, and I think that will be good for you."

"It'll be good for us."

Alicia stared at him but didn't respond.

"I'm serious. I'm opening an upscale restaurant just like I told you. I'm also planning to buy a home not too far from it, and I was hoping you would help me look. You know, once I decide on the restaurant location."

Alicia sighed. "Look, I won't lie to you. I am in love with you, and I do wish I could be with you . . . the right way, but I can't. I'm still marrying Phillip, Levi."

"Baby, how long are you going to keep this up?"

"What?"

"This fantasy you're living. You're not in love with that man, but you're going to marry him?"

"I know you don't understand, but this is the only way."

"But why?"

"I owe him. Plus, Phillip has been there for me. I mean, how could I walk away from a man I treated so badly when he took me back and forgave me for everything? We hadn't been married a year when I started sleeping around on him with you. I never even gave our marriage a chance, and it wasn't like Phillip had done anything wrong in the first place. He's a good man who has always loved me."

"But none of that matters, because you're not in love with him."

"But the other thing, too, is my father, the rest of my family, and the church. Things have been going great, and I just don't have it in me to cause another scandal. If I called things off with Phillip and married you, we would never hear the end of it. Every media outlet locally and around the country will be reporting on Pastor Black's daughter and how she married a drug dealer."

"But I'm not a drug dealer. Not anymore."

"It won't matter. Everyone will still see you as being one, no matter what you say. Maybe years down the road, people will see that you've honestly changed, and they'll stop talking. But even then, some people will start talking about how you *used* to be a drug dealer, how you did time in prison, et cetera, et cetera, et cetera. It'll never end."

"Baby, we all make mistakes, and if God has forgiven me, so should everyone else."

"But they won't."

"So you're more worried about gossip than you are about being happy? You're more focused on other people's opinions?"

"No, I'm just being real."

"What you're trying to do is be logical. You're worried about everyone else and not about you and me. Baby, life is too short to live the rest of our days unhappy, and that's exactly what you'll be forcing us to do if you marry that man."

Alicia looked away from him and toward the ceiling. "You just don't get it. You never will."

"You're right. Not when you're saying you want to walk away from me for good."

"This isn't about what I want; it's what I have to do."

"You're really starting to frustrate me," he said. "This junk is painful."

"I'm sorry," she said, looking at him again.

"Can I ask you something?"

"Go ahead."

"Even if you marry him, do you really think you'll be able to stop seeing me? Making love to me?"

"I do. I know you might not believe that, but I won't commit adultery again."

Levi turned over on his back and laughed. "You never cease to amaze me."

"I'm serious."

He glanced over at her, but his smile vanished. "Sweetheart, what you and I have is forever. You can get married and even move to another country. But I'm the only man you'll ever love."

Alicia sat up, preparing to swing her legs over the side of the bed. But Levi pulled her back down and lay on top of her.

Alicia tried to push him away. "Levi, please stop. I have to go."

Levi kissed her and didn't say a word.

Alicia could no longer think of anything to say, either, and before long, she surrendered. She loved every bit of what he was doing to her, and sadly, she feared Levi was right. What if he actually was the only man she could ever love? What if no other man, including Phillip, could ever make her feel the way Levi was making her feel at this very moment?

She couldn't worry about that now, though. Not when Levi was giving her everything she needed — all the beautiful love and intense pleasure she wanted so desperately.

He gave her what she'd been missing for far too many years.

CHAPTER 18

Melanie pumped her arms back and forth, breathing in and out. It was shortly after six in the evening, and she'd been power walking on the treadmill for forty minutes. She was sweating heavily, her heart rate averaged 165, and she was planning to keep it that way for as long as she could. This wouldn't be hard to do as long as she continued her current pace of 4.8 miles per hour. Melanie also loved how exhilarating it felt when her body released endorphins, and the euphoria alone was reason enough to work out more than once a day.

Melanie lifted the cold bottle of water from the cup holder, took a couple of swigs, and set it back down. Then she picked up the TV selector from the other drink slot, flipped through a few channels, and settled on a rerun of *Good Times*. James and Florida Evans loved and encouraged all three of their children, and while Melanie always enjoyed watching them, there were times when the show made her sad. And rightfully so, given that her own parents had been just the opposite. It was true that Melanie hadn't lived in poverty the way the children on the show had, but Thelma, Michael, and J.J. had still been blessed with a more loving household.

Melanie watched more of the *Good Times* episode and then increased the incline of the treadmill. That way she'd be able to burn more calories. But as she worked harder on her uphill climb and watched more laughter and happy times among the Evanses, a fusion of sweat and depressing tears poured down her face. Maybe she was as messed up as Brad had said she was, and she actually did need professional help. She'd been raised in so much dysfunction, she'd buried most of it in the back of her mind, and she had to think hard just to remember certain events. But for some reason, she suddenly thought about a number of terrible things that had gone on in her parents' household — certain things she'd never told another living soul, except Alicia.

Like, for instance, there was the time she'd heard her mother telling her father that what he needed to do was take a class or something, because his sexual skills were just plain pathetic. Then, to add insult to injury, she'd told him that she needed a man who was packing something a lot bigger than he was carrying. She needed someone who knew how to make her scream. Melanie remembered how at seven years old she hadn't known everything, but she'd known exactly what that had meant. It wasn't long after that when her parents had become swingers. Sometimes they had gone to a swingers club, sometimes to another couple's home, and sometimes they'd invited another couple to their own house. Whenever they did this, they sent Melanie to her room and told her to stay there until they said she could come out. Or they told her she could go spend the night with a friend. Sometimes when Melanie stayed home, however, she would crack her door open, sneak down the stairs to their lower level, and see things she shouldn't have. But until this day, her parents didn't know that.

Melanie's eyes filled with tears again. Her childhood had been beyond disturbing, as her parents would fuss, cuss, and physically fight whenever they got drunk enough. But finally, right before she'd started high school, things had changed. Her dad had been in a near-fatal car accident, her parents had become closer, and they'd stopped arguing, fighting, and swinging for good. Melanie hadn't understood how they could make such a drastic turnaround in the way they felt about each other, but she'd once heard her mother telling a friend that she'd never fully appreciated her husband until she thought she was going to lose him. Then, not long after her dad had been released from a two-month hospital stay, he'd realized how short life was and that all he wanted was to be at peace. What this had basically meant was that her father had made up his mind to go along with whatever her mother said or did. He never disagreed with her, and life was good for them. It was almost as if he no longer had an opinion about anything, not even Melanie's weight. They'd also become "devout Christians," as her mother tended to say, yet she judged, belittled, and made Melanie feel bad every chance she got. It was the reason Melanie had wished all her life that she'd had different parents, and, she was ashamed to say, she still felt the same today.

What was also interesting was how her mother never treated Melanie badly in front of Brad, Alicia, or anyone else she knew. She had, of course, made a few snide comments about Melanie's weight in front of them, but she never spoke rudely or as harshly to Melanie as she did when they weren't around. She acted as though she and Melanie had the best mother-daughter relationship, and like she was the kindest person on Earth. What was sadder was that Melanie had always led Alicia to believe that was true. When Alicia said things such as, "Mel, your parents are the ideal couple" or "Mel, your parents are the kind of people to look up to," Melanie agreed with her, and she sometimes told Alicia she was proud to call them her parents. She wasn't sure why, but she just couldn't admit to anyone, not even her best friend, that her parents basically just lived together and her mother couldn't stand her own daughter.

Melanie heard the home phone ringing but kept up her pace on the treadmill. She wasn't about to stop her workout when she was this close to the end, so whoever was calling would have to try back. But as she continued her stride, the home phone rang again. Still Melanie didn't answer it. She wondered who it could be, especially with them calling back, and it wasn't until the phone rang a third time that she paused the treadmill. She stepped off and ran to answer it, but when she saw her mother's number she rolled her eyes.

"Hello?" she said, practically out of breath.

"Where are you?" her mother yelled. "I've been calling both your phones over and over."

"I was on the treadmill, and my cell is upstairs."

"Well, you need to get over to the hospital. Your dad was doubled over with chest pains, and I'm following him in the ambulance now."

"Oh no. Which hospital?"

"Mitchell Memorial."

"I'm on my way."

CHAPTER 19

Melanie rushed inside the hospital. While she'd witnessed hundreds of medical emergencies at this very location when she'd worked there, she'd never felt as worried or nervous as she did now.

She hurried toward the reception area, but as she looked toward the family waiting room, she saw her mother and her mother's snooty friend Freda.

Melanie walked over to her mom and sat in the chair next to her. "Have you heard anything? Has the doctor been out yet?"

"No, all they keep saying is that they're working on him."

"What happened exactly?"

"Your dad had been complaining of indigestion all day, so he finally took some antacids."

"Has he had problems with that before?"

"Not until the last few days, and that's only because he's been eating pork skins left and right. I told him to cut it out, and that's why I'd been upset with him over the last couple of weeks. But then yesterday and today he didn't go buy any."

Melanie sure hoped this wasn't the reason her mom had been so mad at him she hadn't been planning to celebrate Father's Day. This morning, she'd told Melanie that she'd gotten over it, and this was when she'd called her to see if they were going to dinner on Sunday. Although, when it came to eating fattening junk food, her mother could hold grudges against anyone. It angered her to a point of insanity, and it likely hadn't helped that Melanie's dad wasn't as slim as he used to be. He wasn't severely overweight, but his body wasn't as taut as it had been a couple of years ago, and his stomach hung over his belt.

"What time did the indigestion start?" Melanie asked.

"Late morning, I guess. It was a couple of hours or so after I called you."

"And what about his chest pains?"

"Not until this afternoon, but then they seemed to go away. Until this evening, and that's when he was doubled over, sweating, trying to catch his breath and holding his left arm."

"Was he conscious when the ambulance came?"

"Barely."

Melanie didn't tell her mother what she was thinking, because no matter how little her mother minded hurting Melanie's feelings, she didn't want to upset Gladys any more than she had to. Still, she knew that none of what she'd just heard was a good sign. Her father might have had a heart attack, and maybe blocked arteries were involved. Which meant that by now, they'd likely given him nitroglycerin and heparin. The first would relax his blood vessels and the second would prevent blood clotting. She had so many thoughts and questions, and if she could, she would make her way back to her dad's room and take control of the situation. This was how every medical professional felt when someone they loved was in crisis.

"Do you think it was definitely a heart attack?" her mother asked.

"I don't know. It's hard to say."

"But do you *think* he had a heart attack? That's all I'm asking, Mel."

"I honestly don't know for sure. We'll have to wait until we hear more."

Freda, who was sitting on the other side of Gladys, leaned forward and raised her eyebrows at Melanie. "You went and got all that schooling, and you can't tell your mother anything?"

Melanie swallowed and took a deep breath, because the last thing she wanted to do was disrespect her mother's friend. "First of all, I'm not a cardiologist, and secondly, I wasn't there when my dad was having all those symptoms. And I don't want to guess just to be guessing."

Freda leaned back in her chair. "Hmmph."

Melanie knew it would be too much to hope that her mother would tell her friend that she had no right speaking to her daughter that way. And knowing Gladys, she was enjoying every bit of it. Freda had never liked Melanie, and she knew it was because Freda felt as though Melanie didn't visit her parents often enough. Of course, she was sure Freda had no idea what Melanie's true relationship was with her parents, but even if she had, it wouldn't give her the right to say anything out of the way to Melanie.

They sat and waited another half hour, and Melanie could tell her mother was a wreck. She wore the same look of terror she'd had on her face the night Melanie's dad had been in that car accident. That had been a long time ago, but Melanie had never forgotten how frightened her mother had been. Probably because Gladys had never seemed afraid of anything before or since then.

"I just don't know what I'll do if something happens to Andrew," Gladys said, sniffling.

Freda pulled a couple of tissues from her purse and passed them to her. "Andrew is going to be fine. God is going to see to it."

Gladys patted tears from her eyes and the sides of her cheeks. "I told him to stop eating all that junk, but he just wouldn't listen."

Melanie knew there was a chance her mother might be right, but did everything always have to be about food? Food, food, and more food. Her mother was obsessed.

They sat for a few more minutes, and Melanie prayed her father would be okay. She also wished she could take back what she'd been thinking while watching *Good Times*. That after all these years, she still wished she had different parents.

Melanie stood up. "I'll be right back, Mom."

"Where are you going?"

"To make a couple of calls."

Melanie walked outside the ER entrance and dialed Alicia. She'd already called Brad when she was driving to the hospital, and he'd told her he would be on his way very soon.

Alicia's phone rang until it went to voice mail. Last night at Bible study, Alicia had mentioned something about having to read through the rest of her manuscript, so maybe she wasn't finished yet.

"Hey, Alicia, it's Mel. My dad was rushed to the hospital, and it sounds like he may have had a heart attack. We don't know anything for sure, but I wanted to let you know. Call me as soon as you can. We're at Mitchell Memorial. Love you. Bye."

Melanie went back inside, and after another half hour, the silver-headed cardiologist, Dr. Daniels, introduced himself and led Melanie, her mother, and Freda into a smaller and more private family room.

"Well, Mrs. Johnson," he said. "It's a good thing I hadn't left the hospital yet, because your husband definitely had a heart attack, and he needs a quadruple bypass. The angiogram confirmed it."

Melanie's stomach tied in knots, and her mother and Freda gasped at the same time. Melanie had feared the worst, and it was.

"Your husband is a very sick man, but we're going to do the absolute best we can for him. We have him stabilized, and we'd like to get him prepped so we can get started as soon as possible."

"Is he awake?" Melanie asked. "Would it be possible for us to see him for a couple of minutes?"

"Actually, he's been asking for 'his' Melanie already. That's how I know you're a nurse practitioner. He told me you used to work here, and he's very proud of that. We don't want him talking and moving around a lot, but if you'll follow me, I'll take you back to see him."

Melanie had never heard her father refer to her in such an endearing way, and she was confused by it.

"I'll just wait out here," Freda said, and Melanie and her mother trailed behind Dr. Daniels.

Once inside the ER patient area, they walked down a ways and then went inside Andrew's room. He was hooked up to all the normal equipment. An IV, blood pressure and heart rate monitors, and a pulse oximeter to measure oxygen saturation. His nurse, a thirtysomething woman with black hair, stepped away from the bed so that Gladys could move closer.

"Andrew, can you hear me?"

Andrew opened his eyes, staring at Gladys for a few seconds, and then he turned his head until he saw Melanie at the foot of his bed. He looked back at Gladys and then at Melanie again. Andrew coughed and said, "Mel, I need you to come closer."

She gazed at her father's caramel complexion and short, semi-curly salt-and-pepper hair. She was somewhat surprised by his words because he acted as though he had something important to say to her.

"I'm here, Dad."

"Sweetheart, I am so sorry for the way I teased and made fun of you when you were a child. I didn't realize I was doing anything wrong until I saw how much damage your mother and I had done. I know I'm apologizing a little late, but I hope you can find it in your heart to forgive me."

Tears fell from Melanie's eyes. She'd waited most of her life to share at least one genuine, loving moment with either of her parents, and although her father was ill, it had finally happened.

"Of course, Dad. I accept your apology, and I forgive you."

"Thank you for that. I also hope you can forgive your mother."

Melanie didn't look back at her mother because it was much too awkward, but she couldn't imagine Gladys being happy with what Andrew was saying.

"Well, Andrew, honey," her mother hurried to say, "we just wanted to see you before they take you to surgery. God's going to handle this, and you'll be fine."

Melanie leaned over and kissed her father on the cheek. "See you in a while. It'll be over before you know it."

When Melanie stepped back, Gladys moved closer, stretched toward her husband, and kissed him on the lips. "I'll be praying, and I know you'll be back in great health in no time. I love you, Andrew Johnson."

"I love you, too," he said, and then looked at Melanie. "I love you, too, Mel, and I'm sorry I've never really told you that."

"I love you, too, Dad, and it's time for you to relax. We'll be right outside in the waiting area."

"And one more thing," he said. "I've always been very proud of you, and don't you ever let anyone make you feel bad about yourself again. No one, you hear me?"

"Yes, but sshhh. You need to keep quiet now, Dad."

He smiled. "My daughter, the nurse practitioner."

When they left the room, Melanie's emotions were bittersweet and she felt a little weak in the knees. So much had caught her by surprise, and she was still trying to process everything. Her father was genuinely sorry. She could see it in his eyes, and she would do anything to have more time with him.

As she and her mother walked back to the main family room, Melanie saw Brad walking through the sliding doors. But the closer he strutted toward her, the fuzzier he appeared, and she felt strange and weaker than she had a few minutes ago. As soon as she'd gotten in the car heading to the hospital, she'd actually felt a bit more exhausted than normal, but now she could have sworn she was going to pass out. And that's exactly what she did.

CHAPTER 20

Melanie glanced down at the IV needle buried in the crook of her arm and cringed. She knew she'd lost consciousness, but was filling her body with all these fluids really necessary? Either way, Melanie didn't like it because all this meant was that she was gaining her weight back little by little. She'd taken an over-the-counter diuretic this morning, but now she would have to take another when she got home tonight. She'd have to take two tomorrow.

She heard a short knock on her exam room door and then saw Brad and Phillip walking in.

"Hey, baby," Brad said. "So how are you feeling?"

"I'm fine," she said. Actually, she still felt somewhat weak, but she didn't see a reason to worry him. "The results from my blood work should be back in a minute, and hopefully I'll be able to get out of here. Any word on my dad?"

"They've started his surgery, and so far so good."

"How's my mom?" she asked, not surprised that her mother hadn't bothered to come check on her. There was no doubt that her mom was worried about Melanie's dad, but since he'd already gone to surgery, Gladys certainly could have taken two or three minutes to stick her head inside Melanie's room. Then again, most folks did only what they wanted to do, and Melanie's mother was no different.

Brad rested his hand on the bed rail. "She seems pretty nervous, and rightfully so."

"I just can't believe this has happened," she said.

"Right after you passed out, they let me go in and pray with him," Phillip added.

Melanie smiled. "I'm really glad to hear that."

"My father-in-law and Charlotte are on their way, too."

"What about Alicia? I tried to call her earlier."

"So did I," Phillip said, "but you know when she's writing or reading her edits she turns both her landline and her cell phone on silent."

"I'm sure we'll hear from her soon," Melanie said, and looked at Brad, who was staring at her. "What?"

"You know why this happened, right?" he said.

"What? My dad's blockages?"

"No, the reason you passed out."

Melanie didn't like the suspicious tone in his voice or the irritated look on his face.

"Baby, you're not eating enough, and you know it. You also know how dangerous that can be. You're a nurse practitioner."

"Brad, please. I just started my diet this week."

He shook his head, folded his arms, and leaned against the wall. "So you're gonna pretend like you've been eating full meals?"

Melanie ignored him.

Phillip obviously felt the tension between them and said, "I prayed for you as well, and I know God is going to heal whatever caused you to faint the way you did."

"I'm sure it was all because of how hard I'd worked out earlier, and then hearing the news about my dad just made things worse."

Brad looked at her like she was crazy. "I don't believe you sometimes."

"This has nothing to do with the way I've been eating. I know you think it does, but it doesn't."

Brad no longer argued with her, but Melanie knew if she was truthful with herself, she'd have to admit that going three days without solid food might be the cause of her symptoms.

"So, was my dad in pretty good spirits when you prayed for him?" she asked Phillip.

"He was. He told me how he'd apologized to you and asked God to forgive him for all his sins. Past ones and any recent ones. Said he was ready for whatever plan God had for him."

Melanie wondered if her dad had gone into details about their strained relationship or shared with Phillip some of the awful things he and her mother had done when they were younger. Melanie had seen a number of people confess everything when they thought they might die, and while her father certainly had that right, she wasn't ready for Phillip or anyone else to know the truth about her childhood. She wished she could face the truth head-on and talk about her pain openly, but she was too ashamed and she didn't want anyone looking at her differently.

A few minutes later, Melanie's assigned ER physician, Dr. Romalati, knocked and entered the room. Melanie smiled because she'd had the opportunity to work with Dr.

Romalati in the past, and he had a great sense of humor. He was one of the nicest doctors she knew.

"So, how are you feeling? Are you alive? I mean, you look alive, but I can't tell for sure, so I figured I'd better ask."

Melanie laughed. "I'm fine, Dr. Romalati. Just wanna get out of here is all."

"Well, first things first. We got your lab work back, and both your potassium and sodium levels were far lower than I like to see them. Have you been doing anything out of the ordinary this week? Climbing Mount Everest maybe, or swimming across Lake Michigan?"

They all laughed.

"No, but seriously," Dr. Romalati continued. "A person's electrolytes usually aren't thrown off so noticeably unless there's a reason."

"Well . . . I've been going to work as usual and working out, but that's it. Nothing out of the ordinary at all," she said, casting her eyes at Brad. He stared at her with no emotion, and she hoped he would keep quiet. It was true that drinking three 160-calorie shakes wasn't a lot, but there was no need to disclose any of this to the doctor. She also knew she hadn't been drinking nearly enough water, especially with the way she'd revved up her workouts to twice a day, not to mention the diuretic she'd taken. She remembered, too, how her left foot had cramped up a couple of nights straight, and this morning she'd gotten a charley horse in her calf, all signs of low potassium.

Dr. Romalati seemed stumped. "Well, that really bothers me, because if you haven't changed your eating habits or workout regimen, I can't imagine why your potassium is so low. And I don't have to tell you that low sodium means dehydration, so something's not right."

Brad obviously couldn't take her lies anymore. "Baby, why aren't you telling Dr. Romalati the truth? You know you've been drinking shakes for breakfast and dinner and only having a salad for lunch. You've been doing that four days straight. And working out twice a day instead of once."

If Melanie hadn't heard him with her own ears she wouldn't have believed her own husband could betray her like this. Now Dr. Romalati and Phillip both knew she'd been lying the whole time, and she could barely look at him.

"That's not it" was all she said.

Dr. Romalati sighed. "Well, it very well could be. Are you eating at least twelve hundred calories? Because that would be pretty hard to do with two shakes, unless your salad has a lot of meat and high-calorie salad dressing in it. Or you're eating some snacks in between."

"I'm getting more than enough to eat."

"Why are you trying to lose weight?"

What a stupid question, Melanie thought, but she answered him anyway. "Because I'm overweight."

"You're far from being overweight, Melanie. You're not even close to it."

"I just need to lose another six pounds. That's all."

Dr. Romalati seemed dumbfounded, but thankfully, he changed the subject a bit. "Are you drinking more than eight glasses of water per day? Because with the additional workout you're doing, you need a lot of fluid."

"Yes," she lied again.

"It's a good thing we started this IV, because that'll help tremendously, and your nurse will also be in to give you some potassium. Then, for the next few days, I want you to nix the diet and shakes altogether so you can eat normal meals for breakfast, lunch, and dinner. I'll also be writing you a potassium prescription so you can take it for the next five days."

Melanie didn't like all these questions and

instructions, especially since she'd already told Dr. Romalati she was fine. Of course, now that Brad had blabbed about her diet and workouts, Dr. Romalati knew the truth, and he wouldn't likely believe anything else she said this evening. He would die if he knew about the diuretic she'd taken. Good thing that not even Brad was privy to that.

"So can I be discharged?" she asked.

"Not just yet. Your heart rate was a bit high, so I want you to have an EKG. I'm sure this is only because of your sodium and potassium levels, but I also want to make sure nothing else is going on."

Melanie didn't think this was necessary, but she knew Dr. Romalati's decision was a done deal. He would never take no for answer, so she didn't bother arguing.

"Do you have any questions?" he said.

"No, but I can leave as soon as you have my EKG results, right? Well, not leave, but get dressed so I can go check on my dad."

"Yes, if all checks out, you'll be ready to go. Also, I'm sorry to hear about your dad, but he's definitely in good hands with Dr. Daniels."

"Thank you."

"You take care of yourself, Melanie, and it was good to see you," he said, patting her on the shoulder and shaking Brad's and

Phillip's hands on the way out.

Melanie ignored Brad. She wouldn't so much as look at him, and Phillip seemed caught in the middle of a firestorm.

Thankfully Phillip's phone rang, and he hurried to answer it. "Hey, baby . . . Yes, I'm here with Melanie and Brad now . . . Yes, he's already in surgery and Melanie is fine. I'll let you speak to her," he said, passing over the phone.

"Hey, Alicia."

"Hey, Mel. Girl, I am so sorry I missed your call. I didn't check my phone until just a few minutes ago when I finished working."

"No problem, I understand. Are you done now?"

"Yes, finally, thank God. But enough about me. What's going on with your dad? And why did you pass out?"

"I'm fine. My electrolytes were low, but it's nothing serious. My dad, on the other hand, isn't doing too well. They're giving him a quadruple bypass."

"Gosh, Mel, I am so sorry."

"I'm really worried about him, so please keep him in your prayers."

"I will, but I'm also heading over. I should be there in about an hour and a half."

"I hate for you to have to drive that far

when you've been working all day."

"Don't say another word. I'm on my way."

"Thank you, and drive safely, okay?"

"I will. See you soon."

CHAPTER 21

Alicia got onto I-90 West, heading to Mitchell. She hated that she'd missed Melanie's call and was just now on her way to the hospital. If that hadn't been bad enough, Phillip had also left her a message, and she'd lied to both of them, claiming she'd been working. She couldn't have felt worse, knowing that what she'd actually been doing was lying in bed with Levi all day. She'd only planned to stay a couple of hours, but then after they'd talked and made love again, they'd dropped off to sleep. When they'd awakened, Levi had ordered carry-out from a nearby restaurant, and they'd watched a movie. After that, they'd made love a third time. Finally, when she'd realized that it was definitely time for her to go, she'd checked her phone and listened to both Alicia's and Phillip's messages. She'd purposely not checked her phone at Levi's because she hadn't wanted to feel guilty, which was exactly what would have happened had she noticed a missed call from Phillip.

Of course, her seeing Levi for as many hours as she had today still hadn't been enough for him, because five minutes ago he'd called her and they were on the phone now.

"This is what I get for being with you when I know I shouldn't," she said.

"Sweetheart, why are you beating yourself up over this? The important thing is that your friend is fine, and you're on your way to be there for her."

"Yeah, hours after she tried to contact me."

"It wasn't like you knew her dad was going to have a heart attack."

"That's beside the point. Her dad is in surgery, and something also happened to Mel. She passed out, and if anyone should be there for her, it's me."

"You apologized and told her you were working, so I'm sure she understands."

"What you mean is that I lied to her. I've been doing that a lot lately, and we both know why."

"But it's not like you have to. Just tell everyone the truth, and we won't have to sneak around like this."

Alicia turned on her left signal and changed lanes. "No one can ever know about us."

"After spending nearly a whole day with me, I guess you're still in denial."

"No, I'm not. I already admitted to you that I'm in love with you, and that I wish I could be with you. But I'm still marrying Phillip. I'm doing what's right."

"You're putting someone else's happiness before your own."

"Maybe, but I still know it's the right thing."

"I won't accept that."

"It's not like you have a choice."

"You know, I have to say again that I never once expected you to act this way. All those years I was locked up, the one thing that kept me going was the fact that you still hadn't gotten remarried. I always knew that you still loved me, and that when we saw each other we would connect like we'd never been apart. And we did. But now you're telling me you're going to walk away from true love just so you can be miserable?"

"It's called sacrifice and being unselfish."

"It's called crazy and insane. You must be out of your mind if you think you'll be able to pull this off. You'll marry that man, try to be happy for maybe a couple of months at most, and then you'll come looking for me. Of course, I'll be sitting here ready and waiting. After that, we'll get together, make love like there's no tomorrow, and sooner or later, you'll get caught again. Your new husband will find out about us, and more damage will be done to him than the last time."

Alicia wanted him to stop this. He was draining her word by word, and she wasn't sure how much more she could listen to. She loved him, hated him, and wondered how she was going to live without him.

"I need to call Melanie to see how things are going."

"Are you driving back tonight?"

"I don't know. I doubt it."

"When will I see you again?"

"Can't say."

"What about tomorrow on your way back home?"

"No, I don't think so. Thanks to you, I've missed all this time reading my manuscript, so I really have to buckle down all day tomorrow. Plus, Phillip will be at my condo for the entire weekend."

"Will you at least call me?"

"I'll see."

"I'll say a prayer for your friend's father."

"I appreciate that. Talk to you later."

"You're just gonna hang up?"

"What else?"

"You could tell me you love me."

"Good-bye, Levi."

Alicia ended the call. She was too distraught to talk to anyone, so instead of calling Melanie the way she'd planned, she drove the rest of the way in silence. She thought about everything imaginable, but what she kept coming back to was Levi's prediction of what was going to happen if she went ahead with her marriage. Would she honestly be that unhappy with Phillip? To the point where she would go right back to seeing Levi? She didn't want to believe that, but the whole idea of it terrified her. No matter what decision she made, she wouldn't win.

When Alicia arrived at the hospital, she parked what seemed like half a mile from the ER entrance, and she was glad she had on a sweat suit and athletic shoes. When she walked inside, Phillip stood, walked over, and hugged her. Gladys, Freda, Curtis, and Charlotte all sat in the same row of chairs.

"I'm so glad you came," Gladys said as Alicia leaned down, embracing her.

"I wouldn't be anywhere else. Is the surgery still going on?"

"Yes, and the doctor said it could take a while."

"Well, I know Mr. Johnson is going to be fine. He'll come through this very quickly, and he'll be back to normal before you know it."

"I hope you're right."

Alicia hugged her dad, her stepmom, and Freda. "Where's Mel? Hasn't she been released yet?"

"No," Phillip said. "The doctor ordered an EKG, which came back fine, but he wanted her to stay hooked up to her IV awhile longer."

"Wow. Well, I'm going back to see her."

"I'll be out here," he said.

The receptionist behind the window buzzed Alicia back to the ER examination area, and one of the nurses directed her to Melanie's room. When she opened the door, Melanie smiled and Brad got up and hugged her. Alicia was proud to be back in Brad's good graces, because years ago, when everyone had learned about Alicia's affair with Levi, Brad hadn't wanted anything to do with Alicia. He'd told Melanie that she could remain friends with her all she wanted to, but he was through with her. And he hadn't spoken to her for more than two years. Thankfully, he'd gotten over it, and the two of them were friends again.

Alicia set her purse down and hugged Melanie. "How are you?"

"I'm good."

"Are you sure?"

"No, she's not," Brad said matter-of-factly. "She's also angry with me for telling the doctor the truth."

Alicia raised her eyebrows. "About what?"

"That crazy diet she's on. I wish she'd get off of it before it kills her."

"Why are you blowing this so out of proportion?" Melanie shouted.

Brad turned toward the door. "I'm going back out to the waiting room. Alicia, maybe you can talk some sense into your friend while I'm gone."

Brad closed the door behind him.

"Mel, what is he talking about?"

"Nothing."

"I remember you saying on Saturday that you wanted to lose weight, but what are you eating?"

"Do we have to do this?"

"Yes. You passed out and your blood work didn't come back normal, so yes, I wanna know what's up."

"I'm drinking two shakes a day and eating a salad," she said.

"And what else?"

"That's it."

"Why are you doing this to yourself again?"

"What do you mean *again*?"

"Starving yourself."

"I don't wanna talk about this anymore."

Alicia frowned. "You don't have a choice."

"I know what I'm doing."

"Apparently you don't, because if you did, you wouldn't be lying here in a hospital bed."

"All I want is to get dressed and go wait for my dad," she said.

"Oh, so now you're going to ignore what I'm saying?"

"Look, I appreciate your concern, and please don't take this the wrong way, but this is *my* body. It's my life. It's my business."

"Excuse me?"

"I'm so sick of people telling me what I should and shouldn't be doing. Especially people who don't know a thing about being overweight. People who have perfect lives with no issues."

"And what is that supposed to mean?"

Melanie repositioned her IV tube and folded her arms. "Nothing. I think we should stop before we say something we'll regret."

"All this anger because I asked you about some diet you're on? You're not overweight, Melanie. You haven't been in years, and if you can't see that, something's wrong with you."

"Are you saying I'm crazy?"

"I'm saying you need help."

"You know what, Alicia, get out."

Alicia took a step back, half laughing. "Yeah, right, Mel."

"I mean it. Get out of here, and don't come back."

Alicia had been sure Melanie was joking, but the outraged look on her face told a different story. Alicia wanted to ask her what was going on with her, but she could tell it would only make things worse. Something was very wrong with Melanie's mental state, and the sad part of it all was that she looked like she'd lost a whole size since Saturday. Her neck was too skinny and her face was much narrower. But for now, all Alicia could do was pray for her, and that's exactly what she did.

Chapter 22

They all filed into the large hospital conference room, waiting for Dr. Daniels: Melanie, Brad, Gladys, Freda, Alicia, Phillip, Pastor Black, and his wife, Charlotte. One of the surgical nurses had come to the waiting area to let them know the surgery was over and that Dr. Daniels would be out to speak to them as soon as he could. Melanie hoped her dad was doing better than expected and that his recovery would be successful and quick.

Everyone sat in silence, and it was good to have them there, praying and showing unwavering love and support. Especially Pastor Black and Charlotte, because they were like second parents to Melanie. It was sort of funny how Charlotte was Alicia's stepmom, yet she was only eleven years older than Melanie and Alicia. Even more interesting was the fact that Melanie was also very close to Alicia's mother, Tanya, whom Melanie called Mom as well. Tanya was one of the best women Melanie knew, and she would have given anything for her own mother to be as kind.

Melanie scanned the room. She accidentally locked eyes with Alicia, the one person she wished had stayed home. How dare Alicia judge her and talk to her the way she had when she'd first arrived at the hospital. She'd had no right, and Melanie wasn't happy about it.

After another ten minutes, Dr. Daniels walked into the room and took a seat at the head of the table. "Good evening, everyone."

They all greeted him, waiting for the report.

"Well, it was a tough job, but we got it done. We're having to breathe for Mr. Johnson right now, and the next twenty-four to forty-eight hours are crucial. It's never simple when we have to unblock four arteries, but what I can tell you is that I've done it many times before, and I've done it very successfully. I did the best I could, and now it's in the hands of the good Lord."

"Amen," Pastor Black and Phillip acknowledged. Everyone else nodded in agreement.

Melanie didn't always hear doctors speak

this way, but it gave her a good feeling when she met doctors who hadn't allowed their vast knowledge of science to diminish their strong belief in God.

"Does anyone have any questions?" Dr. Daniels said. "Mrs. Johnson?"

"No, I don't think so," she said.

"Anyone?" he asked again.

"Can we see him for just a few minutes?" Melanie asked.

"Someone will come and get you and your mom as soon as the nurses get your dad situated, but after that, I really want him to get some rest."

"Thank you, and we understand," Melanie said.

Dr. Daniels scooted his chair away and got up. "I guess that's it for now, but I'll be in first thing in the morning to see him. Which actually won't be long, because it's already midnight and I have a six thirty a.m. surgery to perform."

"Oh my," Gladys said. "We already appreciated everything you've done for my husband, but hearing that makes us appreciate you that much more. Thank you for everything."

"Of course. As I said to you and Melanie earlier, I'm glad I was still here when the

181

ambulance brought him in. You all take care."

"You, too, and thank you again, doctor," Melanie said.

"You're quite welcome."

Gladys clasped her hands together and rested them on the table. "I guess all we can do now is wait." Then she looked at Melanie. "Do you think your dad will make it? You know a lot more about this kind of thing than any of us."

Melanie wasn't sure why her mother was putting her on the spot like this when Dr. Daniels had already explained how important the next two days would be. "I've seen lots of bypass patients who have gotten well and lived very healthy lives."

Gladys shook her head in disgust. "I just wish he'd stopped eating all those ridiculous pork skins the way I asked him. I begged him, but he wouldn't listen."

"I'm sure it was much more than that," Melanie tried to tell her. "With Dad having four blocked arteries, it would have taken a good while for that much plaque to build up. This didn't happen just because of what he's been eating over the last few weeks."

"He's been eating all sorts of things he shouldn't for a long time. Now he might die because he wouldn't put a stop to it."

Why couldn't her mother forget about all that and simply pray for her husband to get better? Nothing was ever good enough for her, especially if she couldn't control a person. But for once, Melanie just wished she would keep her thoughts to herself. No one wanted to hear any of her ranting. The blank stares she saw on everyone else's faces proved it.

"What we have to do is pray and keep our faith strong," Melanie said.

"Absolutely," Pastor Black added, "and if you don't mind, Sister Johnson, I'd like to have a word of prayer before we leave."

"Of course, Pastor."

Everyone stood up, moved closer together, and held hands.

Curtis closed his eyes. "Dear heavenly Father, we come right now in the precious name of Jesus. Dear Lord, Brother Johnson is fighting for his life, and while we don't have all the answers, what we do know is that You never, ever make mistakes and that You are always true to Your Word. So we ask that You would please heal and strengthen Brother Johnson. Make him whole again. Allow him to recover in a most miraculous way. Then, Lord, we ask that You would give strength and peace to his wife, Sister Johnson, and his daughter,

Melanie, during this very trying time in their lives. We also ask that You would please heal Melanie from any illness attempting to attack her body. And then, Lord, please bless Brad as well, along with everyone else here who loves and cares about Brother Johnson's well-being. I know You are with each of us every step of the way, and we thank You for that, dear God. We thank you for all that You've done, for all that You're doing, and for all that You will surely do in the future. Lord, we ask for these and all other blessings in Your Son Jesus's name, Amen."

"Amen," each of them said.

Pastor Black and Charlotte hugged everyone, said their good-byes, and left the conference room.

Brad walked over to the doorway. "Baby, as soon as you see your dad you need to go home and get some rest. Your car can stay here, and I'll just drop you back off on my way to the office in the morning."

Gladys glared at Melanie and frowned. "Home? I know you're not going to just leave me here all alone. What if something happens while you're gone?"

"Mom, I don't want to, but I'm still feeling pretty weak. Once I get a few hours of rest, I promise I'll be right back."

"Weak?" she said, scowling. "What did they say was wrong with you, anyway?"

This was the first time her mother had asked her anything about the reason she'd passed out, which was beyond hurtful. Normally, her mother made sure to put on a good front for Alicia, Phillip, and Alicia's parents, but not tonight. For whatever reason, she didn't even try to pretend that she loved or had any respect for Melanie. She spoke to her and treated her any way she wanted, and she didn't care who witnessed it.

"My electrolytes were a little off."

"And what does that mean exactly?"

"My potassium was low, and I was dehydrated."

"Oh well," she said, acting as though none of what Melanie had told her was important. "Maybe if you ate right every single day instead of depriving yourself all at once, this wouldn't happen."

Melanie didn't bother looking at Alicia or Phillip because she was far too embarrassed. "I'll be back in a few hours, Mom."

"You do whatever you want," Gladys said, grabbing her handbag.

Freda got up and followed behind her. "Don't you worry about a thing, Gladys. I'm not going anywhere. I'll be right here for as long as you need me."

Melanie wanted to tell Freda to mind her own business the same as she'd told Alicia earlier, but she kept her mouth shut.

Gladys and Freda walked out of the room and so did Brad and Phillip, but Alicia stopped Melanie at the doorway.

"Mel, wait. Let me talk to you for a minute."

"What is it?"

"I just wanted to say how sorry I am. Here you weren't feeling well, and I come into your room questioning you and telling you what to do. I only said the things I said because I love you, but I truly apologize."

Melanie barely looked at Alicia for more than a second. "Don't even worry about it. Just forget the whole thing. I know I have."

Alicia reached her arms out. "Truce?"

Melanie hugged her loosely enough to let her know her heart wasn't in it. "I just told you I've already forgotten about it."

"I'm glad," Alicia said. "I'm staying in town tonight so I can get some sleep, but I'll call you before I head back to my condo. I still have to read through the last few chapters of my manuscript."

"Thanks for coming," Melanie said as politely as she could. She loved Alicia, but she honestly didn't like her right now. There was something else Melanie thought about, too. When Melanie had spoken to Alicia earlier on the phone, Alicia had told her she'd read the last page of her edits and was finally finished. She'd talked about how this was the reason her phone had been on silent. So why was Alicia lying? Although, knowing Alicia, if she was suddenly taking a long time to return phone calls and not telling the truth about it, she was up to something. It was the only time she did this kind of thing, and Melanie could only imagine what was coming.

CHAPTER 23

It was seven a.m., and while Alicia and Phillip had gotten to the house right around one this morning, she hadn't slept more than twenty minutes here and there. Her mind had raced from one thing to the next, and guilt-ridden tears had streamed onto her pillow. She just didn't know how she could lie next to Phillip in their own house, in their own bed, knowing she'd spent most of yesterday with Levi, holding him, kissing him, and making love to him like he was her husband. If only Levi didn't make her feel so good, she could walk away and forget about him. But he *did* make her feel good, and if things were different, she would marry him the way he wanted. In a perfect world, they would build their dream home, have two beautiful children — a boy and a girl — and grow old together. If she hadn't already committed to another man, she'd be free to do what she knew would make her happy.

But no matter how she tried to weigh things, one simple fact remained — the one fact she'd replayed hundreds of times in her head: She couldn't and wouldn't hurt Phillip. She had to marry him whether she wanted to or not. It wasn't that she didn't love Phillip, it was just that she wasn't *in* love with him the way a woman needed to be in love with a man she was planning to spend the rest of her life with. She'd thought loving him as a person was enough, and it actually had been before Levi had emailed her last Saturday, letting her know he was out of prison. What a mess this all was, but she knew what she had to do. Ending things with Levi wouldn't be easy — she could finally admit that now — but it was her only option. Plus, it wasn't like Phillip wasn't a wonderful man, because he was, and he loved her with all his heart. She knew that much for sure, so maybe in time, she would love him on the same level that she loved Levi.

Phillip yawned, stretched his arms and body, and opened his eyes. When he looked over at Alicia, he smiled. "How long have you been awake?"

"A while."

"I'm glad you decided to spend the

night . . . or I guess I should say morning, since we got in so late. The drive back to your condo would have been exhausting."

"I know. I'm glad I stayed, too."

"I wonder how Mr. Johnson is doing," he said.

"Yeah, me too. I'm also worried about Mel. She's not herself, and this weight thing is getting out of control again."

"Until Brad and I talked last night, I had no idea. You'd never told me about that before."

"Probably because it hadn't crossed my mind in years. When we were in college, she would sometimes starve herself for days and then when she couldn't take it anymore, she would binge on every kind of food she could get her hands on. She did this the whole four years we were away, but once we graduated, she seemed to mellow out and she didn't struggle with that any longer."

"Maybe she got better for a while, but now Brad says she's working out longer, and he doubts she's eating a thousand calories a day."

"But she's not overweight at all. She's as thin as any woman would want to be, but for some reason she can't see it."

"Brad wants her to get help, but I guess she got mad when he suggested it."

"Just like she got mad at me last night. I didn't tell you this on the way home, but she told me to get out of her room. It was almost like I didn't know her. She acted like we were enemies."

"I'm sure the pain she was feeling about her dad had something to do with it, too. She's under a lot of stress right now."

"Maybe, but there's no way Mel can keep going without food. That's just plain crazy."

Phillip raised his arm toward the headboard. "I was also a little shocked by the way her mom was talking to her, and she never went into Melanie's room even once. Are they mad at each other about something?"

"Not that I know of. I mean, when we were younger her mother would constantly make comments about her weight, but that was a long time ago."

"Well, I do wonder if there's a lot we don't know, because when I went in to pray with her dad, he told me he'd apologized to Melanie and asked God to forgive him for all his sins."

"Really? Apologized for what?"

"I don't know, and when I mentioned it to Melanie, she seemed embarrassed and like she was afraid her father had told me a lot more."

"I do know that Melanie's parents were a lot different before I met her, because she told me a little about it. But once her father recovered from some car accident, everything changed and her parents became good people. They've always been wonderful to me as well."

"Yeah, but you know the saying. You never know what's going on behind closed doors."

"That's true, but Mel is like a sister to me, and if there were major problems between her and her parents I would know about it."

Phillip leaned closer to the center of the bed, gazing into Alicia's eyes.

"What's wrong?" she asked.

"Nothing. Can't I admire the woman I love?"

"And you just decided to do that right in the middle of our conversation?" she said, laughing.

"Kinda. You're such a beautiful woman, and I loved you from the first time I laid eyes on you. Now you're going to be my wife again."

Alicia smiled but wasn't sure how to respond.

"I know you must be tired of hearing me say that over and over, but I can't help it. For the first time in years, I'm truly happy and content. I feel like I have everything now, and not many people can say that."

"I agree. We're very blessed."

Phillip held the side of her face and kissed her with more passion than usual but then pulled away. "Okay, I'd better get out of this bed before we do something we'll regret. Although I know you'd be fine with that, wouldn't you?" he said, laughing. "If we could make love right this very second, you'd be on top of the world."

"You know I would be," she said, forcing a smile and hoping Phillip couldn't tell how insincere she was.

"Well, just remember, only two months to go and I'm all yours. Every part of me."

When Phillip went into the bathroom, Alicia got up, walked over to the chair where her tote sat, and pulled out her phone. It was a good thing she'd gotten into the habit of keeping her phone on silent with no vibration, because Levi had just called her ten minutes ago. He'd also sent her a text that said, "Where are you? I miss you. Call me."

Alicia dropped her phone in her bag and fell across the bed, face-first. She'd never felt so trapped or defeated in all her life, but she had to do the right thing. Do right by Phillip. Live happily ever after with the man everyone wanted her to be with.

She settled her mind, got back out of bed to get her phone, and dialed Melanie. With the way she'd acted last night, Alicia wondered if her friend would answer.

"Hello?" Melanie said.

"Hey, Mel. How are you?"

"Hanging in there."

"How's your dad?"

"About the same. I called the nurse's station maybe an hour ago."

"I'm sure it'll take a little more time before he progresses."

"That's what I'm praying for."

"So am I. We all are."

Melanie didn't say anything further, and their silence was unsettling. It felt strange and uncommon, and while Alicia had considered easing into another conversation about Melanie's eating habits, she knew this wasn't the right time. But oddly enough, Melanie was the one who had questions for her.

"So, when we were on the phone last night, why did you tell me you'd finished reading your manuscript?"

"What do you mean?"

"That's what you told me then, but right before we left the hospital, you said you still had a few more chapters to go."

Alicia swallowed the huge lump in her throat. Gosh, had she actually told Melanie two different stories? But even if she had, why was Melanie confronting her about it? Why was she acting as though she'd caught her in something and couldn't wait to interrogate her?

Alicia made up another quick lie to appease her. "I did finish reading it, but I still need to type in my changes and additions. I always mark up my manuscript as I go along, and then I have to incorporate everything on my computer."

"Oh, I see." Melanie said, almost sounding sarcastic.

Alicia ignored her and changed the subject. "So when are you going back to the hospital?"

"I'm getting ready now."

"I really wish I could spend the day here with you, but I have to get back home so I can finish up my work. I'll be calling you, though, and I'll definitely get to see your dad when I come back for church on Sunday."

"How come you didn't bring your laptop and manuscript with you?"

Wow. Just wow. Melanie had turned into a real piece of work this morning, and Alicia was getting a little tired of it. She knew

Melanie was going through a lot, which was the reason Alicia was being tolerant, but she could only take so much attitude and rudeness.

"Well, for one thing, when I heard that you'd passed out and that your dad was having emergency surgery, my work was the last thing I thought about. All I knew was that I needed to get here."

"Oh yeah, that's right," she said.

"Is Brad still dropping you off at the hospital? Otherwise, I can come get you before I head back home."

"Yes, he's in the shower now, but thanks."

"Okay, well, I'll let you go, and kiss your dad for me."

"I will."

"And Mel?"

"Yeah."

"I'm really sorry again about the things I said last night. You're my girl, I love you, and I just want you to be all right."

"I know that. I love you, too."

Alicia set her phone down, and though she wondered why Melanie still wasn't acting herself, she soon thought about her drive back to Covington Park. She was already promising herself she wouldn't call Levi, and she wouldn't stop by his friend's house to see him. She would head straight to her condo so she could read the manuscript she hadn't looked at for the past two days. She so needed to get that finished, because she knew Phillip would be driving over, just as he did every Friday when he left the church. She had to get as much reading done as possible so she could spend all of tomorrow and Sunday with him. Then, on Monday, she would finish reading completely and would type everything in. Monday was Phillip's day off, but she would just have to come up with some other lie to explain why she needed another full day of work with no distractions. She would then be able to email the finished product to her editor on Tuesday, and all would be good.

She would also take some time on Tuesday to check in with their wedding planner. There still wasn't much to do at this point, but Alicia wanted to touch base with her to make sure nothing had been missed. Regardless of how she'd been feeling as of late, thanks to Levi, Alicia wanted her and Phillip's wedding to be flawless. Not because she was nearly as excited about getting married as she had been, but because Phillip deserved it. He'd earned the right to have the best of everything, including a loyal wife, and Alicia would give him that. She would forget her own desires and learn how to be happy with the existing conditions. She would pretend Levi was a mere figment of her imagination.

CHAPTER 24

No matter what explanation Alicia had tried to come up with, Melanie knew something was wrong. Alicia had sounded sort of squirrely, and she'd paused for a couple of seconds before answering Melanie's question. Most people who lied didn't realize they were doing that. But as of yesterday, Melanie had begun doing a bit of pausing and lying herself to her ER doctor, so she knew firsthand how a person acted when they weren't telling the truth.

Melanie heard Brad shutting off the water in the shower, so she knew once he shaved he'd be getting dressed pretty quickly. She still had on her robe, but it wouldn't take her long at all to slip on the pair of jeans and sweatshirt she'd already laid out. The temperature was going to be in the eighties today, but the air-conditioning at the hospital last night had been pretty cold, and she wanted to be prepared for it. There was no doubt that her mother would think she should have worn something more presentable, but Melanie was planning to stay for a few hours and wanted to be comfortable.

She looked at the clock. Since it was still too early to call her office to let them know she wouldn't be in today, she took a deep breath and called her mother. She wasn't looking forward to speaking to her, but Gladys was still her mother and it was only right that she check on her.

Gladys answered on the first ring. "So when exactly are you going to get back over here?"

"When Brad gets dressed, he'll be dropping me off."

"Well, it's good to know that you're in no real hurry."

"Mom, I really needed to get some rest, and I do feel a lot better."

"Yeah, but it's like I told you last night, if you ate right every single day and not just when you want, you wouldn't gain any weight, period. You also wouldn't have to resort to some crazy crash diet. All that up-and-down stuff is just plain silly. Especially when I've taught you so much better than that."

"I do eat right, and I work out, too. But I'm not you, Mom."

"Isn't that the truth, because if you were me you'd be using a lot more common sense."

Melanie squinted her eyes. "Why are you always so mean to me?"

"Look, what time are you going to be here? It's bad enough that you left in the first place. Your dad's doctor came and talked to me and Freda about an hour ago, but you're the nurse practitioner. You're the one who understands all that medical lingo. But noooo, you were more worried about going home and getting in bed."

"Mom, I'll see you in a little while, okay?"

"Whatever, Melanie. Come or don't come. Good-bye."

Melanie opened her mouth to respond, but Gladys had already hung up. Her mother had always been unloving and disapproving, but now she was being down-right cruel. She seemed mad at the world. Although, maybe this was the only way she knew how to deal with her husband's illness and the fact that he wasn't doing so well. Melanie was afraid, too, but instead of being angry she was trying her best to remain prayerful and positive. She also didn't understand why her mother was being so unsympathetic about her collapsing at the hospital or about her struggle with her weight. It was as if her mother didn't love her, and that she spent most of her days looking for reasons to criticize and hurt Melanie. It was senseless, and while Melanie had become as immune to her mother's comments as she could, she wondered why Gladys had always been so tough on her. She wondered why her mother had never loved and nurtured her only child. Maybe it was because Gladys had grown up in foster care and had never met her own parents. There were times when Melanie had wanted to do a background check on her mom and search for her biological grandparents, but her mother had made it clear that she never wanted to lay eyes on the "lowlifes" who obviously hadn't cared enough about her to raise her.

Brad walked into the room with a large bath towel wrapped around him and sat on the bed next to Melanie. He hugged her, and Melanie wondered if this was his subtle way of saying he was sorry for squealing on her to the doctor.

But how wrong she was.

Brad wrapped his arm around Melanie's waist. "Baby, I know you won't want to hear this, but you need help."

She scooted away from him. "For what?"

"Your eating disorder."

Melanie laughed out loud. "You must be kidding."

"I'm very serious. You have a problem, and I would be less than a husband to sit back and watch you starve yourself. Which is exactly what you're doing."

"Where is all this coming from?"

"You have to ask? You're not eating. You fainted in the ER last night. You were dehydrated, and I found these inside the vanity," he said, pulling her box of diuretics from inside his towel.

"What were you doing in my drawer?"

"The same reason you were in mine the other day. I wanna know what's going on."

"And you think losing ten thousand dollars — no, wait, make that twenty thousand dollars — is the same thing as me taking a couple of pills?"

"I'm not saying it's the same thing. I know what I did was wrong, and I've owned up to it. But you're in denial."

Melanie got up and stormed down the hallway. "I don't even wanna talk to you anymore."

She slammed the bathroom door and let her robe drop to the floor. For the first time in years, she hadn't gotten on the scale as soon as she'd gotten up, and it was all because she'd been afraid to see how much weight she'd gained from the IV. So, this morning, she'd gone to the bathroom and come back out to call to check on her father. But now, Brad had made her so furious, she needed to know how much damage had been done so she could take care of it.

She stepped on the scale and wanted to cry. She was up five pounds. Five whole disgusting pounds, the four she'd lost this week plus a new one. She'd known this was going to happen, but somehow seeing it with her own eyes made it too real to deal with.

She looked at her body in the mirror that spanned the double-sink vanity and shook her head. What a disaster. Here she'd stopped eating solid food so she could lose more weight and do it quicker, yet she'd ended up dehydrated and had been pumped with fluids. As she gathered her thoughts and composure, however, she realized all she needed to do was take two diuretics and drink her three shakes. She would do this today and tomorrow, and at the very least, she'd be down those five pounds by the time she got up on Sunday or Monday. She'd been worried about what she would eat on Father's Day, but sadly, dinner was no longer happening.

She would also take the potassium pills Dr. Romalati had prescribed for her, so she wouldn't have to worry about that, either. Her father would get well, she would lose the weight, she and Brad would settle their differences, and life would return to normal. There was, of course, this awkward tension between her and Alicia, but she knew that would work out, too.

In a few weeks, her problems and emotional concerns would be a distant memory. It would feel as though none of it had happened.

CHAPTER 25

Alicia scanned through a few SiriusXM channels until she found Kirk Franklin's Praise. She'd been driving for nearly an hour, heading back to Covington Park, and she needed to hear something inspirational. Something that would help her stop thinking about Levi and do the right thing. She couldn't, shouldn't, and wouldn't see him today. Instead, she would drive straight home and get back to work.

She switched lanes and saw that her father was calling.

"Hey, Daddy."

"Hi, baby girl. What's going on?"

"Just on my way home."

"Have you spoken to Melanie? How's Brother Johnson?"

"I talked to her a couple of hours ago, but there's still no change."

"I'm sorry to hear that. I said another prayer for him this morning, and I'll continue to do so throughout the day."

"It was really nice of you and Charlotte to stay so late last night."

"Of course. Brother Johnson is a wonderful member, but he's also your best friend's father."

"This is really hard on Melanie. She's not saying much, but I can tell she's worried out of her mind."

"I'm sure she is, and that's totally understandable."

"I wish I could be there with her today, but I really have to get my manuscript read."

"How are you in general, though?" Curtis asked. "Is everything okay?"

"I'm good," Alicia said, but she wasn't sure she liked where their conversation was going. She knew her father well, and his tone sounded suspicious.

"I hope that's true, because you seemed a little preoccupied at Bible study this week. Then last night at the hospital you weren't much different."

Alicia bit her bottom lip. "I'm fine, Daddy. Really."

"Baby girl, I've seen you like this before, and since I've never been one to mince words, I'm just going to say it. The last time you acted this way was when you were having that affair with Levi. And don't tell me he's still in prison, because I saw D.C. on Monday, and he said Levi was released last Friday."

Alicia had known her father would eventually find out, either from D.C., a man her father knew well and who was also good friends with Levi, or from someone else. It was just that she'd been hoping he wouldn't learn about Levi's release so soon.

"Daddy, I can't believe you would think something like that."

"Look, you're a grown woman, and I can't control what you do. But I won't condone it, either."

"You're worrying for nothing, Daddy."

"Really? So Levi hasn't tried to contact you? Not in the whole week he's been home?"

Alicia hated having these kinds of conversations with her father, because she didn't want to keep lying to him.

"Daddy, it's like I said. You're worrying for nothing."

"Why won't you answer the question?"

"Because it's silly."

"What's silly about it? You were in love with that man, and now he's out. Not to mention, you're acting like something's troubling you."

"All that matters is that I love Phillip, and

we're going to be married."

"You're clearly not going to tell me the truth, so I'll just say this. The last time you messed around with Levi, things turned out horribly for you. Have you forgotten that you were arrested like a criminal? Have you forgotten how heartbroken Phillip was? How badly you hurt him?"

"Of course not, and I would never do that to him again."

"I hope not, because even the kindest of people can only take so much. Sometimes people will react in ways you never thought possible. It's called temporary insanity."

Alicia shook her head. Her father was so dramatic, and he would say just about anything to get his point across.

"I'm not doing anything wrong," she said. "Everything's fine."

Curtis paused a few seconds, and she knew he didn't believe her. "I just don't wanna see you ruin things for you and Phillip, so if you don't love him you need to tell him."

"Daddy, please. I *do* love him. You know that."

Curtis sighed. "I'm going to let you focus on the highway, but I hope you hear what I'm saying. Oh, and just so you know, it was after I saw D.C. that I decided what Bible study would be about on Wednesday night. I know from personal experience that temptation is nothing to play with, and that the devil really does have more tricks than you can imagine. I did a lot of wrong in the past, and a ton of people were hurt in the process. So, baby girl, I'm begging you not to go down that road. Leave well enough alone while you still have a chance. Stay away from that man, and be prayerful."

Alicia had wondered about her father's chosen topic, and her suspicions had been correct.

Curtis continued. "This is the kind of thing you have to pray your way out of, which is the reason I made sure to focus on Matthew twenty-six, forty-one. You can love Phillip and tell yourself you don't want to be with Levi, but because the flesh is weak, you won't be able to control yourself. Temptation will consume you, and it'll have you doing all kinds of terrible things you shouldn't."

"Everything is fine, Daddy. I mean that."

"I'm going to keep you in my prayers."

Alicia heard her phone beeping and saw a blocked number display across the screen on her dashboard. Her stomach stirred with angst, as there was no doubt it was Levi. She wouldn't dare tell her father she had to hang up because of another call, but thankfully, he told her he had a meeting to get to.

"You take care of yourself," he said.

"I will, and I love you, Daddy."

"I love you, too."

Alicia pressed the Accept button on the screen. "Hello?"

"Finally," Levi said. "Why didn't you call me back?"

"I was at the hospital pretty late, and I spent the night in Mitchell."

"What about now?"

"I'm headed home."

"Are you stopping by here first?"

"No. I have a lot of work to do, and there's something else you should know, too. My father knows you're out, and he thinks we've been seeing each other."

"We have."

"That's not funny, Levi."

"And I'm not laughing. I'm just being real, and anyway, who told him I was home? D.C.?"

"Yep."

"Well, it's not like D.C. knows anything, because I would never tell him about us."

"I know you wouldn't, but my dad still knows. I could tell by the way he was talking."

"Why don't you just tell your dad the

211

truth and get it out of the way? I've always had the utmost respect for him, especially after he decided the church could no longer accept my financial contributions because of where it came from. That's when I knew he was working really hard to do the right thing. He never treated me like a drug dealer, though, and now that I've changed for the better, I think he would be proud."

"My dad will never be okay with you and me being together. He loves Phillip like a son, and he blames both of us for hurting him."

"It might take some time, but once your dad sees how happy we are, he'll be fine."

"No, he won't. He'll never hate you, because he doesn't hate anyone, but he will *never* give us his blessing."

"Let's just say he doesn't. To me that shouldn't mean a thing, because this is about us. Our happiness is the only thing that should matter."

"I wish it were that easy, but it's not. This is so much more complicated."

"It doesn't have to be."

Alicia's phone beeped again, and this time it was Phillip. "Hey, I have to go."

"Why?"

"I have another call."

"Who is it?"

"I have to go. I'll talk to you later," she said, pressing the button and answering her other line. "Hey."

"Hey, baby. You almost home?"

"Yep, not far to go at all."

"Good. I just wanted to make sure you got there safely. I miss you already, and I'm glad you stayed."

"I am, too."

"Did you pick up something to eat?"

"No, I'm just gonna fix a salad and get to work."

"Well, happy reading, and I'll see you this afternoon. I love you, baby."

"I love you, too. Have a good day."

Alicia turned into her subdivision, pressed the garage door opener, and drove inside. She turned the car off and leaned her head against the headrest. Her emotions were in an uproar, and she couldn't stop thinking about her father's words. She also knew he'd been right about everything he'd said, so she got out of her vehicle, went into her condo, and dropped down on her knees in front of the sofa. She locked her hands together and closed her eyes.

"Dear Lord, I come before You, begging you to forgive me for all my sins. Lord, I know I have been wrong when it comes to all the things I've done with Levi, but I can't help the way I feel. I'm in love with him, and I'm to the point where I think about him all the time. But I don't want to do that anymore. I don't want to feel that way, and I don't want to sleep with him or see him ever again. So I'm asking You, Lord, to please remove all carnal feelings I have for him. I'm asking You to let me not just love Phillip but be *in* love with him. Lord, I also ask that You would please encourage Levi to move on so he can find someone else to love more than he loves me. Someone he can spend the rest of his life with. That way, I can marry Phillip the way I'm supposed to, and I won't have to worry about Levi trying to contact me. I ask You, Lord, for these and all other blessings in Your Son Jesus's name, Amen."

Alicia opened her eyes. Tears streamed down her face, but she knew she'd made the right decision. Not only for herself but for Phillip and everyone who cared about them. The two of them would get married, and God would take care of the rest. He just had to . . . and Alicia trusted and believed He would.

■ ■ ■ ■

THREE MONTHS
LATER

■ ■ ■ ■

CHAPTER 26

Today marked the one-month anniversary of Alicia and Phillip's second wedding. They were finally man and wife again, and while Alicia had prayed things would get better — that she would fall hopelessly in love with Phillip and forget about Levi — she was still struggling with a mixture of feelings. Even now, as she lay in bed making love with Phillip bright and early on a Thursday morning, she couldn't stop thinking about Levi and how much better he'd made her feel. To her, intimacy with Phillip was nothing more than repetitive sex, and she had to mentally prepare whenever he wanted her. It also took every ounce of pretending she could muster until he finished. To be fair, it wasn't that Phillip was awful in bed, because he wasn't. It was just that she didn't love him the way a wife should love her husband. She also knew that prayer could and would change things, but she purposely no longer prayed about any of what she was experiencing. She'd stopped praying because, deep down, she didn't want to love Phillip any more than she did, and God forgive her, she didn't want to forget about Levi. She no longer wanted Levi to find another woman to fall in love with, either. She wanted him to keep loving *her,* and it was all she could do to not run to him as fast as she could.

It had been three months since the last time she'd seen him, and though it had been the hardest thing for her to do, she hadn't responded to a single one of his text messages, phone calls, emails, or Facebook communications. There had been times when his loving words had affected her so much that she'd reread them over and over and cried like a child. Then, about a week before the wedding, he'd begun pleading with her to end things with Phillip before it was too late. He'd begged her not to make the mistake of a lifetime, but she hadn't listened. She'd continued on with her plans, because it had been the right thing to do — for Phillip — and she had to live with it. She'd sort of hoped that when Phillip had learned Levi was out of jail he might question whether they should still get married, but interestingly enough, he hadn't seemed to worry about Levi at all.

Phillip lay on his back out of breath, and Alicia could tell he was satisfied and happy out of his mind. She, on the other hand, was relieved it hadn't taken him as long as it usually did.

"I could make love to you every day of the week," he said, turning toward her and caressing her hair.

Alicia played along, turning and facing him on her side, acting as though she couldn't agree more. "It was a long time coming, and I feel the same way."

"Going without was tough, but now we finally get to make up for lost time."

"That we do," she said, forcing a smile.

"Next to God, you're my everything. You're my wife, my best friend, my heart. I couldn't love you more if I tried."

"I love you, too, baby."

Phillip leaned closer, kissing her, and Alicia hoped he wasn't planning for round two, because she wasn't in the mood for it. Thankfully, he pulled away.

"Well, as much as I hate to get up, I really need to get dressed so I can head over to the church. Your dad asked me to deliver the message for the eight o'clock service on Sunday, and I need to finish writing my sermon. That way, we'll be able to spend the entire weekend together."

"Good."

"I was thinking we could maybe drive over to Chicago tomorrow to spend the night at the Peninsula."

"Really? Why?"

"Well, it *is* our one-month anniversary."

Alicia loved the Peninsula, and while they'd flown to the Caribbean the Monday after their wedding for their honeymoon, they'd decided to stay in Chicago on their wedding night and also that Sunday. But she wasn't in the mood for spending time there this weekend. "I was just hoping we'd be able to enjoy some time at home together. Is that okay?"

"Of course. It was just an idea, but you know I'm fine wherever we are as long as we're together."

"Maybe we can go next month," she said, trying to sound excited.

"It'll be a lot colder in October, but it's not like we'll be out all that much, anyway," he said, winking at her.

"Knowing you, I'm sure we won't."

Phillip kissed her again and sat up on the side of the bed. "So, what do you have up for today?"

"Not a lot. I need to answer some of the email from my readers, but that's about it. I might see what Melanie's doing for lunch. The last three times I invited her, she took a rain check."

"She looks like she's lost a lot more weight. I was shocked when I saw her at church last Sunday, and Brad is at his wit's end."

"I don't know what else to do, because every time I even hint around about her weight, she gets mad."

"All we can do is keep praying for her."

"I guess so."

After Phillip got dressed, Alicia fixed him breakfast and he left for the church. Alicia sat in her office in front of her computer, glancing at their wedding photo. The ceremony had been absolutely beautiful and just as flawless as Alicia had envisioned. Melanie and Brad had served as their matron of honor and best man, and Alicia's father had performed the ceremony. It had been a joyous, happy day, but it hadn't taken more than a few hours before reality had set in for Alicia. They'd made love that evening, and she hadn't felt any chemistry or passion.

Alicia signed into the email account her readers used to contact her and saw thirty new messages. She read the first few, smiling the whole time. She had the absolute best readers, and no matter what was going on in her life, their kind words and comments made her day. It felt good knowing that she'd written something that wasn't just entertaining, but also helpful to her readers in one way or another. They could relate to the stories and the characters, and Alicia always prayed for that.

She responded to every single email and then signed on to Facebook. There were a good number of responses listed under the status update she'd posted yesterday about her upcoming novel, so she thanked those readers, too, and answered their questions. She also saw that she had Facebook messages and opened those. There were only four of them, but her nerves sort of got the best of her when she saw one from Levi. He hadn't sent her anything since last week, and she couldn't deny that she'd missed hearing from him. She hesitated before clicking on his message but finally gave in.

Hi Beautiful,
I pray all is well with you. I'd actually made up my mind last week not to contact you again, but the truth of the matter is, I miss you too much to give up. Even with you going through with the wedding and not responding to any

of my messages, I still know in my heart that I'm the man you want to be with. I'm the man you love . . . the man you will love until death. At first I didn't understand how you could deny yourself from being happy, but to some degree, I do get why you thought you had no choice but to honor your commitment to your husband. You've always talked about how much you owe him, and I finally had to realize that if the tables were turned, I would maybe feel the same way. Still, none of this changes the love you and I have for each other. What you and I have is one of a kind, and no matter how many months, days, and weeks have passed, I can't move on without you. I've tried . . . unwillingly and involuntarily . . . but I've still tried . . . and it's not working. A part of me knows that continuing to pursue a married woman is wrong, but how does a man walk away from a woman he connected with so perfectly and contently? How does anyone go on without his or her soul mate? For a long time, I didn't want to believe that so many people got married for reasons other than being in love, but now I know it actually happens. And the reasons are infinite. Convenience, children, financial status, comfort, familiarity, general companionship, and the list goes on. But how awful it must be for any human being to wake every morning and go to bed each night with someone they don't love. Or maybe if they do love and care about them, they don't share any passion for their spouse. They don't know what it's like to not want to live without that person. Anyway, I guess I'm sort of going on and on, but I also wanted you to know exactly how I'm feeling right now. Yes, you're married, and yes, I'm wrong for still trying to convince you to leave your husband, but it's like I've told you before. We all only have one soul mate, and sweetheart, you're mine. I'm also yours, and nothing will ever change that. So what I'm hoping is that one day soon, you'll realize that the only way you will ever be free, the only way you'll ever genuinely be happy, is by telling your husband the truth.

I'll let you go now, sweetheart, but know that I am here and that I will always love you.

Levi

Alicia was devastated and warmly touched

all at the same time. Tears flooded her face nonstop. She was speechless, yet in awe of every word Levi had written. Why hadn't she simply had the courage to be honest with Phillip? Why had she given up on a lifetime of happiness just to be miserable? How could she go on living a lie? The biggest lie of the century.

CHAPTER 27

Melanie stepped on the scale, waiting for the numbers to register. When they did, she nearly jumped for joy. Not only had she lost the ten pounds she'd been struggling with for years, she'd lost twenty. She was officially a size six, and for the first time in her life, she weighed only 145 pounds. She was beyond proud of herself, and though it had been a long time coming, she couldn't have been happier.

She turned toward the mirror in the bathroom, admiring her body. All the flab and bulges were gone, and she no longer minded seeing herself naked. She was finally making great progress, and once she lost just another five pounds, she'd be good. Sixes would be loose on her, and she'd be able to fit some fours if the clothing included a certain amount of spandex. Not to mention, her mother and others would never have to feel ashamed of her. As it was,

Gladys hadn't made any snide remarks about Melanie's weight in more than a month, so Melanie knew she was pleased with the way she looked. Her mother had been pushing her to get back into her eights, but Melanie had done better.

If only her marital life could be just as fulfilling, she'd have everything. But sadly, things had never been worse between her and Brad. He'd taken on yet another daunting case, and he'd lost another twenty thousand dollars in the stock market. He was completely out of control, and she wasn't sure how much more of his recklessness she could take.

Melanie slipped on her robe and walked down the hallway to their bedroom. Brad buttoned up his shirt and cast his eyes at her through the mirror — something he seemed to do more and more, now that they weren't on the best of terms.

"So you don't have anything to say?" he said.

Melanie was taking a vacation day, so she got in bed and turned on the television. She didn't even bother looking at Brad, and she couldn't wait for him to leave.

He turned and stared at her. "So I guess you didn't hear me?"

"Nope," she finally said.

"All because I lost some money that has nothing to do with you."

Melanie flipped through channels, ignoring him.

"You really have a lot of nerve," he said, wrapping a red tie around his shirt collar. "You're practically killing yourself, yet you're judging me like you're some saint."

If Melanie could have thrown something at him and gotten away with it, she would have. But she flipped through more channels, pretending she heard nothing.

Brad leaned against the dresser. "Just look at you. Your face is so thin, you look like one of those anorexic supermodels. Your neck is smaller than a ten-year-old's, and your butt has all but vanished."

Melanie tossed him a dirty look. "You're just worried that other men might finally be interested in me. When I was overweight, that was the least of your worries, but now you know I look ten times better. And don't get me started on how little you and I see each other. You're gone all the time, doing God knows what, and I'm sick of it, Brad."

"In case you've forgotten, I have to work, Melanie. I can't be here every evening right at five or spend all my weekends having a good time. We're representing one of our biggest clients, and I need to stay focused."

"So how much more money have you gambled away this month?" she said, changing the subject. "You've already messed over forty thousand dollars, and I know that's not the end of it."

"First of all, I don't gamble. And secondly, we're not talking about me. We're talking about your anorexia."

Melanie laughed like he was a comedian. "Anorexia! Now I know you've lost your mind."

"Laugh all you want, but you're sick, Mel. You can't see what everyone else sees. You look pitiful and malnourished, and if you keep this nonsense up you'll be laid up in a hospital."

"You're the one who's sick. You're throwing away all your savings, and when it's over you'll have nothing. Actually, I think you're doing a lot more than trading stocks. You're probably gambling just like I said. So tell me, Brad, what is it? Horses, casinos, the lottery? Whatever it is, you're addicted to it and I suggest you join a twelve-step program."

"I'm not addicted to anything."

"Then how do you explain throwing away forty thousand dollars in four months? Are you saying that's normal?"

Brad narrowed his eyes. "It's my money,

and I can do whatever I want with it."

"You know what?" she said, tossing the remote onto the bed. "You're right. It is your money, so from now on we're separating everything. I'm also taking every dime of mine from both of those money market accounts we have together." Brad didn't know it, but she'd been checking the balances of those two accounts every few days, making sure he wasn't dipping into them as well.

Brad turned away from her. "You do whatever you feel you have to. That still won't change the fact that you're anorexic. You're sick, and you need to be admitted to a treatment facility."

"The only sickness I'm dealing with is you," she said, standing up and storming out of the bedroom.

She rushed downstairs to the kitchen and pulled her shake from the refrigerator. She was to the point where she looked forward to drinking each of them. They tasted just that good, and she'd also gone back to eating a salad. Not at lunchtime the way she had before, but for dinner. Her third shake of the day had become her nighttime snack. She hadn't planned on eating any solid food until she was sure she could maintain her weight, but a couple of weeks ago when she'd found herself feeling a little light-headed at work and unable to concentrate, she'd changed her mind. She still took her potassium pills and multivitamins and drank plenty of water, but eating salads had made her feel that much better. She didn't eat small salads either, because what she'd discovered was that eating a large one with cucumbers, carrots, mushrooms, and lettuce hadn't stopped her from losing weight. She was sure that her discipline toward working out twice per day was also helping.

Brad walked into the kitchen, fully dressed in a navy blue pinstripe suit. He laid his briefcase on the island and poured a cup of coffee. Melanie had set the timer last night so that it would automatically brew this morning, but now she wished she hadn't. After all the nasty things Brad had said about her, she didn't want to do anything for him. He'd actually had the audacity to say she looked sickly and anorexic. What a joke. Brad was a joke, too, and it was the reason she laughed in his face. He picked up his coffee cup and gawked at her like she was crazy. But Melanie laughed louder, and soon he walked out to the garage and slammed the door behind him. This tickled Melanie even more, because Brad no longer fazed her. He could lose every nickel to his name for all she cared. She hadn't wanted their marriage to turn out like this, but she wouldn't spend any more time worrying about Brad and his addiction. She wouldn't keep defending her weight loss to him, either. She would focus only on what made her happy — whether Brad liked it or not.

CHAPTER 28

Melanie turned onto her parents' street and drove toward their house. When it came to the changing of seasons, there was nothing better than autumn colors. The leaves on every tree were transforming from green to brown, orange, gold, yellow, or burgundy, and there were lots of variations of colors in between. Some had already fallen to the ground. Melanie loved summer, but she also enjoyed sunny, semi-cool days like today when the temperature was just under fifty and she could wear ankle boots and a leather jacket. She hadn't been able to wait until she could pull out her sweaters again, either, one of which she was wearing today. A chocolate-brown one to be exact, which perfectly matched her brown jacket and boots.

She drove into the driveway and turned off her ignition. She leaned her head back, gazing at the brick house and thinking of childhood memories. She had lots of them, and sadly, most were humiliating and heart-breaking. Her parents had done things to embarrass her, her mother had criticized everything about her, and her father had called her terrible names. She was sure — at least she hoped — there had been some happy times, but for the life of her, she couldn't remember any. It had been that appalling, and what she recalled more than anything was how badly she'd wanted to run away. Then, by the time she'd reached her senior year of high school, she'd counted down the days until graduation. She'd done so because she'd known that once she graduated, it would only be two months before she left for college. She'd finally been able to escape, and she'd made sure to never come home on weekends. Sometimes she hadn't even come home for holidays, and during all her summer breaks she'd worked two jobs just so she wouldn't have to spend much time with her parents.

What was interesting was that after all these years, she still wasn't thrilled about being here. Only difference now, as well as over the last three months, was that she'd become closer with her dad, and she could tell he needed her. He'd survived open-heart surgery but was still off work, and he would be for at least another month or so.

Melanie got out of her car, walked up the sidewalk to the front door, and rang the bell.

It took a few seconds before her mother opened the door. She looked at Melanie and turned away without speaking. She'd been doing this as of late, but Melanie wouldn't let it bother her.

Melanie closed the door and went into the family room, where her dad was.

"Hi, sweetheart," he said, smiling and sitting in a large recliner.

"Hi, Dad. How are you?"

"Oh, I'm makin' it, I guess. I still get pretty tired when I get up, though."

Melanie didn't have the courage to tell him that gaining twenty pounds right after having a quadruple bypass wasn't helping. It was as if he'd literally taken each of the pounds Melanie had lost and poured them into his own body. He ate all the time, and no matter what she or her mother said, he wouldn't quit. Of course, her mother had lost all respect for him as a man and as her husband. The other thing Melanie thought about was her former patient Mrs. Weston, the one she'd changed the blood pressure medication for back in June. Just a month ago, she'd had a massive heart attack, and unlike Melanie's dad, Mrs. Weston had passed away.

"You're on a lot of different medications, so that might be causing some of the problem," Melanie said. "Your beta blocker and one of your hypertension pills are known to cause fatigue, and your statin drug, too."

Gladys walked in on their conversation, and Melanie knew it wouldn't be pretty.

"Maybe if you stopped eating like some sumo wrestler and got off your big, fat behind, you'd feel a whole lot better. It was bad enough that you'd already started gaining weight before your surgery, but now you look ridiculous."

Melanie wanted to cry for her dad. His face squealed hurt and humiliation, but he glanced over at the television and didn't say anything. That didn't stop Gladys, however.

"When are you going to start eating the right things, Andrew? I mean, what is it you want? To have another heart attack? Keel over and die next time? What?"

"Gladys, please leave me alone."

"What I wish is that I could leave you, period. You disgust me. I don't even like looking at you anymore, and I'm not sure what you expect me to do about sex. You're too heavy to lay on me, and I doubt you can get it up with all that medication you're on. It's been three months, and this is so unfair to me. If all those blocked arteries hadn't been your own fault, I might have some sympathy for you, but they *were* your fault. You ate whatever you wanted, just like your daughter always did from the time she was born. Even as an infant, she drank bottle after bottle of milk. She never got enough. It was almost like she didn't know she was full, and now you're acting the same way.

Melanie could barely breathe. First her mother had berated her dad to a pulp, and now she was doing the same thing to Melanie — except she was talking about Melanie in the third person. She acted as though Melanie was a non-entity and wasn't in the room. Her mother was flat-out crazy.

"And don't get me started on the money situation around here. Short-term disability was one thing, but now that you've been off ninety days, you'll have to use your long-term benefits. You haven't had a regular payroll check since you got sick, and all because you didn't take care of yourself."

Andrew suddenly spoke up. "Weren't you on your way to the store?"

Gladys placed her hand on her hip. "Excuse me? How dare you sit your roly-poly butt over there, trying to dismiss me."

"I just don't wanna hear it, Gladys.

Enough is enough."

"You're right about that. Enough is *definitely* going to be enough if you don't drop some of that weight and get back to work."

Melanie shook her head.

"Oh, so now you're ready for me to leave, too, I guess. I forgot that you and your daddy here have become thick as thieves."

"Mom, why do you do this? Why are you always so angry?"

"Just shut up, Melanie," she said, grabbing her handbag and leaving the room. Not long after, Melanie heard the back door closing.

"I am so sorry, sweetheart," Andrew said.

Melanie sat in the chair across from him. "Don't worry about it, Dad."

"But I do worry about it, and I'm not just talking about today. I'm talking about the way your mother has treated you all your life, and how I never did anything to stop her. That's why I apologized to you that night in the hospital and asked you to forgive me. I didn't wanna die without making amends."

"And I told you then that I forgive you."

"I know that, but you didn't deserve all that name-calling from me and all the nasty criticism from your mother. And then when you were much younger, we said and did everything in front of you. I'm so ashamed of that, Mel. We were wrong, and if I have to spend the rest of my life trying to make things up to you, I will."

"I'm just glad I can be here for you now."

"I'm glad, too, and I'm very proud of you. There's something else I need to say to you, though, and I'm not sure you'll like it. But it's important, and it needs to be said."

"What's that?"

"You've lost a lot of weight, and you don't look healthy. I know you think you're doing the right thing, but it's time to stop now, sweetheart."

Melanie wasn't sure how to take her father's words. She didn't know whether to be enraged, shocked, hurt, or all of the above.

"I'm sorry to have to say these things, but sweetheart, you need help. You lost down to a good size years ago, but your mother had you thinking it still wasn't enough."

"Have you been talking to Brad?"

"No, but I can imagine he's feeling the same way."

"Look, Dad, I'm fine. And the only reason I don't look the same to you is because you've never seen me at the size I'm supposed to be. I'm well within the standard weight range for a woman who's five-nine."

"That may be, but you don't look like you're eating enough food."

Melanie didn't want to upset her father by questioning him any further, but she knew Brad had to be behind this. He'd called her father and put him up to this mini-intervention.

"Sweetheart, please don't be mad at me. I just don't want you to get sick, and I want you to be happy."

"I promise you I'm okay."

"I know you think you are, but you're not. I know the signs of an eating disorder when I see them. I've lived with this kind of thing for years."

"How?"

"I'm talking about your mother. She's struggled with anorexia the whole time I've known her, and that started way before you were born."

Melanie frowned. "Mom's not anorexic, she's just always watched her weight and been a healthy eater."

"I know it seems that way because she eats regular food, and as much as I hate to say it, she taught you at an early age that this was normal. But she rarely eats more than a thousand calories. And whenever she does, she skips food altogether the very next day. She's done that for years."

"But when we've gone to lunch, I've seen her eat regular meals. She might only eat half of it, but it's still solid food."

"Yeah, and you can bet that she hadn't eaten anything for breakfast, and she certainly didn't eat anything else for the rest of the day."

Melanie had a hard time processing what her dad was saying. None of it added up.

"She's obsessed with her weight, and now that I'm way too heavy, she can't stand the sight of me," he said. "To tell you the truth, I've always loved food and lots of it. But it never made me gain weight until this year. I'm older, and things have changed."

Melanie was at a loss for words. Was her father right about her mother, or was he one of those people who thought every woman who cared about the way she looked was anorexic? Because from what she could see, her mother looked great. She was an awful human being, but she looked fabulous in everything she wore. Melanie also couldn't understand why Brad and her dad thought she looked sickly, because it was obvious that Melanie had never looked better. She was down two sizes, and she was finally happy with herself. Or at least she would be once she lost a bit more. Only five more pounds, and she would be good.

CHAPTER 29

Alicia had spent most of yesterday crying on and off and trying to figure out what to do next. There was no doubt that what she should have done was block Levi's cell number and Facebook account, and also his email address. This was something she should have followed through on back in June when he was first released. She'd told herself a couple of times that she would, but that had all been nothing more than a bunch of idle thinking. She didn't want to end all communication with Levi. Not now, not ever. But she feared that if she continued reading and listening to his messages, it wouldn't be long before she went to him. Each of his words had tugged at her heart and made her long for him, but none had affected her as much as the note he'd sent her yesterday. Levi had laid everything out with all the right logic and sentiments, and she couldn't argue with any of what he'd written. He was definitely her soul mate, and he was the only man she loved with her entire being. They were connected in a way she couldn't explain, and no matter how hard she tried, she would never share that same kind of chemistry with Phillip. He was a good man with a good heart, but she couldn't control who she loved. No one could do that, and anyone who claimed otherwise was lying.

What she'd also learned was that not everyone's soul mate would be the ideal choice. Take Levi, for example. Here he was a former drug dealer who'd served time in prison, and Alicia was a college-educated writer and a pastor's daughter. They'd come from totally different backgrounds and had lived completely different lives, yet they could relate to each other on every level. If only she could have fallen in love with Levi before marrying Phillip the first time . . .

Alicia wondered how many other women secretly felt the same as she did: married to men who were great in almost every regard, but whom they weren't in love with. She had a feeling there were thousands who fell into that category. She was sure, too, that there were just as many men who didn't love their wives. These people were merely living in the house together, believing they had no other choice. Most of them had lost out on being with their true soul mates because they'd feared what others might say. This was part of the reason Alicia hadn't been able to break off her second engagement to Phillip so she could marry Levi. No one would have understood or approved of their relationship.

Alicia glanced at her watch and saw that it was almost ten. Phillip had been gone for more than an hour, and she'd had no idea so much time had passed. It felt as though she'd only been sitting there for ten minutes, meaning she'd done more fantasizing about Levi than she'd realized. She jumped when her cell phone rang because if it was Levi, she wasn't sure she was strong enough to ignore him today. Thankfully, when she picked it up, she saw Brad's number.

"Hey, Brad," she said.

"Hey, how are you?"

"I'm good. What's goin' on?"

"Well, you know if I'm calling you in the middle of a Friday morning, it's pretty bad."

"Oh no. What's wrong?"

"It's Mel. She's steadily not eating and steadily losing weight, and she won't hear anything I'm saying."

"Phillip and I were just talking about that yesterday. She's lost a ton of weight, and she doesn't realize how small she is."

"She doesn't see it at all, and when I got to work this morning I went on Google and discovered something called BDD. Body dysmorphic disorder. I also think she's anorexic."

"I've heard of BDD, but I never thought Melanie might have it. I just thought she was self-conscious about the way she looked because of how heavy she was when she was younger. And even more so now because of the way her mother talks to her. Mrs. Johnson has Melanie thinking a size ten is huge."

"Her mother has played a huge part in this, but I still think she has BDD and anorexia. This morning when I told her how sickly she looked, she was livid. Totally defensive."

"She was the same way with me in June. Remember when she passed out the same night her dad was having surgery?"

"Yeah, she was already in trouble then, but I didn't realize how bad it was until now. Her personality is even different. She flies off the handle about everything. Anyway, I was hoping you would go and talk to her."

"I can try. I'll call her later to tell her I'm coming by tomorrow."

"I'll be at the office most of the day, so that'll be a good time. If I'm there, she'll swear we're ganging up on her."

"I just wish she knew how beautiful she was before she started losing so much weight," Alicia said.

"So do I."

"What does she eat for breakfast?"

"She drinks a shake."

"What about lunch and dinner?"

"She claims she has a salad for lunch, and unfortunately, I've worked so many hours over the last few weeks, I haven't been home to see what she has in the evening."

"Well, she can't be eating all that much. Not with losing so many inches and pounds."

"I think she's eating only enough to survive."

"Gosh, that really scares me, Brad."

"It scares me, too. This is serious, and something has to be done."

"I'll definitely go over and talk to her tomorrow. I wish I could get her to meet me for lunch, but I know that's out of the question. She stopped doing that a while ago."

"She doesn't want to go to restaurants, because she doesn't want us to see how little she eats."

"I really wish we'd paid more attention to what was going on. I mean, I knew she wasn't eating enough, but I never expected things to turn out the way they have."

"Neither did I. But hey, I have to get going. Alicia, thanks for listening."

"Of course. Mel is my girl, and you know you can call me anytime."

"Will do. Talk to you later."

"See ya."

Alicia hated having to confront Melanie, because there was a chance it might end their friendship for good. Alicia still hadn't forgotten how angry Melanie had been that night she'd practically thrown Alicia out of her room. But if losing her as a friend meant saving her life, then so be it.

She picked up her phone to call Melanie but noticed that she had another Facebook message. She clicked on the icon and opened it.

Hi Beautiful,
I really thought I would hear from you by now. Especially after pouring my heart out to you the way I did yesterday. Maybe you're hoping I'll just give up, but sweetheart, that's not going to happen. Giving up on us would be like giving up on life, and I can't accept that. I

have a lot of plans, but none of them will mean anything if you're not coming along for the ride. Actually, I think I've done a lot better than most would expect. I haven't once tried to see you, even though I could easily have found you or "accidentally" run into you anytime I wanted. I also haven't left you any voice messages except during the week when I know your husband is at the church. So I think you know by now that I'm not trying to make trouble for you. I just want to see you face-to-face. If it'll make you feel better, we can meet at a public place. Whatever you want. Just tell me where, and I'll be there. Oh, and by the way, I know you've read every last one of my inbox messages here on Facebook, because it always shows the exact time you opened it.

You take care, sweetheart. I'll love you always.

Levi

Alicia closed her Facebook app and took a deep breath. She needed to get dressed and get out of there. She had to find some way to keep her mind off Levi. Just about anything would do, but it didn't take long for her to consider something she hadn't done in years: venturing out on one of her fabulous shopping sprees. Right after Phillip had divorced her the first time, she'd completely stopped spending beyond her means. But today, maybe a bit of retail therapy was what she needed. Something to relax her mind. Something to keep her from being reckless and irrational.

CHAPTER 30

The sun shone brightly, and Alicia was happy to be out and about. It was somewhat chillier than she'd thought, and she was glad she'd worn a black turtleneck sweater and jeans. She'd also thrown on the black lambskin leather jacket Charlotte had given her last Christmas, along with a pair of black pointed-toe, high-heeled boots she'd bought for herself around the same time.

She sat at the stop sign at the entrance of their subdivision readjusting her sunglasses, then drove onto the main street. It had been an hour since Levi had sent her that last in-box message, and she was hoping she wouldn't hear from him again. At least not today, anyway, because she needed to spend some time alone, enjoying the day and clearing her head.

Alicia pushed the audio command button on her console. "Call Phillip."

The system in her vehicle responded.

"Dialing Phillip, please wait."

After a few seconds, Phillip answered. "Hey, my beautiful wife. What's up?"

"I'm heading to the mall."

"Really? Which one?"

"Oakbrook."

"Your favorite."

"You know it is. I love Woodfield, too, which is a closer drive from Mitchell, but Oakbrook is on a different level. And before you even start thinkin' it, I won't go crazy when I get there."

Phillip laughed. "You said it, I didn't. But I *am* glad to know that. There was a time when you shopped like a drug addict."

"Yeah, I definitely had a little bit of a problem. I learned a tough lesson from it, though."

"But that's all in the past now, so no worries."

Alicia thought about the way she'd forged Phillip's name on preapproved credit card applications without his knowing it. She'd received the cards, maxed them out, and hid the statements. The memory of it all still made her cringe, and it was her father who'd paid off the balances so Phillip's credit wouldn't be ruined. She had, however, paid her father back every penny.

There was a short silence, and Alicia knew

Phillip was also thinking about the deceitful thing she'd done.

"I haven't shopped just to be shopping in a long time, and I'm looking forward to it."

"Nothing wrong with that."

"I hope you don't mind because with it being Friday, I might not get back until early evening. It's eleven now, so I won't even get there until noon or after."

"You'll probably get caught up in rush-hour traffic, too. But that's fine. You enjoy yourself."

"I plan to."

"I hope you still have some energy when you get home, though."

"I'm sure I will," she replied, trying to sound enthused. "Oh, and hey, Brad called me earlier."

"He told me he was going to, and I meant to tell you that this morning before I left. This thing with Melanie is a lot worse than we thought."

"Yeah, it is. I'm going to call her and go over there tomorrow afternoon."

"I hope she hears you, because she can't keep going the way she's been."

"Not at all," she said.

"I had a cousin once who was both an-orexic and bulimic, and she died. I'm not sure I ever told you about her."

"You didn't."

"It was years ago, before you and I met."

"How old was she?"

"Twenty."

"Gosh, that's really sad."

"Eating disorders are very serious, but you don't hear much about them. And even more so when you're talking about adults. It's much more common with teenagers, but it sounds like Melanie has been struggling since she was a child."

"She has been, but I never thought she needed professional help. It never crossed my mind."

"You just have to be there for her. We all do."

"For sure."

"Well, I guess I'd better get going. I have a few more things to do, and then I'm going to take a late lunch."

"I'll see you tonight."

"I love you, baby, and be safe out there."

"I will. Love you, too."

Alicia ended the call and turned on SiriusXM. Kem's latest single was playing on the Heart & Soul channel, and like with every other song he'd made, Alicia loved it. But the more she listened to the lyrics and the way Kem sang them, she found herself thinking and fantasizing about Levi. She'd just hung up with Phillip a few minutes ago, telling him that she loved him, but now she was longing to hear Levi's voice. Longing to simply see his gorgeous face and alluring smile.

She quickly switched the channel to a random talk radio station. It wasn't even one she'd listened to before, and she didn't care. All she wanted was to make sure she didn't hear any more love songs.

It was only four o'clock, and Alicia had already made her rounds. She'd shopped in Neiman Marcus, Nordstrom, White House Black Market, and Tiffany's, and she'd found a few things she loved in all four places. A to-die-for silver necklace with matching earrings, a winter-white Armani sweater, two pairs of riding boots: one black and one brown, a navy blue leather jacket, a black off-the-shoulder wool sweater, and a pair of dark indigo boot-cut jeans. Today had been a good day and well worth the trip.

Alicia walked away from the mall, heading toward the parking lot. She was sort of hungry and debated whether she should lock her bags in her car and get something to eat. But when she thought about how late she'd get home, she decided against it.

If she left now, she would at least beat some of the work traffic, even if not all of it.

She strolled down the long aisle, passing rows of cars, but as she walked closer she could tell her eyes were playing tricks on her. They had to be, as they saw a man dressed in all black the same as she was stepping out of a silver Mercedes-Benz parked next to hers — and he looked like Levi. She definitely had to be dreaming. Or maybe she was fantasizing about him again without trying.

She kept walking, but when she arrived at her car, she knew Levi was as real as always. She pressed the trunk button on her key fob, acting as though she didn't recognize him.

Levi leaned against his own vehicle with his arms folded. "Let me go ahead and apologize now for having you followed. I'm sorry, but I just couldn't go another day without seeing you."

Alicia set her bags inside the trunk one at a time. "Levi, you know you're wrong for doing this."

"What did you expect me to do? I've been sending you message after message, and you wouldn't respond. I mean, how do you think that made me feel?"

Alicia felt her hands shaking, but she

pressed the button and shut her trunk.

"Baby, I'm sorry to catch you off guard like this, but there was no other way."

"How did you know where I was?"

"I told you, I had you followed. Not to check up on you, but so I could eventually meet you somewhere. And when my guy told me you were at the mall, I drove over here and waited."

"And how long has your *guy* been following me?"

"A couple of weeks."

Alicia hated herself for not being upset with him. She knew she should've been, but shamefully, a part of her was glad Levi had taken matters into his own hands.

"Can I talk to you?" he said, and Alicia was happy she had on sunglasses, so he wouldn't see how nervous and excited she was. Levi looked even more handsome than usual, and Alicia's heart felt as though it were beating through her chest.

"It's getting late, and I have to get home."

"Just come sit in my car for a few minutes. That's all I'm asking."

Alicia didn't move. She wanted to, but she knew nothing good could come from being closed up in a vehicle with Levi. As it was, the chemistry between them was so intense, a mere stranger could see how in love they were with each other.

Only problem was, Alicia was married.

"Sweetheart, please. Just let me talk to you."

"Levi, why are you trying to make things hard for me?"

Levi walked around to the passenger side of his vehicle and opened the door. "Only for a few minutes. I promise."

"I don't think so."

"Well, I told you I'm not giving up. So if we don't do this now, I'll have to meet up with you somewhere else."

"Is that a threat?"

"Actually, it is. Not the kind that'll harm you, but I'm being honest. If you won't talk to me here, we'll have to do it down the road."

It wasn't even worth arguing with him anymore, so Alicia strutted over and sat inside the car. Levi shut the door and walked back to the driver's side.

When he got in, he raised his sunglasses and rested them on his head. "Still as gorgeous as ever, I see."

Alicia felt like jumping out of her skin, and she wasn't sure how much longer she'd be able to stand this.

"Remember when I said you'd come looking for me two months after you got married?"

"Yeah, but as you can see I didn't."

"Yeah, well, it's only been a month, and you would have eventually."

"And your point?"

"I couldn't wait that long. I needed to see you now. I feel like some silly schoolboy, and I don't like it. There are days when my heart hurts so badly, I feel sick."

"I'm sorry to hear that."

"And you don't feel the same way? You haven't missed me at all?"

"Even if I have, it doesn't matter."

"It does matter, so just tell me."

"Look, Levi, I'll be honest. Walking away from you and marrying someone else was one of the hardest things I've ever had to do. But what's done is done, and we can't change it."

"No marriage is permanent unless both parties want it to be."

Alicia looked toward the passenger window and closed her eyes.

Levi turned her face back to him, removed her sunglasses, and caressed the side of her face. "Girl, don't you know how much I love you? I would do anything for you. You hear me? Anything. And I know your feelings haven't changed, either. Being without you these last three months has been straight torture."

Alicia tried to stop her tears from falling, but she couldn't.

"You're miserable, too," he said. "So why are we suffering like this?"

Alicia turned her entire body toward him and laid the side of her head against the backrest, gazing into his eyes. Levi wiped her tears with his hand and then leaned over and kissed her. Alicia didn't bother trying to fight him. Instead, she grabbed both sides of his face and kissed him as though they were locked away in a bedroom. Every pent-up emotion she'd been hiding rushed freely through her soul, and at this very moment, she felt at total peace. She was so in love with this man, it frightened her. But what scared her more was the thought of never seeing him again. She couldn't imagine living like that, and she wouldn't.

CHAPTER 31

Alicia pulled into the garage and shut off her vehicle. She'd sworn she wouldn't betray Phillip again, but a couple of hours ago, history had repeated itself. Levi had asked her to follow him to the house he was renting, which was still about an hour from Mitchell, and she'd done so without hesitation. She'd wanted to go — wanted so desperately to be with him — and they'd made beautiful love throughout the evening. But now it was nearly ten o'clock, and she had to face Phillip. She'd spent the entire drive rehearsing her alibi, and thankfully, she'd already spoken to him right before leaving Levi's. He'd called to see where she was, and she'd told him she was browsing around at the bookstore in Schaumburg. She hadn't been able to tell whether Phillip had believed her or not, but he hadn't questioned her any further.

If only she hadn't driven over to Oakbrook

Center, Levi never would have gotten a chance to see her. If only she hadn't laid eyes on him, kissed him, and realized how much she'd missed him. But she had. She was wrong, there was no denying that, but she loved him and couldn't wait to see him again.

She walked inside the house and saw Phillip sitting at the speckled-black island. He glanced over at her and then back at the television. Alicia knew this wasn't good, so she immediately slid into fix-it mode.

"Hi, baby," she said, dropping all her bags on the kitchen counter. "I am so sorry I was gone so long. I shopped for a lot longer than I'd planned, and then once I ate, I went to the bookstore."

Phillip wouldn't look at her. "Yeah, you already told me that."

Alicia went over and hugged him from behind. "Baby, please don't be upset. I know I said I wouldn't get carried away at the mall, but I did. The old me showed up, but I promise you it won't happen again."

Phillip scanned all her bags and shook his head.

Alicia held him tighter. "Baby, please say something."

"Like what? Please don't turn into the shopping addict you used to be? Please don't shop for all eternity?"

Alicia hated upsetting Phillip, but she was relieved to know that he hadn't suspected she was sleeping around. He was angry about all the money and time she'd spent at the mall.

"I won't make a habit of this," she said. "You know I haven't done anything like this in years, and then once I stopped at the bookstore, time just sort of got away from me."

"So is that all you bought?"

"Yes."

"I hope that's true, because lying and hiding stuff won't work. I love you, but I won't tolerate that like I did before."

"And you won't have to. I'm not saying I'll never go shopping again, but it'll be a long time."

Phillip kept his eyes locked on the television and didn't respond.

Alicia rested the side of her face against his. "I'm really sorry. I just needed to get out of the house and do something fun. Can you forgive me?"

"And I don't have a problem with that. I want you to enjoy yourself, but I also don't want any problems."

"I understand, and I'll be mindful of that from now on. Okay?"

"I'm serious."

"So am I," she said, releasing him. "Have you eaten?"

"I had leftovers from last night."

"You wanna watch a movie?" she asked, trying her best to act normal.

"I'd rather be doing something else."

Alicia hoped he wasn't talking about sex. "Oh yeah, like what?"

"Do you have to ask?" he said, scooting his chair back and pulling her toward him.

"Phillip, stop. I need to get my things upstairs and put away."

"Why? It's not like they're going anywhere."

He spread his legs farther apart and pulled her between them. "You really had me worried, you know that?"

"I know, and I'm sorry."

"I just don't want things to go back to the way they were."

"And they won't. You might not believe me, but I'm not obsessed with shopping again."

Phillip stroked her flowing hair back with both hands and held on to it while kissing her. After a few seconds, she pulled away, but Phillip's desire for her became more ravenous and he kissed her more voraciously than before. Alicia wasn't sure what to do.

The last thing she wanted was to have sex with her husband only hours after making love to another man. Phillip had no clue what had gone on, but Alicia's conscience was tearing her up inside.

"I missed you," he said between breaths and steadily kissing her. Alicia kissed him back, but she wanted him to stop.

"I missed you, too."

He kissed her again, but then he eased her away from him and stood up. "Let's go into the other room."

"For what?"

He smiled playfully. "You know."

"I've been gone all day, so let me take a shower." Alicia had already taken one at Levi's, but for some reason she felt like she needed another.

"Uh-uh. I wanna make love to you now," he said, taking her hand and leading her into the family room. He pulled his sweater over his head and then removed hers. Alicia went along with what he wanted, but she wasn't sure how she'd get through this. Sleeping with her husband and her lover all in one night was unbearable. Although, it suddenly dawned on her that if she continued making excuses, Phillip might suspect she'd been up to more than just shopping. She couldn't allow that, so she had to think of something fast. And she did. By the time they'd stripped away the rest of their clothing, Alicia kissed Phillip like she couldn't get enough of him. She kept her eyes closed the entire time, pretending he was Levi.

CHAPTER 32

"So when are you gonna ask your husband for a divorce?" Levi asked.

Alicia was headed over to Melanie's, but she'd called Levi a few minutes ago. She'd enjoyed her time with him yesterday, and she also wanted to see him again, but asking Phillip for a divorce wasn't part of the plan. She didn't like sleeping with two men and practically living a double life, but what other choice did she have? It was true that she didn't know how she could keep this up, but going to Phillip with the truth and confessing that she wanted out of the marriage wasn't an option. He would never understand, his world would be shattered, and Alicia didn't want to be the cause of that.

"Sweetheart, why aren't you saying anything?" he asked.

"No reason."

"Well, when are you planning to tell him?"

"You know I can't do that."

"Okay, wait a minute. You're joking, right?"

Alicia sighed. "Baby, please don't do this."

"Do what?"

"Pressure me about Phillip."

"I don't believe this. Not after everything you said to me yesterday."

"And I meant every word. I really do love you, and you're the only man I want to be with. But that doesn't change the fact that I'm married."

"And being married doesn't change the fact that you're in love with me. That you're living a lie with your husband."

Alicia pulled up to a stop sign, looking both ways. "Why can't we just enjoy each other?"

"Because that's not enough for me, and you need to make a decision."

Alicia wondered where all this was coming from. Why Levi's tone sounded much different than it had when she'd seen him.

"Look, I don't wanna fight with you, so why don't we talk about this later?" she said.

"Whatever."

"Why are you so angry?"

"Like you said, let's just talk about this later. Are you coming by when you leave Melanie's?"

"You're an hour away."

"And?"

"I can't be gone all evening again. Phillip will think something's up."

"What about just for a couple of hours?"

"It'll take that long just to drive there and back."

"So you're not coming?"

"I wish I could. Maybe Monday."

"Even though that's your husband's day off?"

"Then Tuesday."

"That's three days from now."

"I know, but I can't get away before then. We have church tomorrow, and my mom and stepdad are driving down for dinner."

"I really thought you were ready to make things right."

Alicia didn't know what else to say. She'd thought being with him and admitting how much she loved him would be enough, but it wasn't. "Hey, I'm almost at Melanie's, so can I call you when I leave?"

"Yeah, all right."

Alicia waited for him to tell her he loved her, but he didn't. "I wish you wouldn't be so mad."

"What do you expect?"

"For you to understand."

"Just call me back."

"Fine," she said. "I love you."

"I love you, too."

Alicia ended the call, and she could tell Levi still wasn't happy. He'd been so different yesterday, content and glad to be with her. But today he wanted more, and she had to talk him down from that.

Alicia drove down Melanie and Brad's street and turned into their driveway. When she grabbed her purse and got out, she saw the garage door rising.

"Hey, how are you?" Brad said.

"I'm good. You leaving?"

"Yep. Need to head to the office for a while. You can just come through here if you want."

Alicia was glad she'd parked in front of their third garage door and not the double one, so Brad could back out okay.

"Is Mel in the kitchen?"

"No, she's upstairs, but you can go on in," he said, then added in a whisper, "And thanks for doing this."

"Of course. I'll see you later."

Alicia walked inside the house. "Mel?"

"Hey," she said. "I'll be right down."

Alicia set her bag on the island, looking around. When she spotted the refrigerator she walked over and opened it. There must have been forty shakes divided between two rows. Ten packages of four. Alicia also saw two bags of butter lettuce, which she loved, but she didn't see much else. That is, unless you counted all the condiments and bottles of water. There weren't any eggs, milk, juice, or yogurt, all of which she'd seen plenty of times in Melanie and Brad's refrigerator, so things had definitely gotten worse.

Alicia closed the door and sat down at the island.

"Hey, girl," Melanie said, walking into the kitchen and hugging Alicia.

"Hey," she said, relieved Melanie hadn't caught her snooping.

Melanie took a seat across from her. "So what are you up to today? I was glad you called this morning."

"Nothing, really. Just wanted to come by to hang out for a while. We haven't done that in weeks."

"I know. I've been working a lot of hours and spending a lot more time with my dad."

"How is he doing?"

"Okay, but he won't watch what he eats."

"I can tell he's gained weight. I noticed it the last couple of Sundays at church."

"He really has, and I hope he does something about it."

"Have you tried to talk to him?"

"I want to, but I don't have the heart. Not

when my mother is already making him feel bad enough."

Alicia still couldn't get over some of the things she'd heard Mrs. Johnson say and do over the last three months. She was a whole different woman. Although, Alicia was starting to believe Phillip's philosophy. Maybe this truly was the way things had always been behind closed doors.

"Your poor dad."

"Yeah, I know."

Alicia could tell Melanie wanted to say more, but as usual, she didn't. "So what's new?"

"Girl, you don't even wanna know. And hey, can I get you a bottle of water or something? I meant to go to the store to get some juice and soda, but I never got around to it."

"No, I'm fine. But what's going on?"

"Well, for starters, Brad lost another twenty thousand dollars."

"What? Are you serious?"

"Yeah, and I'm getting pretty tired of it. Yesterday, I'd decided I wasn't going to let him worry me, but when I woke up this morning it was the first thing I thought about."

"And he lost this money in the stock market, too?"

"That's what he says, but I think it's something else."

"Like what?"

"I don't know, maybe gambling."

"Has he ever done that before?"

"Years ago, but it was never a problem. He used to like betting on horses."

"Now I kinda remember that. But he never did that all the time."

"No, but maybe now he's caught up."

"I hope not. Maybe it really is stock related."

"I don't think so."

"Why?"

"Just a feeling I have. He's still gone all the time, too, and when he is here, all we do is argue or ignore each other."

"I hate hearing that," Alicia said, thinking how when Brad had called her yesterday she'd had no idea they were having so many problems. He'd made it seem like all he was concerned about was Melanie's weight-loss issues.

"Yeah, well, if he loses any more money, I'm going to get to the bottom of it. Because it's not like I've seen any proof that he's lost it from trading."

Alicia sat listening and the more Melanie talked, the more Alicia hated to bring up the real reason she'd come by to see her.

"So how are things with you and Phillip?" Melanie asked.

"Everything's great."

"I'm really happy for you guys. I never told you how worried I was back in June, and I'm glad everything worked out."

"Worried about what?"

"Levi being out of prison. I really thought he was going to cause trouble, but God had a different plan."

Alicia had no idea why Melanie was suddenly bringing up Levi, and she sort of resented it.

"Well, I guess we've both been a little worried about each other," Alicia said before she could stop herself.

"Really? What were you worried about?"

"You.

"Why?"

From the time Melanie had walked into the kitchen, Alicia had noticed how thin Melanie's face was. The jogging suit she wore also looked way too big, but Alicia had pushed it out of her mind for the time being.

"Mel, I hope you don't get upset with me, but you have to start eating again."

Melanie raised her eyebrows. "What do you mean? I eat every day."

"But not enough. You've lost a huge

amount of weight, and you don't look the same."

"Oh my goodness, first my dad and now you? Brad has been lying to both of you, and you actually believe him?"

"Mel, this has nothing to do with Brad. I'm looking at you right now with my own eyes, and you've lost way too much weight."

Melanie folded her arms. "Please tell me you're kidding."

"I'm not. Mel, do you think I would say anything at all unless I thought it was absolutely necessary? I've loved you like a sister for years, and I don't want anything to happen to you."

"Like what?"

"I don't want you to become physically ill. Or worse, end up in the hospital."

"Hospital? Yeah, it's just what I thought. Brad has gotten to you big-time. He was talking that same nonsense yesterday."

"Mel, look at how big your clothes are. Everything you wear to church is way too loose, and so is that sweat suit you're wearing now."

Melanie shook her head, dismissing Alicia. "Is that what you came over here for? Was this so-called visit some sort of trick?"

"No, I really wanted to see you, but I also want you to get some help. What if you really have an eating disorder?"

Melanie stood up. "Wow, so my mother spent years insisting that I needed to lose weight, and now you're telling me I need to gain it back? You must be out of your mind."

"Mel, do you think I would come to you like this if it wasn't for your own good?"

"I don't know, you tell me. Or maybe you just hate that I'm finally smaller than you."

"What are you talking about?"

"Don't play dumb. I've always weighed more than you, but now that the tables have turned, you don't like it."

Alicia stared at her in shock. "You're really messed up, aren't you?"

"No, I'm fine, you're just jealous."

Alicia half laughed. "I know you don't believe that."

"I'm positive of it, and I think you should leave," she said, walking over to the door and opening it.

"You know, I'm getting a little tired of you kicking me out of places. You did this same thing when you collapsed in the ER, but I let it go."

"Well, that makes two of us, because I'm tired, too. I'm sick of you being in my business."

"Why can't you see what you're doing to yourself?"

"Why are you judging me? Did I judge you when you ruined your marriage to Phillip?"

"Oh, so we're going there?"

"I'm just being honest."

Alicia wanted to set her straight, but she knew Melanie was sick, so she stayed as calm as possible. "Mel, let's not do this. Why won't you just let me help you?"

"Are you deaf?" she said, frowning. "How many times do I have to ask you to leave?"

So much for keeping composure. "Girl, please," Alicia said, picking up her handbag. "You won't ever have to ask me again. I'm done with this."

"As you should be."

Alicia got up and walked over to the doorway. She and Melanie locked eyes, and Melanie slammed the door behind her. They'd never gotten this angry with each other before, and while Alicia was glad to be leaving, she drove away sad, furious, and in tears.

CHAPTER 33

Three hours had passed since Alicia had stormed out of Melanie's house, yet Melanie was still beside herself. She was livid, and she had a mind to call and let Alicia have it once and for all. They'd been the best of friends for years, but Melanie wasn't about to let Alicia judge her and tell her what to do when Alicia had done all kinds of unspeakable dirt. She'd married Phillip and had treated him like nothing. He'd been the best husband any woman could hope for, but Alicia had nearly ruined his credit and slept with a drug dealer. She'd even gone so far as falling in love with Levi, and the only reason she'd stopped seeing him was because he'd gone to prison. Melanie also wondered whether Alicia was telling the truth about not having any contact with Levi since he'd been released. Because it wasn't like Alicia had been the one to tell her Levi was out. Brad had heard about it from Phillip, and when Melanie had asked her why she hadn't told her, Alicia had shrugged it off like it was no big deal. She'd claimed that Levi was the least of her worries, and that this was the reason she'd forgotten to mention it. Melanie had wanted to believe her, but she still hadn't forgotten the night of her father's surgery when it had taken hours for Alicia to return any of their calls.

There was no way Alicia would make the same mistake twice, though. She was selfish and a little spoiled, but not even she would sleep with the same man who'd broken up her marriage the first time. She wouldn't do something that crazy.

Alicia had, however, brought her behind over to Melanie's and accused her of being mentally ill. Unlike Brad and Melanie's dad, Alicia hadn't used the word *anorexic,* but she had thrown out the term *eating disorder,* which was the same thing. What incensed Melanie more was the fact that Alicia and Brad had clearly been discussing her behind her back. What kind of best friend did that? Melanie had always thought she could trust Alicia with everything. Alicia was her sister, BFF, ride-or-die chick, and confidante to the end. Or so she'd thought, but now Melanie was rethinking their friendship.

She'd also thought she could trust her own husband, but he'd turned against her as well. He was the reason her dad and Alicia had confronted her in the first place.

"How dare he," she said, picking up the phone and dialing Brad. It rang multiple times until she heard his outgoing voice message.

"Hi, this is Brad Richardson. Unfortunately, I can't take your call right now. But please leave a detailed message, and I'll get back to you as soon as possible. Thanks so much, and have a great day."

"Brad, I know you're probably ignoring my call on purpose, but thank you for telling all those lies about me to my dad and Alicia. You've got a lot of nerve, and you can bet this conversation isn't over. And when are you bringin' your lowdown behind home, anyway? I can't believe you did this to me. You're such a liar, and you can't be trusted. Actually, instead of coming home, why don't you find somewhere else to stay tonight, because I don't wanna see you. Bye."

Melanie ended the call and dropped the phone on the island. Brad made her sick. But that was okay, because Melanie wouldn't let anyone — not Brad, Alicia, or her dad — impede her progress. She'd lost twenty whole pounds, and in no time, she'd be down to 140.

Melanie got on the treadmill, power walking at top speed for an hour, and then thought about her dad. So after drinking a full bottle of water and allowing her heart rate to return to normal, she called him on his cell phone.

"Hello?" he answered.

"Hi, Dad."

"Hi, sweetheart. What's up?"

"Something's been bothering me, and I wanted to talk to you about it. But not in front of Mom, though."

"She's gone, so go ahead."

"Is it true that you and Mom are struggling to pay bills? She seemed really upset yesterday, and that worries me."

"Honey, we are having a bit of a time, but don't you think twice about it. Once I go back to work, we'll be fine."

"But we don't know when that'll be. You could be off for another month or longer."

"I'm sorry your mother burdened you with this. She never should've talked about our finances in front of you."

"No, but I'm glad she did. I don't want you going back to work before you have to, so just come by my office on Monday. That way Mom won't have to know anything."

"Why?"

"I'm giving you a check."

"You really don't have to do that."

"I know, but I want to."

"What will I tell your mother once she sees that all the bills are paid?"

"I don't know. Tell her whatever you want, but you can't afford to be stressing over money. Not with your heart condition."

"You're such a good daughter. Especially with the way we treated you."

"You're still my parents, Dad, and you don't have to keep apologizing for that."

"I feel like I do. I sit here day in and day out, thinking about everything I said. All the mistakes your mother and I made."

"It's in the past."

"Bless you."

"Just call me Monday when you're on your way, and I'll meet you out in the parking lot. I hope ten thousand will be enough."

"No, no, no, that's way too much. We don't need all that."

"You never know how long you'll be off, so I want you to take it."

"I sure do appreciate it."

"You're welcome. I'm going to get off of here, but I'll see you at church tomorrow."

"See you then, and I love you."

"I love you, too."

Melanie felt good about helping her dad, but after a few minutes she thought about Brad and the way he'd betrayed her, and her joy turned to rage.

She picked up her phone and called him again. It rang until his voice mail answered again. She had a mind to drive over to his office so she could *make* him talk to her. She knew that was his place of business, but she didn't care about that. She'd long been tired of Brad's legal cases taking priority over their marriage, anyway, so maybe showing up unannounced was the best way to handle things. Maybe confronting him at work, especially if some of his partners were there, would get his attention.

Melanie dialed him one more time, and when he didn't answer she ran up the stairs to shower and change clothes. If she hurried, she could be at Brad's office within an hour. But as she walked into her bedroom, the doorbell rang. She frowned when she realized it might be Alicia. She sort of hoped it was, because if Alicia was planning to harass her about her weight again, Melanie wouldn't hold back this time.

She went down the stairs, through the long corridor, and peeked out the window. Melanie wondered why two police officers were standing there.

She opened the door. "Yes?"

"Are you Melanie Richardson?"

"Yes, I am."

"Ma'am, we're sorry to have to tell you this, but your husband was in a pretty bad car accident. He's been taken to Mitchell Memorial, and you should get there as soon as possible. If you'd like, we can drive you."

Melanie heard every word the officer was saying, but she couldn't respond to him. She couldn't move or think because her body went numb.

CHAPTER 34

By the time Melanie had slipped on her shoes and thrown on her jacket, her nerves had settled some, so she'd driven herself to the hospital. That's what she'd thought, anyway — that she hadn't needed the officers to take her. But now as she drove through the parking lot searching for an open spot, her nerves flared up again. What if Brad was in critical condition? What if he died? She was so sorry for the things she'd said to him over the last few weeks and the nasty voice messages she'd left him this afternoon. It was just that she'd been so upset about the way he'd betrayed her.

Melanie found a parking spot one row away from the hospital, got out, and strolled quickly to the entrance. There was a twenty-something woman standing at the reception window, and the waiting room was busier than usual. There were also a couple of babies crying, and Melanie hoped they soon quieted down because all the noise was making her more anxious.

Melanie waited behind the woman who was still answering questions and looked toward the sliding doors to see if Phillip or her dad had arrived. She'd called both of them while on her way, and she needed them. Normally, her nursing background kept her medical worries at bay, but strangely enough, she was scared out of her mind about Brad. She'd felt the same way the night her dad had gone into surgery, but for some reason, this felt worse.

When the woman walked away to take a seat, Melanie stepped forward.

"Hi, my husband, Brad Richardson, was just brought in by ambulance."

The middle-aged receptionist checked her computer. "Yes, the doctors are in with him now, and I'll let them know you're here."

Melanie reluctantly walked over to the waiting area and sat down. She felt restrained, the same as she had when her dad had been rushed to the ER. It was hard knowing she was medically qualified to work side by side with the other nurses and doctors who were taking care of Brad. But she also knew they couldn't allow her to see him unless he was stable, and that they'd want to have a solid diagnosis before updating her.

She pulled out her phone to see if she had any missed calls from her dad or Phillip, but when she looked up she saw them walking in.

Andrew seemed almost out of breath. "I got here as fast as I could, sweetheart."

She stood and hugged him. "Thank you, Dad, and why don't you sit down."

Her father didn't argue, and Melanie hugged Phillip.

"What happened?" Phillip asked.

"All I know is that someone ran a red light and hit Brad. That's all the officers told me."

"I've been praying for him ever since you called, and I know he'll be fine."

Melanie hoped Phillip was right, because suddenly, none of their problems and none of what they'd been bickering about mattered. All Melanie wanted was for Brad to be okay so they could make up and start their marriage fresh. It was amazing how even when a person had done things to hurt you, it didn't affect you quite as profoundly when you thought you might lose them.

"I wish they'd come out and tell us something," Melanie said, leaning her head against the wall.

"I'm sure we'll hear something soon,"

Andrew said, patting her thigh.

It was then that Melanie thought about something. Where was her mother?

"Where's Mom?"

"Oh . . . She's home . . . She said she wasn't feeling well."

Melanie didn't question him any further, but she knew her mom was lying about being ill. There wasn't a single thing wrong with her, and the reason she hadn't shown up was because she never saw a reason to support Melanie with anything. Melanie also knew that her mother wasn't happy about how close Melanie and her father were getting.

Phillip pulled out his phone when he heard it beep, but it must have been his email signal. "I tried calling Alicia, but I couldn't get her. What time was she over at your place?"

"Maybe four hours ago."

Melanie could tell he didn't know about her and Alicia's fight, so she didn't say anything.

Phillip scrunched his eyebrows. "That's strange. Her phone went straight to voice mail, so let me try again."

Melanie wasn't too happy with Alicia right now, so she honestly couldn't have cared less whether she answered or not. Still, because she saw a hint of worry in Phillip's eyes, she hoped Alicia wasn't doing something she shouldn't. Just this afternoon, Melanie had been thinking about this very thing, but once again, she told herself Alicia wouldn't stoop to such levels.

Phillip dialed Alicia's number. "It's still going straight to voice mail."

Melanie acted as though she didn't hear him, because if she looked at him or made any comments, she feared that Phillip might detect her suspicions. There was no way Alicia would have another affair, and certainly not with Levi. She was capable of acting out in other shocking ways, but she wouldn't sleep with another man. Melanie replayed her thoughts, trying to convince herself she was right, but the gnawing questions in the pit of her stomach made her uneasy.

Another half hour passed, and one of the ER nurses walked over to the waiting room. "I'm looking for the family of Brad Richardson."

Melanie stood up. "I'm his wife. Is he okay?"

"We've got him stabilized, but if you'll follow me, Dr. Romalati will explain more.

Melanie felt a bit relieved when she heard Dr. Romalati's name, then she turned to her dad and Phillip. "I'll let you guys know what's going on as soon as I can."

"We'll be here," Andrew said.

Phillip nodded. "Tell my buddy we're praying for him. I'm also getting ready to call my father-in-law."

"Thanks," she said.

When the nurse swiped her hospital badge to open the door, Melanie followed her toward the ER nurses' station. She saw Dr. Romalati right away.

He reached out his hand. "Melanie, how are you?"

"I've certainly had better days."

"I'm sure. Well, as Gina probably told you, we have your husband stabilized, but he hit his head pretty hard against the driver's-side window. And he has a concussion. Of course, those are very common, but when we did the scan we noticed a little brain swelling, so I want to keep him sedated until it's gone. It's not a lot of swelling, but we'll keep him under with propofol just to be safe. I'm guessing we'll be able to bring him out of it by tomorrow evening. At the latest, the day after."

"And there wasn't any bleeding?" she asked.

"No, that's the best news of all. He does have quite a few bruises, but nothing was broken. Brain swelling is nothing to play with, but he certainly could have ended up much worse. The woman who hit him was intoxicated, and her daughter didn't make it."

"Oh my God," Melanie said. "The officers didn't tell me that. How awful."

"It's very sad, and this never should have happened. If only people would stop drinking and driving. Brad is very blessed to be alive. If she'd hit him on the driver's side instead of the passenger's, we might be having a very different conversation."

"Thank God that didn't happen."

"In a few days, I think Brad will be fine. I'm sending him to neuro ICU, though, so we can monitor him closely. But you can go in to see him now . . . although first, please tell me how you're doing. You know, with your sodium and potassium?"

"Good. Haven't had any more problems."

"That's good to hear," he said, eyeing her from head to toe. "Are you eating three meals a day?"

Melanie liked Dr. Romalati, but this wasn't the time to be asking her about her diet. Brad had been hurt, and that's all they should have been discussing.

"I am," she said. "I hope you are."

Melanie half expected him to comment

on her weight loss, but he didn't and she was relieved.

"I'll let you go in to see your husband, and then I'll be back to check on him before we send him to the ICU. His room is two doors down," he said, pointing.

"Thank you for everything, doctor."

"You're quite welcome," he said. "You hang in there, and take good care of yourself."

Dr. Romalati sounded more worried about her than he did about Brad, but Melanie ignored his comment and walked down to her husband's room. When she opened the door, she saw one nurse jotting down his vitals from the monitors and another adjusting his blankets, making sure he wasn't too cold. They both smiled at Melanie but didn't say anything.

Melanie walked up to the side of the bed where neither nurse was standing. She read the monitors, glanced at his IV bags, and looked at Brad again. His face was swollen and bruised pretty badly, and so was his left arm. Melanie stared at him, and tears filled her eyes. She truly loved her husband, and she didn't want to live without him. *Please, God, let him be okay. Please heal his body completely.*

Melanie caressed the top of his hand, the

one he didn't have a needle in, and she thanked God that Brad hadn't been killed. She also thanked God for allowing this tragedy to open her eyes. She no longer cared about all the money Brad had lost or the things he'd said about her to her father and Alicia. She just wanted him to get well. And when he did, Brad and their marriage would be her top priority.

CHAPTER 35

After falling out with Melanie, Alicia had called Levi as soon as she'd driven out of the subdivision. Her emotions had scurried in far too many directions, but Levi had talked her down and reminded her that Melanie was ill. He'd insisted that Alicia needed to remember that and recognize that folks with eating disorders were sometimes just as defensive as drug addicts. He'd also explained that the reason Melanie was lashing out at her and Brad was because she was in denial. It had taken Alicia a while to settle her anger, but because Levi's voice had soothed her soul and given her peace, she'd ended up driving to his house. She'd had such a stressful afternoon that she'd needed to see him. Needed to lie in his arms the way she was now. Then, the manner in which he'd made such beautiful love to her had left her spellbound. It was as though she'd been hypnotized and not much else mattered except the two of them.

Alicia lay as close to Levi as she could, with her stomach touching his side. Her head rested in the fold of his arm.

"Thank you," she said.

"For what?"

"Being there for me today. Helping me get through a very tough time."

"That's what I'm here for, and I'm glad you called me."

Alicia wondered what time it was, and she almost didn't want to know. As it was, she'd shut her phone off, making sure all incoming calls went to voice mail. There was no doubt that Phillip had tried contacting her more than once, but she was already brainstorming what lies she would tell him when she got home. He wouldn't be happy, not with her spending so many hours away from him two days in a row, but somehow she would get him to believe her story.

"I wish I could stay here forever," she said.

"If you hadn't gotten married, you could. You really made things difficult for us."

"I realize that now, but it won't stop us from being together."

Levi didn't say anything.

"Right?" she said.

"I was serious about what I asked you today. So when are you getting a divorce?"

"Baby, why do you keep bringing that up when you know it's not that simple?"

"Because I've done a lot of thinking and a lot of soul-searching. What I thought about most was how I keep telling people that I've changed. How I'm living the way God wants me to live. Yet at the same time, I'm sleeping with a married woman."

"Wow, so does that mean you're dumping me?" she said, walking her fingers across his chest and chuckling.

"I know you think this is some kind of joke, but I'm serious. I won't keep doing this to Phillip, to myself, or to God."

For the first time ever, Levi had spoken Phillip's name. It was almost as if he was purposely acknowledging him in some way. Alicia had no idea why he was being so deep all of a sudden. When she'd arrived, he'd been watching a pastor preaching on one of the Christian networks, so maybe he'd heard something that made him feel guilty.

"Why can't we just lie here and enjoy ourselves?" she said.

"Because we have a lot to talk about. You have a decision to make, and things won't be right until you do."

"Maybe in time," she said, hoping this would satisfy him.

"That's not good enough. Do you remember when we were seeing each other before, and I told you I wouldn't keep being with you if you didn't get a divorce?"

Alicia sighed loudly.

"Well, I meant it then, and I mean it even more today."

"Why can't you try to understand what this is like for me? I really hurt Phillip the last time, and I don't think he could take something like that again."

Levi pulled slightly away from her and turned her cheek so that she was looking at him. "I love you with every ounce of my being, but I won't keep sleeping with another man's wife."

"And you just decided that today, I guess."

"I've been thinking about it all along. When I first got out, I was just happy to see you and spend time with you. But when we got together yesterday I was sure you were planning to tell Phillip the truth. The way we made love, all the things we professed to each other . . . I thought it was a done deal. Until you showed me something different on the phone today."

"Baby, please try to understand. I love you too much to lose you."

"Then, sweetheart, do the right thing. Handle your business."

They lay there in silence for what seemed

an eternity. Alicia finally asked him a question.

"So have you decided on a location for your restaurant?"

"Yeah, I think so. It's about five miles north of Mitchell's city limits, so I'll also be looking for another house to rent. Something closer to there."

Alicia had been hoping he wouldn't complain about her changing the subject, and she was glad to move on to a better conversation. Levi was excited about opening his new establishment, though, so he never minded talking about it.

"I can't wait to see it."

"It's very nice and spacious, which is what I need. I've also interviewed three different chefs from the Chicago area, because in addition to great customer service, great food is the key to a successful restaurant. You can't have just a few delicious items. Everything on the menu has to be perfect."

"Very true."

"To get a top chef with experience, I'll have to pay them very well, but it'll be worth it," he said, pulling his cell phone from the nightstand when he heard it ringing. "Hmmm, I wonder what D.C. wants."

Alicia sat straight up, staring at him. Levi had assured her he wouldn't tell anyone about them, but just the fact that D.C. knew her father made her nervous.

"Hey, man, what's up?" Levi said. ". . . Not much, just chillin' at the house . . . Really? Why? . . . Is that right? Well, I can't help you with that one . . . wish I could, but you know the deal . . . No problem, man, and let's try to hook up in the next couple of days. Grab a bite or somethin' . . . Tomorrow's good for me, too . . . I'll just drive over to Mitchell and we can decide when I get there . . . See you then . . . Be safe, man."

Levi set his phone down, and Alicia breathed freely. Thank goodness D.C. hadn't been calling about her.

Levi looked at her. "I hate to tell you this, but your dad is looking for you."

"What? D.C. told you that? What did he say?"

"That your dad asked him to call me to see if I knew where you were."

"This is crazy. What else did he say?"

"Not much. When I told him I couldn't help him with that, he was through with it. I will tell you this, though. D.C. is a good friend, and I don't like lying to him. Not telling him something is one thing, but lying to him is something different."

"But you know we have to keep this between us."

"For how long?"

"For as long as we need to," she said, looking at the clock on the nightstand. "I didn't realize it was so late. I really have to get going."

Levi picked up the remote and turned on the television.

"Did you hear me?" she said, wondering why he hadn't pulled her closer and kissed her the way he normally did. There had never been a time when she'd told him she was getting ready to leave that he hadn't stopped her and made love to her again. But now, he barely looked at her.

Alicia lay back down, kissing him until he pushed her away.

"I don't like this," he said.

Alicia sat up again. "What are you talking about?"

Levi sat up, too, stacking two pillows behind him. "You and I spending a few hours together whenever we can and you running back home to a husband you don't love."

"What changed since yesterday?"

"I told you, I thought you'd made up your mind to tell Phillip the truth."

"At some point I will, but I can't say when. It's gonna take some time."

"Baby, that's all fine and well, but I won't

keep doing this forever. You're going to have to make a choice, and I'm giving you a month. Either divorce your husband and marry me, or forget about us altogether."

"Oh, so all that talk about how you were never going to give up on being with me and how you didn't want to live your life without me . . . what was that?"

"I meant it. I didn't give up on trying to see you, which is why we finally saw each other yesterday. I also don't want to live my life without you, but I will if I have to."

Alicia swung her legs over the side of the bed and got up. She wrapped the silk robe around her body, the one Levi had surprised her with, and tied it. "Well, isn't this an interesting turn of events. You knew what my situation was, so if you couldn't deal with it, why didn't you just leave me alone?"

"Because we're in love with each other. You wanted me to find you, and that's why you're here."

"You're wrong for this."

"No, we're both wrong. So you need to leave your husband or we have to end things."

Alicia's heart ached already. Why was Levi doing this?

She walked around to his side of the bed

and sat facing him. "Baby, why can't we just —"

Levi interrupted her. "I meant what I said. I love you, but if you don't take care of this, I'm done. I won't continue doing to another man what I don't want done to myself."

They gazed into each other's eyes. Alicia had never heard him speak with so much conviction. She could tell he'd never been more serious about anything — at least not with her, and his words struck her greatly. She tried not to cry in front of him, but when she did, he pulled her close and held her. As always, she felt loved and protected, and she didn't want to leave him. But sadly, she didn't have a choice. Regrettably, her home was with Phillip.

CHAPTER 36

Alicia pressed the power button on her phone more than once, making sure her battery was dead. She'd just pulled into the garage, but before she'd left Levi's, she'd turned on her phone and seen two missed calls from Phillip and two from her dad. She'd also seen that her battery was still at 70 percent. So, for a few minutes, she'd sat in Levi's driveway, browsing her Facebook newsfeed and reading various articles on Twitter. By the time she'd started up her car, her battery had drained to 60 percent. This was when she'd clicked open her iHeartRadio app, found a great R & B station, and played it the whole way back to Mitchell. She hadn't been sure her plan would work, but thankfully, by the time she'd stopped at the mall and purchased a few items — to prove she'd been shopping — she'd successfully run down her battery and driven home.

Alicia had also taken a shower at Levi's, washed her face, held a cold towel across her eyes, and reapplied her makeup. That way Phillip wouldn't be able to tell she'd been crying. It was good, too, that she'd known so many of the songs she'd heard on iHeartRadio, she'd sung her way out of sadness.

Now all she had to do was put on a happy face and prepare herself for all the questions Phillip would be asking as soon as he saw her.

She grabbed four shopping bags, walked up to the door leading to the kitchen, turned the key, and went inside.

Phillip stood there waiting for her. "Where in the world have you been? Didn't you get my messages?"

"No, baby, I'm sorry. My phone has been dead for hours."

"What about the charger in your car?"

"I couldn't find it. I never have to use it, so I must have misplaced it."

"Where have you been?" he asked in a louder voice.

She set her bags down for effect. "Baby, please don't be upset . . . but I went shopping again. I went to see Melanie, she and I got into it, and the next thing I knew I was over at Woodfield."

"For nine hours? Because it sounds like you left Melanie's around two o'clock."

Alicia wanted to ask why Melanie had told him anything at all, but she didn't want to take a chance on making him more furious.

"I got caught up, and I'm sorry. I know I said I wouldn't do this again, but Melanie really upset me."

"Well, while you were MIA, Brad was in a serious car accident and a child died. Her mother was drunk driving and ran a red light."

"Oh no," she said, leaning against the counter. "Is Brad okay?"

"No. He has a concussion and brain swelling, so they have him heavily sedated."

"Dear God. And that poor child."

"That's why I kept calling you. That's why I left you those messages, but some good that did."

"I'm really sorry."

"What's wrong with you? Why are you all of a sudden shopping again?"

"I told you, Melanie and I got into it. I should've just come home."

"Yeah, that's exactly what you should've done."

Alicia hated having to defend herself about shopping, but it was better for him to believe she'd been at the mall for hours than to suspect the truth.

"Did you just leave the hospital?" she asked.

"About an hour ago, but you really need to call Melanie. And why did the two of you fall out? Because she never said a word to me about it."

"Remember, I told you Brad wanted me to talk to her about all the weight she's losing. I brought it up, and one thing led to another."

"Well, you need to check on her. Not tomorrow but now."

Phillip was angrier than Alicia had seen him in years. Their quarrel tonight reminded her of all the horrible arguments they'd had the first time they were married.

"Can I use your phone? Mine is still dead."

"Your charger is right over there," he said, glancing toward the electrical outlet near the toaster.

Alicia pulled her phone from her tote and plugged it in. When it came on, she dialed Melanie, but she didn't answer. It wasn't as though Alicia expected her to, anyway, not with the way they'd spoken to each other earlier.

"I'll just have to try her later."

"Your best friend's husband could have

died today, and you're not going to the hospital? Not to mention Brad's my best friend who I love like a brother."

"Visiting hours are over."

"Not for emergencies."

"Melanie won't want me there."

"Well, I'm going back, but you do what you want," he said, walking away from her and going upstairs.

Alicia was staying home, and she was glad Phillip had left the kitchen for the time being. He seemed so through with her, but she would explain and apologize for the next week if that's what it took for him to get over this.

She dialed into her voice mail system and listened to the messages her dad and Phillip had left her. She'd purposely not played them when she'd first discovered them, because she'd wanted her plan to seem as genuine as possible. That way, if, for instance, Phillip walked back into the kitchen without warning, he'd see her checking her messages the same as anyone would do as soon as they realized they'd missed a few calls. But when she heard the last one from her dad, she deleted it. His tone was stern and terse, and he sounded as though he was expecting the worst. There was no way she was calling him back tonight. She would just wait and see him at church in the morning. Her dad wasn't always tactful, but he would never question or accuse her of anything in front of others. She knew she'd have to talk to him at some point, but it would be on her own terms and not until she was ready. It wouldn't be a second before that.

CHAPTER 37

Normally, the eight o'clock service wasn't as full as the one at eleven, but today, a lot of Deliverance Outreach members had gotten up early. Although, Alicia was sure it had something to do with her dad announcing last week at both services that "my son-in-law will be delivering the eight a.m. message next Sunday, and I'm asking that you all come out to support him." This didn't happen at every church, but whenever her dad asked his congregation to do something, they were usually in agreement.

Service wouldn't be starting for another twenty minutes, so while Alicia, Charlotte, and most everyone else had taken their seats, many parishioners quietly chattered amongst themselves.

"It's great that so many people came out this morning," Charlotte said, crossing her legs and pulling her black knit skirt closer to her knees.

Alicia nodded. "I was just thinking the same thing."

"Phillip always gives such a great teaching sermon, and everyone loves him."

"I know. He's definitely a wonderful speaker."

"So, how's Brad? Did you make it out to the hospital last night?"

"No, I didn't, and I haven't spoken to Melanie yet, either."

"Why, what's wrong?"

"It's a long story. I'll tell you about it later."

"We were out there for a while yesterday evening, so I hope he's doing better."

"Me, too," Alicia said. "And I've been praying for him."

"And that poor baby that died. It's so hard to believe a mother would drink and then subject her child to so much danger."

"It's very sad."

Alicia looked up when one of the male ushers walked toward them.

"Sister Sullivan," he said to her. "Your dad would like to see you in his office."

Alicia wanted him to go away, but he stood there waiting.

"Thanks," she said.

"You're welcome," the man said, finally leaving.

Charlotte looked at her. "Is everything okay?"

"I guess."

"Something's wrong. What is it?"

Alicia wanted to tell Charlotte everything, but she couldn't. If anyone would understand what she was going through, it would be her stepmother. However, Alicia was too ashamed to tell her about Levi. "Nothing, but I'd better go see what Daddy wants."

Alicia got up, walked across the front of the sanctuary, and went into the hallway leading to her father's office. As it was, Phillip hadn't said a word to her since returning from the hospital late last night, and he had driven to church without her, so there was no telling what her dad was preparing to say or do. Especially since he'd already left her a not-so-nice message yesterday.

She knocked on the door.

"Come in," Curtis said.

Alicia opened it and went in. "You wanted to talk to me?"

"I do. Please close the door and have a seat."

Alicia did what he asked.

Curtis leaned forward, locking his hands together and resting them on his desk. "So, after all that I tried to tell you back in June.

After I reminded you about the dangers of temptation, you still went out and did whatever you wanted. Even knowing what happened the last time you had an affair with Levi."

Alicia swallowed and looked him straight in the eyes. "I don't know what you're talking about. I haven't done anything wrong."

"Alicia, you and I both know that you're lying. We also know that your phone wasn't off yesterday for no reason."

"There actually was a reason. My battery was dead."

Curtis leaned back in his chair, shaking his head with disappointment. "You were with him Friday night, too, weren't you?"

"Daddy, I'm not seeing Levi, so I'm not sure what else you want me to say."

"You're lying, and I know you're lying. As soon as I called Phillip Friday night, and he told me you'd been shopping over in Oak Brook since noontime, I knew what you were up to. Poor Phillip joked about it, saying he hoped you hadn't returned to your old ways and was spending every dime you had. But my thoughts immediately shifted to Levi. Then, when you wouldn't answer your phone last night, I knew what you were doing. You were with Levi both days, weren't you?"

Alicia rarely got upset with her father, but he was starting to annoy her. "I'm really offended by all these accusations."

"Why won't you just answer the question? Were you with him or not? I already know you were, but I wanna hear you say it."

Alicia stood up. "Daddy, you know what? I'm a grown woman, and I don't have to lie about anything."

"Then why are you?"

She pushed the chair she'd been sitting in closer to his desk. "Is that all you wanted? Because I need to get back to my seat."

"I just have one last thing to say. Whatever you're *not* doing, you need to stop doing for good. Shut it down before you're sorrier than you were the last time. Nip this craziness in the bud before somebody gets hurt."

She hated when her father spoke sarcastically and acted as though he'd never committed a sin in his life. Yes, he'd changed for the better, and yes, he was now faithful to his wife, but he had a past and he wasn't perfect. She also didn't like the fact that he'd summoned her to his office as if she were a child. He had no right doing that, but she wouldn't let her father's interrogation ruin her Sunday. She would enjoy her husband's sermon and look forward to seeing her mom and stepdad for dinner.

After Alicia returned to the sanctuary and praise and worship service ended, Phillip got up and walked into the pulpit. Normally, before he gave any sermon, he squeezed Alicia's hand, touched her in some kind of way, or just smiled at her. But today, he acted as though she didn't exist. She wasn't sure what it would take to soften his rage, but she had to figure it out before the day was over.

Phillip scanned through his electronic tablet and glanced at Alicia. There was still no smile on his face, and if anything, he seemed irritated and as though he didn't want to be there.

"A few months ago during Bible study, my father-in-law taught a lesson entitled Temptation and the Tricks of the Devil. I was really touched by it, and while my original topic for today was The Joy of Forgiveness, I realized last night that God had something else He wanted me to talk about. So, if you would, please turn in your Bibles to Romans six, twenty-three."

Alicia knew exactly what scripture that was, and she wondered why Phillip had suddenly changed his sermon.

"Do you all have it?" he asked.

"Yes," most everyone said.

"And Romans six, twenty-three, reads,

'For the wages of sin is death, but the free gift of God is eternal life through Jesus Christ our Lord.' " Phillip looked at Alicia again and then across the congregation. "So my topic for today is Sin and The Ultimate Betrayal."

Alicia wasn't sure if it was her guilt that was making her take Phillip's topic personally, or if Phillip actually believed she'd betrayed him in some way. Because with the way he kept glaring at her, he seemed to be speaking to her directly. Her father sometimes did that very thing when he wanted to get a point across to Charlotte, or even Alicia for that matter, but she hadn't expected this from Phillip.

"Of course, we all know that the ultimate betrayal in history was when Judas identified Jesus to the Roman soldiers so they could arrest him. But over the years, I've learned that betrayal can occur on many levels. It can also involve grave amounts of sin, and innocent people can be hurt pretty badly. And please don't get me wrong, we've all sinned at one time or another and fallen short of the glory of God, but there ought to come a time when, as Christians, we don't want to commit those same awful sins anymore. And yes, it is also true that we all make mistakes, but when we make mistakes, we also have an opportunity to learn some very valuable lessons. That way, we never, ever make those mistakes again."

"Amen," some of the members said.

"The other thing I've learned is that lying can cause just as much pain as any other sin. Not being honest with the people we love can cause irreparable damage. It can also cause lots of suspicion and total distrust."

If Alicia could run out of the church without anyone seeing her she would. She wasn't sure whether Phillip suspected anything about Levi, or whether he was referring to the way she'd lied to him about going on another shopping spree. Years ago, when she'd gone out and blown all their money on shopping, he had become furious and they'd argued like enemies — every single time she'd done it. But today, she couldn't tell which was which. Was it the shopping he was still so upset about, or did he think she was having an affair again? Surely two days of shopping hadn't made him believe she was sleeping around. But what if it had? What if he knew more than he was saying? What if her father had shared with Phillip his own suspicions? But then, there was no way her dad would betray her that way. He wouldn't do that to his own daughter. Or would he? What if her father was having her followed the same as Levi had? It certainly wouldn't be out of character for him. He had done much worse to others in the past, so anything was possible. But then again, her dad wasn't like that anymore.

Alicia tossed so many thoughts and scenarios through her mind, her head started to ache. Sneaking around, hiding, and lying for two days straight was weighing heavily on her heart, and it was making her insane. One weekend was only a short period of time, but as she sat listening to Phillip, she knew she couldn't go on this way. There was something too unsettling about the pain and the troubled look she saw on his face. She needed to decide who she was going to spend the rest of her life with: her husband or the man she loved so completely. Phillip or Levi? The man who'd never stopped loving her or the *other* man who'd never stopped loving her? Because if she didn't, she knew her father's words would play out in real life. Somebody would get hurt. She wished that weren't true, but it was almost inevitable.

CHAPTER 38

Melanie looked at the accident photo and article write-up in the newspaper and shook her head. That poor, poor little girl. Dead because of a mother who saw nothing wrong with drinking and driving with her own child in the car. From the looks of how demolished her compact car was, it was a wonder the woman driving hadn't died as well. Brad was truly blessed, and it probably hadn't hurt that he'd been driving a large SUV.

She folded up the paper and placed it in her handbag. She stood on one side of Brad's bed, leaning against the wall, and her father stood on the other, holding on to the bed rail. Brad was still sedated and resting peacefully.

"You look a little tired, Dad. Why don't you go on back out to the waiting room?"

"I will. Just thought I'd come in for a few minutes."

Melanie wasn't sure why she was bringing this up right now, but she couldn't stop herself. "So, what was Mom's excuse this afternoon?"

"Said she was tired from getting up so early for the eight o'clock service."

"Really? That's the reason she gave?"

"You know your mother," he said. "Hard to understand some of the things she does."

"I've spent my entire life trying to do everything she wanted, but after all these years, it's still not enough."

"I know, and I'm very sorry about that."

When someone knocked, Melanie and Andrew looked toward the door and saw it opening.

Melanie smiled. "Hey, Phillip. How nice of you to stop by."

"Of course," he said, hugging her. "And thank you for adding me to the visitors list."

"You're like a brother to Brad, and to me, too. He wouldn't want it any other way."

Phillip walked around and hugged Andrew.

"Son, you gave a great sermon this morning," Andrew told him. "It was powerful."

"Thank you, Brother Johnson. I'm glad you enjoyed it."

"I'm sorry I missed hearing you," Melanie said. "I was really looking forward to it."

Phillip looked at Brad for a few seconds. "So how's he doing?"

"Good. Dr. Romalati ordered another brain scan a few hours ago, and the swelling has gone down a lot. They're going to slowly bring him out of sedation early tomorrow morning."

"Praise God."

"Well, hey, you two," Andrew said. "I'm gonna head back out there to sit down for a while."

"Okay, Dad. We'll be there shortly."

When Andrew left, Phillip moved from the foot of the bed to the side of it.

"I'm sure you saw the newspaper this morning," he said.

"I did. Was just looking at it again right before you got here."

"Such a senseless act. This woman has killed an innocent child, and they've already charged her with child endangerment and vehicular homicide."

"There were a couple of other charges, too. It's all very unfortunate. A part of me is angry because of the fact that she could have killed Brad, but I also can't help feeling somewhat sorry for her. Not only is she going to prison, but she'll have to live with what she's done for the rest of her life."

"A lot of folks wouldn't understand it, but

we have to keep everyone involved in our prayers. Including her."

Melanie nodded in agreement, but she sensed something was bothering Phillip. "Are you okay?"

Phillip folded his arms and relaxed his body against the wall. "It's your friend. The old Alicia is back."

Melanie prepared for the worst, but she waited for Phillip to continue.

"She's up to her same old shopping habits again, and it came out of nowhere. You should have seen all the stuff she bought."

"I'm sorry to hear that," Melanie said, glad Alicia's lost time was all about shopping and that it had nothing to do with Levi.

"It's not like I didn't know she'd had a problem, but I thought those days were gone for good. She hasn't been obsessed with shopping in years."

"She really hasn't. Maybe this was just a one-time trip."

"Well, that's the thing. She did it all day Friday and said she wasn't going to do it again. Of course, that was a just a huge lie because she was right back at it yesterday. She also lied about her phone being dead. Swore she couldn't make or receive any calls the whole time she was gone."

"Wow. Not good."

"She also said something about you and her getting into it. I wasn't sure if that was true, though."

"I'm embarrassed to admit it, but we did. We said some really terrible things to each other, and I feel bad about it. Especially after seeing what happened to Brad and realizing how short life is."

"I don't like what she's doing and the problems she's already causing for us. I haven't even spoken to her since last night. Didn't even ride to church with her this morning."

"That's really unlike you guys."

"I'm too upset to deal with her. She got me so worked up, I changed my whole sermon. I'd planned on speaking about one thing, but early this morning I changed my mind and spoke about betrayal."

"I think you need to talk to her."

"I was hoping you would, too. Just to see where her head is. Do you mind?"

"Not at all. Brad's resting, and I'm sure the nurses will be back in soon, so I'll go call her now."

The two of them walked out of the room and left the ICU area. Phillip went into the family room with Melanie's father, and Melanie walked down the hallway and into a tiny conference room. She closed the door and sat in one of the chairs.

Alicia answered on the second ring. "Hey."

"How are you?"

"Not the greatest, and I'm really sorry about yesterday."

"I'm sorry, too. About everything I said and for asking you to leave."

"How's Brad?"

"Good. They're going to bring him out of sedation tomorrow, and he'll probably get to come home in a couple of days or so."

"That's wonderful. Thank God nothing worse happened to him."

"I know."

"They were saying on the news that the woman who caused the accident was on suicide watch."

"Really?" Melanie said. "I hadn't heard that, but Phillip was just saying how we have to pray for everyone. Even her."

"We do," Alicia said, but Melanie noticed her voice trailing off a bit.

"Hey, Phillip is really worried about your marriage. He's kinda down, and I don't know if he's ever asked me to call you about anything. If he has, it was years ago."

"I messed up. I didn't mean to be gone so long Friday, but once I started shopping I couldn't stop. Then yesterday I went again."

"Well, Phillip's not happy about it, and

you need to talk to him."

"I will. You don't know how glad I am that you called."

"I'm glad I called, too."

"I think I'll just head over to the hospital so I can see Brad."

"Sounds good."

"I should be there in about an hour. Maybe less."

"See you then . . . and I love you."

"I love you, too, Mel."

Melanie stood up, preparing to leave the room, but she felt dizzy. She held on to the doorknob, trying to steady herself. At first she wondered what was going on, but then it dawned on her that she hadn't drunk any shakes today. She'd had a couple of bottles of water, but after all that had gone on with Brad she hadn't remembered to drink anything else this morning before leaving the house. Her nerves had also been too shot for her to eat a salad last night, and she still didn't have an appetite now.

She opened the door to the conference room, and while her dizziness had begun to subside, her legs felt weak. She hoped she wasn't getting dehydrated again, but just in case, she would up her water intake for the rest of the day. She would do it until her energy level returned to normal.

CHAPTER 39

Alicia hated that she'd had to call her mom and stepdad to take a rain check on dinner, but given the circumstances with her and Phillip, she hadn't thought getting together with them was a good idea. Not when Phillip would have quickly shown how angry and irritated he was with her. It had just been better for Alicia to cancel, versus setting herself up to hear questions from her mother, because Alicia couldn't handle that. Not today.

Alicia turned off the ignition of her car and pulled out her phone. She'd just arrived at the hospital, but she wanted to try Levi again. She'd called him twice while driving, but he hadn't answered. He didn't pick up this time, either, and since she'd already left him a message earlier, she hung up. It wasn't like him not to answer or at least call her back within a few minutes, so she wondered what was going on. Nonetheless, she deleted all her calls to him from her phone, got out of her car, and went into the hospital.

As she stepped on the elevator, she pulled her phone back out and placed it on silent. She wasn't sure if Levi would be calling back or not, but if he did, she didn't want it to ring when she was anywhere near Phillip.

She walked off the elevator and went down to the family waiting room. Melanie, Mr. Johnson, and Phillip sat in one of the far corners, and a couple of other families were there, too.

Phillip stood up, and when he reached out and hugged her she was relieved. But soon, more guilt inched up her spine because while she'd tried to find comfort in Phillip's embrace, she couldn't stop thinking about Levi. She was still wondering where he was and why he wouldn't answer his phone.

"Hey," Melanie said, standing and hugging her, too. Then Alicia leaned down and greeted Mr. Johnson.

Phillip stood next to her, and Alicia wasn't sure what to say. The connection between them felt awkward, and she detected a certain sense of sadness from him. It was the reason she refused to make eye contact with him and looked at Melanie instead. "Can I go in to see him?"

"Of course. We can do it now."

Phillip and Mr. Johnson stayed behind, and Alicia followed Melanie to the intensive care unit.

"Where's your mom?" Alicia asked, noticing dark circles under Melanie's eyes. She'd sort of wondered about that yesterday, but she'd figured maybe Melanie was just tired and hadn't been sleeping well. The darkness seemed more obvious today, however.

"Home, I guess."

Alicia wanted to ask why, but since Melanie hadn't elaborated she left it alone.

Melanie opened the door, and one of Brad's nurses smiled and walked out.

Alicia moved closer to the foot of his bed. "I can't believe this happened."

"I don't think any of us can, but I'll tell you one thing: Brad's accident has made me rethink everything. Two of his senior partners dropped by this morning. They couldn't go in to see him, but they made it clear that they were here for us. Said they want him to take off as much time as needed to recover. So I decided right then that I was taking a leave of absence as well. Brad and our marriage have to come first now. Life is too precious and unpredictable. Too short to be miserable and unhappy. Even just for one day."

"I don't blame you. I remember when my dad was beaten by those men a couple of years ago, and then last year when Racquel stabbed Matthew. Tragedies like that really make you place things into perspective."

"Brad and I have really grown apart, but that has to change. We can't live like that anymore. If a husband and wife don't make each other a priority, what's the point of being married? Why be together if you barely see each other?"

"I agree."

"I hope things get better for you and Phillip, too, because all the drama just isn't worth it. Not if you really love someone. Even I was letting petty stuff like money come between Brad and me, and it's just not that serious. I know Brad can't continue throwing away thousands of dollars, but I also know I could have talked to him about it a lot differently. Over the last few months, we've yelled and argued so much, I don't even remember the last time we had a normal conversation . . . the last time we even joked around or just laughed about something together."

"I didn't realize things had gotten that bad. I knew you'd said he was still working all the time and you were doing a lot of arguing, but I just thought it was something temporary."

"No, things between us were headed toward divorce. I know that might sound strange, but we just haven't been on the same page lately. We've been going our separate ways, and once you do that for so long, you get used to it. We were never together. But seeing him lying in this bed has gotten my attention. I don't ever want to know what it feels like to be without him," she said with tears in her eyes.

Alicia listened to her friend speaking from her heart and thought about her own situation — how lost she would be if she couldn't see Levi or hear his voice again. But then there was also Phillip, whom she'd caused a lot of distress over the last couple of days. So what was she going to do? Levi had given her an ultimatum, and now she couldn't get in touch with him. What if he'd changed his mind about giving her a month and had moved on already? Alicia didn't even want to think about something that dreadful. At this point, all she could do was call him again when she left the hospital, hoping he would answer. Maybe he'd already tried her back or left her a text message. She wouldn't check her phone in front of Melanie, but it would be the first thing she did when she got back to her car. She didn't want to seem desperate, but she was. She wouldn't be at peace until she talked to him.

CHAPTER 40

It was four a.m. and much too early for most people to be up, but Melanie wanted to get back to the hospital by six. Dr. Romalati was planning to bring Brad out of sedation, and chances were, he'd already asked the overnight nurses to begin the process. Before showering, though, she wanted to go online to transfer the money for her dad from one of her and Brad's money market accounts. She'd actually just written the check a few minutes ago, and since she wouldn't be going to work the way she'd planned, she'd told her dad he could pick it up from her at the hospital.

She pulled up her bank's web site, typed in her user ID and password, and waited for their accounts to display. She scanned all three of them, her checking account and both their joint money market accounts, but she frowned when she noticed the balance on one of them. She clicked the link for it, and her stomach tightened. Brad had withdrawn another ten thousand dollars on Friday. She thought about how she'd checked the account that very morning, but when she clicked on the withdrawal slip she saw a time stamp of 3:08 p.m. She took a deep breath, trying not to get herself worked up. Brad was steadily lying and saying he wouldn't do this again, and worse, he'd begun taking money from their joint savings.

Melanie checked the balance of their other account, and thankfully he hadn't withdrawn anything from that one. She sat there praying for strength and the ability to forgive him, because she didn't want this latest setback to sabotage her new thinking. Everyone made mistakes, and Brad and their marriage were her priority. She had to remember what was important, and now that Brad had nearly lost his life, maybe he would realize how foolish it was to continue playing the stock market, gambling, or doing whatever it was he was caught up with.

She transferred the money for her dad, signed off, and got up from her computer. But no sooner than she'd gotten to her feet, she sat back down. Another dizzy spell had struck her, and she tried to shake it off. She even saw stars this time and somewhat struggled to breathe. But after a few minutes, she felt fine and went into the bathroom.

When she removed her robe, she stepped on the scale and smiled like a giddy child. The readout couldn't have been right, but it had to be because she was staring straight at it. She was 140. She'd lost five whole pounds in only two days, and she had never been more proud of herself. It had taken years to achieve such a huge accomplishment, and she thanked God for giving her the desires of her heart. She'd hoped and prayed all her life to be thin and beautiful, and now she finally was. Everything was falling into place at the same time. Brad was on his way to a full recovery, they'd be able to mend their marriage, and Melanie could finally feel good about herself. She did wish things were better between her and her mother, but just being closer to her dad was helping to make a major difference.

Melanie didn't feel the best physically, but emotionally she felt serene and grateful. She was happy and looking forward to an awesome future.

When Melanie stepped off the elevator, she felt a bit weak, and she wasn't sure why since she'd drunk a shake and taken a multivitamin. She still didn't have an appetite, but she'd drunk it anyway because of how low her energy was. Maybe she was feeling this way because of all the stress and worry relating to Brad. It was certainly possible, so hopefully she'd feel like her old self when he was home.

She walked into the ICU and saw Dr. Romalati leaving Brad's room. He smiled at her.

"Good morning, Melanie."

"Good morning. How are you?"

"I'm good, and so is that husband of yours. He's already awake. Still a little groggy, but he answered all my questions, and he doesn't seem to have any neurological problems."

"Thank God for that, and thank you for everything you've done for him."

"You're quite welcome, and of course I'll be back to see him later this afternoon."

"Have a good day," she said.

"You, too."

Melanie eased open the door and saw Brad watching television. He looked at her and smiled.

She smiled back at him and spoke to his nurse, who was replacing his empty IV bag. "So you're finally awake, I see."

"Yeah, but I feel lost."

"I'm sure," she said, leaning over and kissing him on the lips. "You hit your head pretty hard."

"So I hear."

"How are you feeling otherwise? Any pain?"

"No . . . I mean, my arm and head are sore, but only when I move around. More than anything, I'm exhausted."

"That's to be expected. You'll feel better with each passing day, though."

"I'm also having a hard time remembering what happened. I do remember driving down State Street, but that's about it."

"A woman ran a red light and hit you."

"That's what the doctor told me, but I don't remember anything like that," he said, covering his mouth and coughing. "He says I might never remember, either, and that's already driving me crazy."

"Maybe *not* remembering is a good thing. Maybe it's God's way of protecting your mind from such an awful incident."

"I still don't like it," he said, turning the TV channel from ESPN to the local news. "Was something written up about it in the newspaper?"

"Yeah, but I left it at home."

"What about on TV?

"I'm sure they did, but I didn't see the

news Saturday night or yesterday."

"Maybe they'll have something on this morning."

"Maybe. Sometimes they cover stories from the weekend on Mondays, but why don't you try to relax?"

Brad locked his eyes on the young male news anchor, barely blinking. If they did air the story, they would certainly show all the damage that was done. Not just to Brad's SUV but to the woman's car as well. Worse, they would report that her daughter had been killed, and Melanie didn't think Brad was ready for that. This wasn't something he should be focusing on, and he needed to stay calm. But he continued watching, and just as the nurse walked out of the room, a photo of the crash flashed on the screen.

"Late Saturday afternoon, thirty-one-year-old Jessica Davis ran a stoplight and slammed her compact vehicle into a full-size SUV," the anchor said. "The owner of that SUV, thirty-eight-year-old Bradley Richardson, was rushed to Mitchell Memorial and listed in serious condition. Miss Davis's one-year-old daughter, Brittany Davis, was also riding with her and was pronounced dead at the scene of the accident. Miss Davis, however, was treated at Mitchell Memorial and released to authorities. She has been charged with vehicular homicide, attempted vehicular manslaughter, child endangerment, and failure to yield. As of this morning, no bail amount had been set, but a hearing is scheduled for two p.m. today."

"Dear God . . . no," Brad said with tears streaming down his face. "Please, God, don't let it be true. Please don't tell me she died."

Melanie touched his arm, trying to console him. This was the reason she hadn't wanted him to see any of this. It was too much too soon, so she grabbed the remote and changed the channel to the first thing she could find. But Brad wailed loudly like someone was beating him. He covered his face with his hands and cried with the kind of emotional pain Melanie hadn't witnessed from him before. But when she heard him mouth his next few words, her body fell numb.

"Dear Lord, no," he said, weeping uncontrollably. "Please tell me my baby girl isn't gone. Tell me she's not dead."

CHAPTER 41

Though Phillip had insisted on making love to her, Alicia lay there thinking about Levi and how she still hadn't been able to get in touch with him. He hadn't answered any of her calls or responded to any of her text messages. She'd tried him multiple times before going inside the hospital yesterday and four more times when she'd left, and then she'd sneaked and called him again last night once she and Phillip had made up. Of course, Phillip had wanted to make love to her then, too, but apparently that hadn't sufficed because he'd wanted her again as soon as he'd awakened a few minutes ago. Phillip had slept peacefully and contently, but Alicia hadn't slept more than an hour, tops. She'd even tried to pray herself to sleep, and when that hadn't worked she'd lain there watching each passing minute on the digital clock, all while agonizing over Levi.

She'd stewed and fretted, and then she'd finally gotten up and gone into her office. She'd sent Levi a message on Facebook and then waited to see if he would at least read it. But after sitting in front of her computer for more than an hour, he hadn't. This was so unlike him, and she was starting to wonder if something bad had happened. Maybe he was in some kind of danger. She couldn't bear the thought of losing him for good, so she had to find out what was going on.

Alicia lay there, pretending to enjoy her husband and trying to figure out what she would tell him later today, when she got in her car and headed toward Levi's house. Originally, she'd been happy about Levi renting a home a full hour from Mitchell — that way there was less chance of someone seeing her — but today she wished he lived here. Especially since Phillip didn't have to go to the church on Mondays, and it would be doubly hard to convince him that she had something important to do all afternoon.

Phillip rolled to the side of her, and Alicia barely noticed him.

He took a deep, long breath. "Baby, what's wrong?"

"Nothing, why?"

"You seemed like you were somewhere else. And like you didn't enjoy it."

"No, I'm fine. Just a little tired. I didn't sleep well."

"Why?"

"Insomnia, I guess."

"Are you sure? Because if there's something bothering you, you need to tell me."

"I'm good. Couldn't be better," she said, amazed at how quickly her lies came out.

Phillip turned toward her, smiling. "So do you love me?"

Alicia looked at him. "You know I do."

"I'm glad, because I was really starting to wonder whether you did or not."

"Why?"

"Because of this past weekend. You seemed like you were in a totally different world and like I didn't matter to you."

"That's not true, and I'm sorry you felt that way."

"I just want us to move on and get past this."

"We will. I'm done with the shopping thing. You may not believe me, but I am."

"I hope so, because you know what it did to our marriage the first time."

"I'm a different person than I was then. I slipped a little on Friday and Saturday, and I'm sorry. But I really am okay now."

"Are you happy?"

"About what?"

"Are you happy with me? Glad we got married again?"

"Why are you asking me that? Of course I'm happy," she said, wishing she didn't have to keep lying.

"I guess because you hadn't done anything like this in years."

"I told you, I slipped up. But I'm not planning to go to another mall for a very long time."

Phillip leaned over and kissed her. Alicia kissed him back and hoped he wasn't trying to make love to her again. Her heart just wasn't in it, and she wouldn't be able to bear it.

When their home phone rang, they both glanced toward Phillip's nightstand. It was only minutes after seven a.m.

"Who could that be?" Alicia said.

Phillip reached his arm toward the phone. "I believe it's Melanie. Looks like her cell number, anyway."

Alicia sat up. "Oh my God. I hope it's not about Brad."

Phillip answered the call. "Hey, Melanie, is everything okay? . . . No, she's right here."

Alicia took the phone and heard Melanie sniffling.

"Mel, what is it? What's going on?"

"Can you come over?"

"To the hospital? Of course."

"No, my house."

"Oh, is Brad okay?"

"He can die for all I care, and I hope that tramp of his rots in prison."

Alicia swung her legs over the side of the bed. "What tramp? What happened?"

"I can't do this on the phone."

"I'll be right there," Alicia said, ending the call and getting up.

"What's going on?" Phillip asked.

"I don't know, but it isn't good. Sounds like Brad's involved with some woman."

Phillip frowned. "You must've heard her wrong."

"No, she was pretty clear on what she said."

"Brad wouldn't do that to Melanie."

Alicia went into the bathroom and turned on the shower. Could it really be true? Was Brad having an affair? Like Phillip, Alicia didn't want to believe he'd do something like that, but who was she to doubt anything when she was having an affair herself? How could she judge Brad, or anyone, when at this very moment, she was plotting out a way to get to Levi?

CHAPTER 42

As soon as Alicia walked in, Melanie fell into her arms, crying silent tears. Alicia stood there holding her, tearing up herself and not knowing what to say. After a few seconds, Melanie released her. Alicia shut the door and they walked down the long hallway into the kitchen. Melanie wiped her face with her hands and sat down at the island.

Alicia took a seat across from her. "Mel, what happened?"

Melanie sniffled, closed her eyes, and took a deep breath. "That baby that was killed was Brad's."

Alicia grabbed her chest. "What?"

"You heard me," she nearly whispered. "That little girl was his child."

"Who told you that?"

"The story aired on the news, and Brad was practically hysterical."

"Oh my goodness. And he actually said

she was his daughter?"

"Not to me specifically, but he said it out loud. He was devastated the same as any parent would be."

"Mel, I am so, so sorry."

"Talk about being stupid and naïve. Because not once would I have expected Brad to do something like this. I knew he'd been working long hours for the last couple of years, but an affair? *And* a baby? Just a few months ago he wanted me to stop taking my birth control pills so we could have our own child."

"Did that woman hit him on purpose? I mean, did he explain anything?"

"No, but I left before he could."

Alicia leaned back in her chair. "Gosh, Mel, I'm speechless."

Melanie shed more tears and shook her head. "He really had me fooled. Even with all the hours he worked, I still thought he loved me. And to think I was more worried about the money he was losing, when all along, he was out sleeping with some trick."

The phone rang, and Melanie walked over to the kitchen counter. "It's from the hospital, and I know it's him."

She sat back in her seat, ignoring the call.

"Maybe you should talk to him."

Melanie squinted her eyes. "About what?

That tramp and how she killed his baby?"

Alicia wasn't sure what to say. Not when she wasn't any better than Brad. The only difference was that she hadn't gotten pregnant the way Brad's mistress had.

"You know," Melanie said, "now I'm wondering if Brad was withdrawing all that money for his whore."

Alicia had already thought of that, but she would never admit that to Melanie. Not while she was hurt and upset.

"Yeah, I'll bet that's exactly what he was doing," Melanie continued.

Alicia was still at a loss for words but finally said, "Why don't we go get some breakfast. Anything to get you out of the house."

"I'm not hungry."

Alicia stared at Melanie and couldn't help noticing dark circles under her eyes again.

"Have you eaten anything?" Alicia asked, hoping her words wouldn't make Melanie any more upset than she already was.

"No."

"What about a protein shake?" Alicia got up and went over to the refrigerator.

Melanie watched her with obvious disapproval. "Didn't you hear me when I said I wasn't hungry?" Her tone was short, and Alicia knew she'd gone too far.

"I'm sorry. I'm just worried about you, Mel."

"I'll be fine. Just as soon as I file for my divorce, I'll be good."

"Maybe when some time passes, you'll feel differently. Once the two of you talk."

"You're joking, right? Surely you don't expect me to stay married to a man who's sleeping with another woman. And don't get me started on some baby that was born a whole year ago."

"I'm just saying. With God, anything is possible. Sometimes people can forgive and be okay."

"Well, not me."

"You might feel differently in a few days."

Melanie raised her eyebrows. "Don't take this the wrong way, but I'm not Phillip."

"Okay, wait a minute," Alicia said. "I know you're hurting, but you don't need to take this out on me. I came over here to support you."

"Then stop trying to defend Brad. Stop trying to make it seem like what he did was no big deal. Because it *is* a big deal, and I'm not putting up with it."

Alicia was getting tired of Melanie throwing her past in her face, and she had one more time to mention it. Best friends just didn't talk to each other this way, no matter what either of them had done.

"Why don't you go upstairs and lie down," Alicia said. "Then when you get up, we can go get lunch or do whatever you want."

"Still bringing up food, I see."

"What are you talking about? I'm just trying to be here for you. And since when did talking about food become off limits?"

"The moment you got together with Brad, talking about me behind my back."

Alicia wondered who this woman was — the one sitting in front of her — because it certainly wasn't her best friend. "Mel, you really need to stop."

"Are you saying he didn't ask you to come talk to me? Because I know he did."

"Only because he was worried about you, and so was I. Why can't you see that?"

"You're supposed to be my best friend. Period. Best friends don't plot and plan against each other."

"Nobody plotted or planned anything."

"Of course you did, but it's not like I should've expected anything different. Especially with the way you betrayed Phillip. I've always tried to look past what you did, because you and I were such good friends. But now that you've betrayed me, too, I'm seeing things a lot more clearly. I'm seeing you for who you really are," Melanie said with bitter eyes.

Alicia got up and pushed her chair against the island so forcefully, she wondered if she'd broken it. "I hope you get some help, Mel, and soon. Because you're sicker than I thought. You're anorexic *and* paranoid."

"I wish I'd never called you over here," Melanie fired back.

"Honey, don't flatter yourself. I wish you hadn't, either, and please don't call me again."

"I won't," she said as Alicia headed toward the hallway to leave. "Not ever."

CHAPTER 43

Alicia tossed her shoulder bag over to the passenger seat, quickly sat in her car, and slammed the door. She was beyond livid, but she couldn't stop herself from crying. What was wrong with Melanie? And why was she being so mean to Alicia? It was true that Melanie was dealing with a lot, what with this latest news about Brad's affair and his baby, but Alicia still didn't deserve the way Melanie was treating her. She'd thrown Alicia out of two separate places, and only a few minutes ago she'd glared at Alicia like she hated her. And this was all because Alicia had mentioned *food* too many times? Come to think of it, Melanie had also turned salty when Alicia had suggested that she talk to Brad about what was going on.

Alicia leaned her head back and wiped her face. She'd been trying her best to be patient with Melanie, trying to understand all that she was enduring, but Alicia flat-out wouldn't keep taking this kind of abuse from her. She loved Melanie, and there was no friend she cared about more, but Alicia was tired of getting her feelings hurt.

She looked toward Melanie's house and saw her peeping out the window, obviously checking to see if she was gone. But Alicia ignored her, and instead, she pulled her phone from her bag and called Phillip.

"Hey," he said. "How's Melanie?"

"She's upstairs lying down," Alicia lied. "Have you talked to Brad?"

"Yeah, he called me not long ago."

"What did he say?"

"That he'd tell me everything when I got to the hospital."

"Mel says she's filing for divorce."

"Oh no. I really hate to hear that. Maybe she'll feel differently once she settles down."

"I hope so, but I don't know. She's really upset."

"I can understand why, but I still don't want to see them break up."

Alicia looked at her watch. "Neither do I. Anyway, I'm gonna stay here with Mel for as long as she needs me. Is that okay?"

"Absolutely."

"I'll call you later, though," she said.

"Sounds good, and please tell Melanie I'm praying for her."

"I will."

"Talk to you later, baby. Love you."

"I love you, too," she said.

Alicia pulled out her pressed powder compact, touched up her face, and slipped on her sunglasses. She prayed that Phillip wouldn't have a reason to call Melanie directly, because if he did, he'd discover Alicia wasn't there. Phillip rarely called Melanie for much of anything, though, so Alicia wasn't that worried about it.

She picked up her phone again and dialed Levi, but he still didn't answer. She debated leaving a message, but instead, she backed out of Melanie's driveway, left the subdivision, and headed toward I-90. If traffic was good, she'd be at Levi's in an hour.

Alicia pulled into Levi's driveway and shut off her vehicle. He always parked his car in the garage and kept the door down, so she couldn't tell if he was home or not. She hoped he was, because she wasn't sure how much longer she could go without seeing him. She also needed to know he was okay.

She got out of her car, locked it, and strolled up the brick sidewalk that led to the front door. Levi's house was a brick two-story, and since he wasn't buying it, Alicia could only imagine how high his rent must be. This of course, confirmed that he'd stashed away quite a bit of money the way he'd claimed.

When she stepped closer to the front door, she rang the bell. Interestingly enough, Levi opened it immediately.

"Hey, how's it goin'," he said with no particular expression on his face.

Alicia frowned. "How do you think it's going, Levi?"

He moved to the side so she could walk in.

"I've been calling and texting you like crazy!" she shouted.

He shut the door. "I realize that."

"You *realize* that? Is that all you have to say? What's wrong with you?"

"I needed you to see that I was serious about what I said."

Alicia leaned against the wall of his entryway and folded her arms. "This from the man who claims he never plays games?"

Levi folded his arms, too. "It wasn't a game. I wanted you to see what it would feel like."

"What?"

"Not being able to hear my voice, let alone see me. I wanted you to know how it would feel, having no contact at all."

"Like I said, this from the man who claims

he doesn't play games."

"Not a game. More like a dose of reality."

"I can't believe you made me drive all the way over here."

"You came because you wanted to."

"I came because I had to. For all I knew you were dead."

"Well, as you can see I'm totally fine."

"I didn't deserve this."

"You don't think so?"

"I really don't."

"Well, I did what I needed to do to get your attention. And there's something else, too."

Alicia rolled her eyes toward the ceiling.

Levi continued. "You know how I always do what I say I'm gonna do?"

"Yeah, whatever."

"Well, not this time."

"I don't understand."

"I told you that you had thirty days to make a decision, but I need you to decide now. Either you're going to stay married to Phillip or you're not."

"What's the hurry?"

"I thought about you a lot over the last couple of days, and I know how you operate. You'll ride out the thirty days and then make up some excuse for not being able to choose. And I'm not doing that with you. It may sound harsh, but baby, this is the way it has to be. I'm too caught up with all of this. I can't focus on my business or anything else, and I need to make changes. More than anything, my conscience won't allow me to keep being with you. Not when I know you're married to someone else."

Alicia hated that he was giving her yet another ultimatum, but as she watched him, she knew he was serious.

Levi wrapped his arm around her neck, towering over her and pulling her close. He gazed into her eyes and caressed the side of her face. "Baby, do you understand what I'm saying? I love you from deep within my soul. I would die for you. But either we do this the right way or not all."

Alicia didn't say anything, but soon she dropped her purse from her shoulder. She was exhausted. So tired of all the back-and-forth, all the deception, all the ways she'd been hurting Phillip. Right or wrong, she was tired of running from true happiness and the man she was meant to be with. Alicia also thought about her dad and how he'd talked about someone getting hurt, and she didn't want that. Not when she could prevent it.

She and Levi stood there, still staring at each other. But finally, Alicia spoke.

"Okay."

"Okay what?" he said.

"I'll tell Phillip today. I'll tell him I want a divorce."

CHAPTER 44

Melanie had cried for hours. Brad had called no less than ten times, so she'd finally unplugged the bedroom phone and closed the door. That way she wouldn't hear the other extensions ringing, either. She'd then silenced her cell.

Through all her tears, she'd tried to come to terms with what had happened, but no matter how she attempted to rationalize it, the idea of Brad having an affair and having a baby with another woman wasn't something she could stomach. It wasn't doable for Melanie — it wasn't the kind of thing she could ever live with, and she wouldn't. She knew all about the importance of forgiveness, but more than anything, she knew she would never be able to trust Brad again.

Throughout the morning, she'd felt gut-wrenching pain, tremendous shock, and downright rage. Now, she didn't feel much of anything, and she was on her way to her parents' house. If she'd had her choice, she wouldn't be going anywhere, but because she'd promised her dad that she'd give him a check today, she didn't want to disappoint him. He'd offered to come get it himself, but the more she'd conversed with him by phone, the more winded he'd sounded. So she'd pulled herself together as best as she could, refusing to focus on Brad or the awful falling-out she'd had with Alicia a few hours ago. She'd been annoyed with her for taking Brad's side and suggesting that Melanie "talk to him," and then Alicia had tried in a sly way to suggest that Melanie wasn't eating. First she'd mentioned breakfast, and then going to lunch, and all that had done was remind Melanie of how Alicia and Brad had discussed her behind her back. Melanie wasn't happy about her fight with Alicia, but after learning what she had about Brad's affair, she didn't feel she could trust anyone.

The one positive about her visiting her dad this afternoon, however, was that her mother wasn't home. Melanie rarely enjoyed seeing her, but today certainly wasn't a day when Melanie would be able to deal with her. Although, Melanie still thought it strange and heartless of her mother not to have visited Brad one time since Saturday.

The woman hadn't so much as called her own daughter to see how her husband was doing. Melanie also knew she shouldn't have been surprised. Of course, now Melanie herself didn't want to see Brad, so the whole subject was a moot point.

Melanie rang the bell, and after a couple of minutes, her father opened the door. She hugged him, but when they went into the family room and sat down, he seemed bothered by something.

"Have you been crying?" he asked. "What's wrong?"

Melanie had tried disguising her swollen eyes with makeup, but clearly it wasn't working.

She passed her father the check, and he set it on the coffee table.

"I know something's wrong, sweetheart, so tell me."

Without warning, tears filled Melanie's eyes, and she told her dad everything. She hadn't planned or wanted to, but it was as though she'd needed to confide this to someone other than Alicia. She needed words and compassion from a parent.

Melanie's tears fell faster, and her father struggled to get to his feet. When he did, he went over and tried to console her.

"Sweetheart, I'm very sorry to hear all

this, but everything is gonna be fine. It may not seem like it now, but it will be."

Her father rubbed and patted her back until she settled down. Then he sat back in his chair. "Have you talked to Brad since leaving the hospital?"

"No, I'm through with him."

Andrew sighed. "This thing right here has really caught me off guard. I saw the news coverage this morning and again at noon, but I never imagined that child was Brad's daughter."

Melanie's phone rang, and when she saw Brad's cell number, her stomach turned somersaults. Until now, he'd been calling from his hospital phone, but apparently he'd gained access to his personal belongings. Melanie dropped her phone back in her purse.

"Was that him?" Andrew asked.

Melanie nodded.

"You're gonna have to talk to him at some point."

"Maybe so, but not today."

Her father sighed again. "I tell you . . . this just doesn't seem like something Brad would do."

"Well, he did."

"When will he be getting out of the hospital?"

"I don't know. Maybe in another day or two. Just depends on how he continues to progress."

"Sweetheart, I'm really sorry because you certainly don't deserve this. No woman does."

"It's really hard, Dad. I'm at such a loss for words."

"Have you eaten anything?"

"Yeah," she said, telling her father what he wanted to hear and trying not to become irritated. Why wouldn't everyone leave her alone when it came to food? Melanie wished they'd all get over it and accept that she was fine. She was thin, and that meant she'd never been healthier.

Andrew stared at her, seemingly not believing her, but he didn't say anything else. Then sadly, her mother walked in, and Melanie hated that she hadn't simply dropped off the check and left.

"Hi, Melanie," Gladys said, walking closer to her. "I didn't know you were coming by today. How's Brad?"

Her tone was noticeably cordial, and Melanie was dumbfounded. "He's better."

"I'm sorry I haven't been out to see him. I just haven't felt very well," she said, spying the check on the table and picking it up. "What's this for?"

Melanie and Andrew looked at each other.

Gladys set the check back down. "Melanie?"

"It's to help with bills."

"Oh, really? Well, we certainly need it. Especially since it doesn't look like your father here is *ever* going back to work."

"You don't know that, Gladys," he said.

"Hmmph. With the way you walk around here, huffing and puffing? And steadily gaining more weight? Please."

Melanie knew it was time to go, so she stood up.

Her mother perused today's mail. "Are you heading to the hospital?"

"No," Melanie said.

"Oh, did you just leave there?"

"No."

Her mother eyed her suspiciously. "Is everything okay? And come to think of it, have you been crying?"

Gladys was the last person Melanie wanted to tell her marital problems to, but since her mother was sure to find out eventually, Melanie got it over with.

"That baby that died in the car crash was Brad's."

Her mother frowned. "Who told you that?"

"He did."

Gladys widened her eyes in shock, but interestingly enough, she didn't comment. She simply stared at Melanie like she was some pitiful excuse for a wife.

Melanie grabbed her bag. "Well, Mom, I'm sure you're loving every bit of this, aren't you? The fact that you were right about everything you said."

"I don't know what you're talking about."

"Of course you do. You've always said that if I didn't lose weight, Brad would find someone else. And that's exactly what he did, a long time ago."

Gladys still didn't say anything, which was very odd, so Melanie turned to her father.

"I'll see you later, Dad."

"Sweetheart, you take care of yourself, and I'll call you later. Just wanna make sure you're okay. Or maybe you should stay here for a couple of days."

Melanie appreciated her father's suggestion, but even if she were homeless, she would never sleep under the same roof with her mother. Not for one day.

"Thank you for the offer," Melanie said, "but I'm going home. And please don't worry."

"I can't help but worry," he said. "I just hate this for you."

Melanie glanced at her mother, who stood

there watching, yet she still wasn't ranting or criticizing Melanie the way she normally did. It was completely out of the ordinary for her not to say "I told you so," but Melanie was glad she hadn't. Melanie wouldn't have been able to bear it. Not when, at this very moment, she felt like dying.

CHAPTER 45

Alicia sat in her car taking deep breaths, trying to slow her heart rate. Even the thumping in her chest became more intense, and she was starting to wonder if she could go through with this. After spending the last few hours with Levi, making love to him and promising that she was going to end things with Phillip, she'd suddenly lost her courage. Her mind was still made up, but the guilt she felt stopped her from getting out of her vehicle. She'd been sitting in the garage for at least twenty minutes, and she was glad Phillip hadn't heard her drive up. If he had, he would have come out to check on her, and she didn't want that.

If only she'd listened to Levi three months ago, when he'd told her not to marry Phillip. He'd sworn she'd end up miserable, and she was. If only she hadn't been in denial about the way things would turn out — if she hadn't convinced herself that she could forget about Levi and fall *in* love with Phillip. Had she made the right choice, she wouldn't have to do this awful thing once she entered the house. She wouldn't have to hurt her loving husband, who deserved so much better. Phillip was a good man, always had been, and she wasn't sure what this would do to him. If he'd been an awful, abusive, intolerable person, leaving him would be easy. But Phillip was just the opposite. He was one of the kindest and most trustworthy men she knew, and he had a good heart. He also loved and honored God, and he tried his best to never go against God's Word. For these reasons, Alicia hoped he would recover from what she was about to do.

She took another deep breath and said out loud, "Dear Lord, please forgive me. Please give me strength."

She got out of the car and walked toward the door leading to the kitchen. Still, she hesitated before opening it. She debated whether she should wait until morning to talk to Phillip, because maybe then she wouldn't feel so nervous and she'd have more time to get her words together. While driving home, she'd done a couple of run-throughs of what she would say, but maybe it was best to sleep on it. As it was, it was already after six p.m. Phillip had left two messages for her, and she hadn't called him back. By now, he had surely phoned Melanie, who had probably been thrilled to tell him Alicia wasn't there. Especially now that Melanie believed Alicia had betrayed her.

Of course, if she waited until morning, she would have to lie to Phillip about where she'd been all day and then take a chance on his wanting to make love to her again. It was bad enough that she'd slept with Phillip last night and this morning and also with Levi this afternoon. If her parents knew she'd slept with two men on the same day, they would be horrified. In all honesty, she was disgusted with herself. She'd become nothing more than a common whore, and she was ashamed.

She stood there, still debating, and then finally walked inside. Phillip sat at the island, facing her, with the same look of disappointment and anger he'd worn Friday night when she'd gotten home.

"I know you're mad, baby, but let me explain," she hurried to say.

Phillip glared at her, seemingly deep in thought, and didn't speak.

Alicia sat across from him and set her purse on the other chair. "You're going to kill me, but baby, I'm sorry. I got carried away again, and I didn't realize how much time had passed."

"Is that right?" he said. "What'd you buy?"

Alicia smiled as much as she could. "Well, that's the best news of all. I bought a bunch of stuff I didn't need, but then I returned it. I took everything back because I realized how upset you were gonna be."

Phillip leaned back in his chair and relaxed his arms on the island. "If that's true, show me the receipts. All of them."

Alicia's face turned solemn. "What?"

"Show them to me. For purchases and returns."

Alicia's heart revved up again. What was she going to do now?

Phillip's eyes turned cold, and she could tell he meant business. He wanted to see proof, but she didn't have any.

"Why can't you just believe me?" she said, hating how pathetic she sounded.

"Because you're a liar."

"I'm not."

"Then show me."

"I'm not a child," she said, hoping he would back off.

"No, but you're my loving, faithful, committed wife, and if I want proof I have a right to see it."

"If you don't trust me, then why did you

marry me?" Alicia rambled off whatever she could, trying to turn things in a different direction.

"You really think I'm stupid, don't you?"

"I don't think anything like that."

"So you were at the mall all this time."

"Yes."

Phillip shook his head. Then he picked up his phone and typed in his passcode. He clicked a few icons and slid the phone over to Alicia. "Does this look like the mall to you?"

She glanced at the displayed photo and knew she had to be seeing things. On the screen was an image of Levi hugging her good-bye on his front step, which had happened less than two hours ago. But this couldn't be real. There was no way Phillip had followed her.

"Why are you so quiet?" he asked. "I'll bet you weren't this quiet earlier."

"Phillip, it's not what you think."

"Alicia, don't even try it. You've lied for the last time."

"I can't believe you were following me," she said, feigning outrage.

"I wasn't. I hired an investigator."

"When?"

"Right after I discovered that lowlife was out of prison. By then, he'd been out for a few weeks, so I couldn't help wondering if you'd already been seeing him."

Alicia was starting to feel a bit uneasy, because the more Phillip talked, the less upset he seemed. Almost as though he couldn't care less about what she'd done.

"But silly me," he said, laughing out loud. "I only had the PI follow you for the four weeks leading up to our wedding. I told him to stop when I saw that you really weren't being with Levi. But then after you were gone all day Friday and Saturday, I called him again. He wasn't available, but he put one of his associates on it right away yesterday."

Phillip was explaining things in great detail, and taking this a lot better than she'd expected, but she still thought it was best to wait to ask him for the divorce.

"But what I really wanna know is, did you see Levi when he first got out? Before I hired an investigator?"

"What? No," she said, relieved that she'd cut things off with Levi in June and Phillip couldn't prove otherwise.

"So the first time you saw him was three days ago?"

"The first time I saw him was today." Phillip was trying to trip her up, but he'd just admitted that the investigator hadn't begun following her until yesterday.

"Still lying, I see."

"I'm not."

"You are," he spat, reaching over and picking up a handgun from the chair next to him. He got up and hurried around the island.

"Oh my God, Phillip, what are you doing?"

"Just shut up," he said, grabbing her hair and yanking her head back.

"Phillip, please don't do this. I'm begging you."

He pointed the gun at her face. "I said shut up."

Alicia thought she was going to pass out. She hadn't even known Phillip owned a gun, let alone that he would threaten to kill her with it.

"You made a fool out of me, not once but twice. You practically got on your knees, pleading with me to take you back. And now you're sleeping with that same snake all over again?"

"Phillip, baby . . . I didn't sleep with him. All we did was talk."

Phillip rubbed the gun up and down the back of her head as though it were a water pistol. "They always say nice guys finish last, but not this time, sweetheart. You took my kindness for weakness, and something has to be done about it. Somebody has to pay."

It was all Alicia could do not to urinate on herself. Phillip had snapped, and she was frightened for her life.

"Baby —" she said.

"Don't you call me that!" he shouted. "Don't you ever call me that."

"But I just wanna talk to you."

"About what? Your jailbird boyfriend? Okay, let's talk about him."

"He's not my boyfriend. He's nothing to me."

"Still lying," he said, laughing and pressing the gun harder against her head. But when her phone vibrated, he reached over with his other hand to pick up her handbag. He set it on the island and dug through it until he found her cell. Then he typed in her passcode.

Alicia loathed the day they'd exchanged passcode information, because while she'd made sure to delete all text and call logs between her and Levi, there wasn't a thing she could do about this current message. She hoped the text wasn't from Levi, but she soon learned otherwise.

"Oh, so you were planning to ask me for a divorce?"

Alicia closed her eyes, praying Phillip

didn't shoot.

"Because this text right here says, 'Call me after you talk to him about the divorce. Let me know you're okay. I love you, baby.' "

Alicia didn't bother lying anymore. Instead she said, "Our Father, who art in heaven, hallowed be thy name, thy kingdom come, thy will be done on Earth, as —"

Phillip dropped the phone on the island and yanked her head back again. "Stop all that praying. First you sleep with me, then you sleep with that punk Levi, and now you're saying the Lord's Prayer? All in one day? You're such a hypocrite. Such a low-down whore."

Alicia wanted to plead with him to put the gun down, but she was afraid to say anything.

"Text him back," he demanded.

"For what?"

"Tell him everything went fine, and that you'll call him later. And don't forget to tell him you love him."

Alicia didn't move.

"Here," he said, forcing the phone into her hand. "And you'd better type exactly what I told you or else."

Alicia quickly keyed in the message with jittery fingers, correcting a number of mistakes. But right when she got ready to send it, Phillip snatched the phone from her. He read the text more than once and pressed Enter himself. Then he dropped her phone back in her bag.

"I should kill you right now," he said matter-of-factly.

"Baby, I don't want Levi," she said. "I love *you,* and that's what I went to tell him."

"Stop talking to me like I'm stupid. You didn't have to drive an hour to do that. You could've told him that on the phone."

"I tried, but he said he wouldn't stop calling me unless I told him in person. That's the only reason I went."

"Then why did he just send you that text about divorcing me?"

"I don't know."

Phillip grabbed her purse and pressed it against her chest. "Let's go."

"Where?"

"Don't worry about it."

Alicia believed it was better to stay here than to get in the car with a crazed gunman. "Baby, why don't we stay here and talk. Let's pray about it, and call my dad."

"Your dad doesn't have a thing to do with this. This is about you, me, and your boy Levi. Now, let's go!" he yelled. "Don't make

me ask you again. Don't make me blow
your brains out."

CHAPTER 46

Melanie upped the speed on her treadmill from 4.2 to 4.8 miles per hour. She'd been power walking for nearly a half hour, but every three to four minutes she'd been having to take it down a bit. She felt as though she couldn't comfortably walk at her usual pace, because when she did, she struggled to breathe and her heart beat well beyond the normal range. But in order to burn the necessary amount of calories and feel the release of endorphins to feel better, she needed to finish off the last few minutes at top speed. She was only planning to stay on for thirty minutes, but already she was starting to feel wiped out again. Her face and body were also drenched in sweat, something that didn't usually happen with such severity.

Melanie fought to keep up her desired speed, but when she couldn't, she dropped it back to 4.2. Still, she couldn't seem to catch her breath the way she needed to, so she dropped it to 3.5. When that didn't seem to do much, either, she slowed the treadmill to 2.0. She held on to the rails, panting and waiting for her heart to stop pounding, and when it didn't, she stopped the machine and went up to the main floor. That flight of stairs alone took everything out of her, so instead of continuing up to her bedroom, she walked into the family room and lay across the sofa. When she did, her cell rang. She sat up to look around for it, but the room started to spin and she felt dizzy. She thought she saw flashing lights, but when she squeezed her eyes together, they disappeared. Her phone stopped ringing for a few seconds, and then it rang again. This was when she realized it was coming from the kitchen, and she pried herself off the couch and went to answer it.

"Hi, Dad," she said, pulling a bottle of water from the refrigerator and heading back into the family room.

"How are you feeling?"

"Okay. Just finished working out."

"You sound exhausted."

She lay on the sofa again. "I'm fine."

"Sweetheart, I'm really getting worried. You seemed a little weak today, so maybe you should stop exercising for a while. Just until you feel better."

"I've been thirsty the last couple of days. Probably just a little dehydrated," she said, turning up her bottle of water.

"I really wish you would've spent the night over here. Especially with everything going on with you and Brad."

"I just need to be alone right now."

"But that's not good. Even if you don't wanna come here, why don't you call Alicia? Go stay with her and Phillip."

"Alicia . . . Alicia . . . she's my best friend."

"Yeah, and that's why you should head on over there."

"They live in Orlando now," she said.

"Who lives in Orlando?"

"Alicia and . . . you know his name . . . you know . . . that minister at the church."

"Sweetheart, are you okay?" Andrew said. "You don't sound right."

"I have to get dressed for work. I have a lot of patients this morning."

"Sweetheart, it's not morning, it's evening."

Melanie heard her father speaking, but she couldn't decipher what he was saying. She tried to ask him to repeat it, yet when she opened her mouth, nothing came out. She fought to say something, but soon her eyes fell heavy and rolled toward the back of her head. In seconds, everything went black.

Alicia drove along I-90 East, praying God would stop Phillip before he did something crazy. For an entire hour, Phillip had forced her at gunpoint to circle around Mitchell, but thirty minutes ago, he'd instructed her to head toward the interstate. He hadn't given a single reason for doing so, but she had a bad feeling about it. Especially since Levi lived in that direction.

Phillip poked her harder in her right side with the gun. "I did everything I could to make you happy. Everything."

"I know that, and —"

"Don't you say one more word. Not unless I tell you."

Alicia swallowed hard, trying not to cry.

"Why couldn't you just be faithful to me? Why did you have to turn into a worthless tramp?" he said, poking her with the gun again.

Alicia prayed one prayer after another in silence.

"The first time, you hurt me so badly I wasn't sure I'd ever get over it. And then I was dumb enough to start seeing you again. Even after you ruined our marriage with that drug dealer and married that thug pastor. After all that, I still loved you and took you back. I believed you when you said you were sorry, that you would do anything to be my wife again, and that you could never love anyone else. You lied about everything," he said, sticking the gun in her side, this time much more forcefully.

Phillip took his other hand and turned her face toward him.

"Phillip, please don't," she said, trying not to yell. "It's dark out here, and I can't see the road."

"Stop whining. There's hardly any traffic at all."

"We can still run off the highway."

He let her chin go. "Maybe that's a good thing. Maybe an accident is the answer to our problems. With death, there's no more pain. I just preached about this very thing yesterday. The wages of sin is death."

Alicia mentally prayed the Lord's Prayer over and over and kept driving.

Phillip pointed the gun at her temple. "So tell me. What is it exactly? Is it the way he makes love to you? Is he really that much better than me?"

Phillip had told her not to say anything, so she pretended she didn't hear him.

He jabbed her side with the gun. "Answer me when I'm talking to you."

"It wasn't anything like that. I told you, I didn't sleep with him."

"Liar!" he screamed. "If you lie to me one more time, it'll be the end for both of us."

"Okay, okay, okay," she said, fearing what he might do next. "When I slept with him six years ago, it just happened. I never planned for it, and it certainly wasn't because he was better than you."

"Then why did you keep going back? Like you couldn't get enough of him?"

"I don't know. I made a huge mistake. I was young and stupid."

"You're still stupid."

"I'm sorry for the way I treated you."

"Are you sorry for what you did back then or what you're doing now? Because you and I both know you slept with that fool Friday, Saturday, and today. Just admit it."

"Phillip, please, let's turn around and go home. I'll do whatever you want."

"You don't need to do anything except drive."

"Where are we going? Can I at least call to check on Melanie?"

"If you were so worried about her, why did you ditch her to go be with your man?"

"I told you, it was the only way Levi would leave me alone."

"What did I tell you about lying to me?"

"I wouldn't do that, Phillip. I'm your wife."

"No, you're a dirty whore who doesn't deserve to live. Now keep driving."

Phillip's phone rang, and Alicia glanced over at him by reflex. He pulled it from the holder attached to his belt and answered it.

"Hey, Pastor," he said, raising the gun back to Alicia's head, this time cocking it. "Oh, I'm sorry to hear that," he continued. "Is she conscious? . . . No, Alicia and I decided to get away for the night, so we're downtown Chicago . . . Oh, that's because her phone is off," Phillip said, looking at her.

Alicia wanted to scream as loud as she could. She wanted to tell her father everything, but having a gun pressed against her head stopped her.

"I was just gonna call and tell you I wouldn't be in tomorrow," he said, sounding as innocent as always. "I'll be there Wednesday, though . . . Of course . . . No problem at all. I'll tell her, and you have a good night."

He rubbed the gun down the side of her face. "That's a good girl. See? You kept your mouth shut, and you're still alive."

"What did my dad want?"

"He tried to call you, but your phone kept

going to voice mail."

"You made me turn it off, remember?"

"And it's staying off."

"Why was he calling?"

"Melanie was rushed to the hospital."

"Oh my God, is she okay?"

"I'm sure she'll be fine. Just like last time."

"Phillip, we have to go back."

"You just keep driving. It'll all be over soon enough."

"What does that mean?"

"I already told you," he said, suddenly breaking into tears and sobbing. "The wages of sin is death. It's the only way to fix all this."

For the first time since they'd gotten in the car, Alicia knew for sure Phillip was going to kill her. He was also going to kill Levi. She'd wanted to believe he would snap back to reality, but if anything, he was slipping into a deeper state of insanity. Which meant she had to do something. Anything. If she was going to die, it wouldn't be without a fight.

Alicia pressed on the accelerator, zigzagging her Mercedes from lane to lane, hoping a state trooper saw them.

Phillip cocked the gun again. "You either slow this car down or so help me . . ."

Alicia swerved over to the side of the road

and slammed on the brakes so violently, their heads and bodies jerked wildly. She threw the gear into park, unbuckled her seat belt, and jumped out. She hurried into the middle of the highway, waving her hands, hoping to flag down the next vehicle that drove by. But Phillip rushed over and dragged her back toward the car.

"Let me go," she screamed, but when he pointed the gun in her face, she knocked his arm away so hard, it fell out of his hand. They both dove at it, but when they hit the ground, Phillip landed on top of her. Still, Alicia grabbed the gun, and Phillip tussled with her, trying to take it. He was much stronger than she was, but she held on to the weapon with all her might. They scuffled and fought, and suddenly the gun flew a couple of feet away from them. Phillip stretched his arm toward it, but Alicia wrestled closer to it as well. They scrapped and brawled like the enemies they'd become . . . until the gun finally went off.

CHAPTER 47

Melanie heard beeping monitors and slowly opened her eyes, trying to focus them. Her vision was blurred, but the more she blinked, the clearer her surroundings became. First she saw a ceiling and a bright light, then she looked to her right and saw a salt-and-pepper-haired nurse standing over her, smiling.

"Melanie? Do you know where you are?"

"I'm assuming the hospital."

"That's right. How are you feeling? Are you having any pain?"

"No."

"Good. Your parents are here, but I'll be back to check on you, okay?"

Melanie watched the woman leave and then looked to her left. She wasn't surprised to see her father, but when she noticed her mother she wondered if she was hallucinating.

"Hey, sweetheart," Andrew said.

"Hi, Dad."

"How are you feeling?"

"Tired."

"You really scared us this time," Gladys said. "You have got to start taking better care of yourself."

Melanie wasn't sure how to take her mother's *caring* words, because rarely were they sincere.

"What happened to me?"

"Don't you remember us being on the phone?" Andrew said.

"No."

"Well, we were talking and all of a sudden you sounded confused. You were saying things that didn't make sense."

"How long have I been here?"

Andrew looked at his watch. "Maybe three hours or so. Oh, and we called the pastor, and he said he'll be praying for you."

"What did the doctor say?"

"They're still running tests, but when he was in a little while ago he told us that your potassium and sodium were down to life-threatening levels," her father said. "Your heart rate was sky high, too, and the rhythm was off. He said they'll be doing an ultrasound on your heart tomorrow morning."

"Is it Dr. Romalati?" Melanie asked, not wanting to hear any more of what her father was saying.

"No, you have a different one this time. He's just as nice, though."

"They say you're anorexic," her mother blurted out. "That you likely haven't eaten in days."

"I've had a lot going on."

"But you still need to eat," Andrew said. "You can't go on like this. If you keep this up, the doctor says, you'll be a lot worse off than you are now. He says you'll die."

Melanie looked away from her parents.

"She got this thing from you," Andrew said to Gladys, and Melanie glanced back at them.

Gladys frowned. "Excuse me? What kinda fool talk is that?"

"You've got the same thing. The first year we were married, you used to have some of these same health problems. But somehow you learned how to eat just enough to stay thin and not get sick anymore. You're still anorexic, though, if you ask me. And you pushed this child here to lose so much weight, she didn't know how to stop."

"That's the most ridiculous thing I've ever heard," Gladys said. "You don't know what you're talking about."

"Stay in denial all you want, but I'm tired of being quiet. Melanie needs help, and I'm gonna see that she gets it. I'll tell everything if I have to. Even about that year you made yourself throw up after every meal. You were in the hospital for a whole week behind that."

Melanie stared at them and saw how ashamed her mother was. Melanie waited for Gladys to call her father every vile word imaginable, but all she did was sit there. Earlier today, her mother had been pretty cordial, too, and now she was letting Melanie's father expose her secrets and say whatever he wanted? Melanie wondered what was wrong with her, and why she was being so pleasant. Why her personality had suddenly changed for the better. More important, why she was sitting at Melanie's bedside like a loving, sympathetic mother when she hadn't treated Melanie this way her whole life?

Melanie lay there thinking about her medical condition. Did she really have an eating disorder? She hadn't thought so, but she'd be lying if she said it was normal to feel as exhausted as she had over the last couple of months. Then again, until she'd lost down to her current weight, she'd seen with her own eyes how fat she'd still looked. And anorexia was something that usually occurred when a woman was much younger than Melanie. She knew that much just from the little she'd studied about it in nursing school.

Melanie's parents sat there, not saying anything else, and Melanie lay there with her eyes closed, thinking about Brad. How could he do something like this to her? Pretend that he was so in love with her when all along he was sleeping around with someone else? Melanie also thought about Alicia and how sorry she was for the way things had turned out between them. She'd been angrier than ever with her, but now as she lay there wondering if something was wrong with her heart, her issues with Alicia didn't matter. She just wanted to apologize, because she needed her best friend to be there for her. She was going through so much, so fast and all at once, and Alicia was the only person who could help her through it.

Melanie wiped tears from her eyes, but then there was a knock at the door.

"Come in," she said.

The door eased open, and Brad rolled inside with his wheelchair.

"What are you doing here?" Melanie said.

Gladys stood up. "We should go, Andrew, so they can talk."

"No," Brad said matter-of-factly to his

mother-in-law. "You're part of the reason all this happened."

"I know you're not gonna blame all this on me?" Gladys shot back.

Melanie was confused. "Brad, what does my mother have to do with you having an affair? And how did you even know I was here?"

"One of the deacons of the church saw your parents, and I called down to see if you were here. I just took a chance, but how are you feeling?"

"I want you out of here. Just get out."

"Not until I say what I came to say. Look, I know I was wrong. What I did was the worst, but Jessica meant nothing to me. Nothing at all, except she got pregnant. I never slept with her after that, but I wanted to be a father to my baby. So, last year, I helped her with medical expenses, bought everything the baby needed, and I gave her child support. You didn't know it, but that's where most of that thirty thousand dollars went. And Jessica was fine with our arrangement until a few months ago, when she said child support wasn't enough. She wanted ten thousand dollars a month or she was telling you everything."

"Andrew, let's go," Gladys said.

"No," Andrew declared. "I wanna hear

every bit of this."

Brad secured the wheels of his chair with each safety latch. "And that's why I've been withdrawing money every single month. But when you and I kept arguing about my so-called stock losses, and I saw how much it was tearing us apart, I told Jessica I was done. I told her I would give her a reasonable amount, but that was it. That's when she told me that it was your mother's idea for her to blackmail me in the first place."

Melanie looked at her mother and so did Andrew.

"I'm leaving," Gladys said, heading toward the door.

But with Melanie's room being so small, Brad quickly released the wheels on his chair and backed it against the door.

Gladys stepped closer to him in a huff. "Please move out of my way, Brad."

But he ignored her. "Yes, that's right. Your mother here found out about the baby, and she told Jessica that if she *didn't* blackmail me, she would tell you everything and Jessica wouldn't get another dime. Said she and the baby would never see me again. So for the last five months, your mother has collected half of every ten-thousand-dollar check I gave Jessica."

Melanie tried to register all that she'd

heard. "Mom, is that true?"

"I don't have to explain anything. And anyway, if you'd lost weight like I told you, this lowlife husband of yours never would've had an affair in the first place. I kept telling you what would happen, but you wouldn't listen."

"Lord have mercy on your soul," Andrew told his wife. "Gladys, you've done some pretty awful things in your life, but nothing as foul as this. You betrayed your own daughter for money?"

Gladys rolled her eyes at him and then told Brad, "Will you *please* move out of my way?"

Brad gazed at Melanie with pleading eyes. "Baby, I'm sorry. I was going to tell you as soon as I got home on Saturday. But after I told Jessica she wasn't getting another dollar, she lost it. She kept calling my phone, and next thing I knew she was flying through a red light."

Melanie glared at Brad and then at her mom, blinking back tears. "Both of you make me sick. And I want you out of here."

Brad leaned forward. "Baby, I know you're hurt, but you have to forgive me. Please don't end our marriage. Give me a chance to make things up to you."

Tears flowed down the sides of Melanie's

face. "If you don't leave, I'm calling security."

"You don't have to call anybody on me," Gladys replied. "I'll leave on my own."

"I still don't believe this," Andrew said. "You've been doing all that complaining about me not working, yet you've collected twenty-five thousand dollars?"

"That's *my* money," she said. "It's put away, and that's exactly where it's gonna stay. All those bills are *your* responsibility."

Melanie watched her mother acting as though she hadn't done a thing. Then she looked at Brad and pressed her call button for the nurse. She would get her mother and Brad out of her room one way or the other.

"Are you staying or going?" Gladys asked Andrew.

"You go ahead. I'm not leaving Mel all alone."

"Suit yourself," she spat.

Brad finally wheeled himself away from the door, and Gladys strutted out of the room.

"Baby —" Brad started, but Melanie cut him off.

"Brad, there's only one thing I want from you and that's a divorce."

"Baby, I made a mistake. I'm not perfect,

and you know how much I love you. This whole thing has been eating me up inside ever since it happened, and I'm sorry I hid it from you. Just let me fix this. I'll do anything you want."

"Please leave," she said.

Tears fell from Brad's eyes, and while Melanie still loved him, she didn't feel sorry for him. He had deceived her, and now he had to live with the consequences. She would suffer as well, but their marriage was over.

EPILOGUE

Three Months Later

Day in and day out, Alicia struggled to get out of bed. No matter how many times she went to sleep and woke up, her reality never changed. Phillip was gone, and he was never coming back. The two of them had fought over the gun, but when Phillip had finally gained control of it, he'd accidentally shot himself. Alicia remembered screaming at the top of her lungs, holding him and begging God to save him. But after being transported by helicopter to the nearest Chicago trauma center, he'd died in less than an hour. His mother had lost her only child, and Alicia couldn't correct Phillip's fate. She hadn't physically pulled the trigger, but as far as she was concerned, she'd killed her husband. Her father had warned her that someone would get hurt, which was the reason she'd finally made up her mind to divorce Phillip. But she'd waited too long, and her plan had failed miserably.

What bothered her more was the fact that she never should have remarried Phillip in the first place. Especially since she'd known all along that her heart and soul belonged to Levi. She'd wanted to believe she was doing the right thing, but now she knew that for the last three months she'd done everything wrong — and that a once kind, loving, innocent man was dead. Phillip had been her husband, one of her father's favorite people, and a minister the entire congregation adored. He'd been everything he knew how to be for her and so many others, but Alicia's mistakes had cost him his life. She'd pushed him too far this time, and he'd become someone she hadn't recognized. It was still hard to fathom the way he'd spoken to her that night, the way he'd pulled a gun on her, the way he'd decided without a doubt that the only way to fix things was to kill her and Levi. It had been as if he'd forgotten about his love and honor for God and that he'd given up on life altogether. For days, Alicia had wondered if he'd been planning to kill all three of them. Her, Levi, and himself. She couldn't be sure, but the deranged, unhinged look in his eyes had made her believe it. His demeanor had been violent, and the idea of taking someone's life hadn't seemed to bother him. Months before, her father had insisted that even the kindest of people could only take so much, and Alicia was sorry she hadn't listened.

But this was all because she'd hurt him in the very way she'd tried so hard not to. Her actions had been selfish, to say the least, and hardly anyone sympathized with her. Not family, friends, or church members. Her parents and stepparents tolerated her and told her they still loved her, but sadly, not even her brother Matthew picked up the phone to call her. When she called *him,* he always answered, but their conversation was awkward and short-lived. Actually, the only person who treated her the same was Levi. For the first month after Phillip's death, she'd refused to see him because her guilt wouldn't let her. But the more she'd talked to him on the phone, the more she'd realized how much she needed his love and compassion. This was also the reason she'd moved out of her and Phillip's house in Mitchell and rented an apartment about twenty minutes away. She'd considered moving back to Covington Park, but since Levi was spending a lot more time in Mitchell preparing for the grand opening of his restaurant, she'd decided to stay.

At the moment, however, she was sitting in the reception area of an inpatient facility for eating disorders in Wisconsin. Melanie had agreed to admit herself three weeks ago, but only after she'd fainted again and ended up back in the hospital. In the past, her heart had beat too fast, but last month it had slowed way too much, and her heart muscle was damaged. It was then that Alicia and Melanie's dad had begged her to get professional help, and this time she hadn't argued.

A young female staff member escorted Alicia back to a small visiting room, where Melanie sat on a sofa. She and Alicia both smiled when they saw each other and hugged like they hadn't connected in years.

"I'll leave you ladies to your visit," the young woman said, closing the door behind her.

Alicia and Melanie held each other tightly, not wanting to let go. Finally, they sat down.

"I'm so embarrassed," Melanie said, pulling two tissues from the box on the basic wooden table and passing one of them to her best friend.

Alicia sniffled. "Why is that?"

"I treated you so badly. I said some really awful things to you, and all you were trying to do was help me."

"You were sick, Mel. I knew something was wrong, but I didn't realize things had gotten so out of control."

"Neither did I. I've been ill for a very long time, and what scares me is that I could have died, yet I couldn't see what I was doing to myself."

"But now you're getting the help you need, and you're going to be fine."

"I still have a long way to go, but I've learned so much about myself over these last three weeks. When I first got here, I thought I was too sane for a place like this. Can you believe I had the nerve to look down on people who purge? To me, bulimia was much worse than what I was doing. But now, I know I was in just as much trouble as everyone else here. I was starving myself to death. Literally."

Alicia kicked off her leather ballerina shoes and drew one of her knees onto the sofa. "I think I was sort of in denial, too. I knew you weren't eating enough, but I didn't want to believe things were so bad."

"Well, they were, and I'm sorry for purposely trying to hurt you."

"That's all in the past. Although, it wasn't like you said anything wrong."

"How do you mean?"

"I never should have slept around on

Phillip. The first time or the second. He's dead, and everyone hates me for it."

"When it first happened, I was upset with you, too. But when I collapsed this last time and you came to the hospital, I knew I needed you. I knew that you and my dad are all I have."

"You still haven't heard from your mom?"

"No, and I don't want to. My therapist wants me to talk to her and find a way to forgive her, but I'm just not ready for that. Same thing with Brad."

"Are you still filing for divorce?"

"I am. It's the one thing I'm absolutely sure of. About a month after Brad's accident, I met him for dinner a couple of times, but the pain was just too great. Even when he would call me on the phone — which he did daily — all I could think about was the affair and the baby he had behind my back. I could never trust him again, and I just don't have the strength to stay married to someone like that."

"I'm really sorry, Mel."

"Don't get me wrong. I love Brad and I love my mother, but I have to move on. Even my dad is planning to do the same thing. He just can't take my mother's cruelty anymore. But what about you? What's going on with Levi?"

"I love him, Mel. I love him with all my heart. But I feel guilty . . . you know, because of Phillip."

"Look, I loved Phillip like a brother, and I certainly wasn't happy about your affair with Levi. I'm just being honest. But if there's one thing I've learned, life is shorter than most of us realize. We have to do everything we can to be happy."

"My mom and dad are so disappointed in me."

"Maybe, but they'll eventually get over it. And even if they don't, are you gonna stop being with someone you love? Someone you were willing to risk everything for?"

"I don't want to, but . . ."

"Then don't," Melanie said.

"I've prayed and asked God to forgive me, and I know He has. But it's just so hard knowing that everyone blames me for Phillip's death."

"I can imagine, but it'll all work out. You and I just have to be here for each other."

Tears rolled down Alicia's face, and Melanie leaned over and hugged her. Melanie was the one in treatment, but she seemed stronger than Alicia. Actually, it had always sort of been that way, and Alicia was grateful for her best friend. They were sisters for life, and nothing would ever change that.

They would help each other through their pain, and that gave Alicia a great sense of peace. But more important, it would be God's love, mercy, and grace that would sustain them. Her father had taught her this many years ago, and she knew he was right. Alicia had sinned and fallen short of the glory of God, but from today on, she would follow His Word much more diligently. She still had a lot to learn and lots of changes to make, but she sincerely wanted to be a better person. And it was for these reasons that she knew she would be fine. She knew God would take excellent care of her.

ACKNOWLEDGMENTS

As always, I thank God for Your mercy, grace, and abundant blessings; without You, not a single thing is possible, and I never forget that. To my wonderful husband, Will — thank you for absolutely everything; This is our 25th year together, and I love you with every part of my being. To my brothers, Willie, Jr. and Michael — thank you for always supporting your big sister; I love you both so very much. To the rest of my loving family — I love you all: Tennins, Ballards, Lawsons, Stapletons, Robys, Youngs, Beasleys, Haleys, Romes, Greens, Garys, Shannons, Normans, and anyone else I may be forgetting! To my first cousin and fellow author, Patricia Haley-Glass, who is also my dear sister, to my best friends, who are also my sisters: Kelli Tunson Bullard and Lori Whitaker Thurman and my cousin and sister, Janell Green — I love the four of you ladies with all my heart. To my spiritual mom, Dr. Betty Price, whom I love so very much — I can't thank you enough for all the genuine love and support you have given me. To my publishing attorney, Ken Norwick, for such great representation. To the best publisher in the world, Grand Central Publishing: Beth de Guzman, Linda Duggins, Elizabeth Connor, Jamie Raab, Stephanie Sirabian, the entire sales and marketing teams, and everyone else at GCP. To my amazing freelance team, Connie Dettman, Shandra Hill Smith, Luke LeFevre, Pam Walker-Williams, and Ella Curry — thank you all for everything! To all the wonderful booksellers who sell my work, every newspaper, radio station, TV station, website, and blog that promotes it, and to every book club that consistently chooses my books as your monthly selection — thanks a million!

Finally, to the folks who so graciously make my writing career possible — **my wonderfully kind and hugely supportive readers**. I love you with everything in me, and I am forever grateful to **ALL** of you.

Much love and God bless you always,
Kimberla Lawson Roby

E-mail: kim@kimroby.com
Facebook: www.facebook.com/kimberla
  lawsonroby
Twitter: www.twitter.com/KimberlaLRoby

READING GROUP GUIDE

1. Phillip gives Alicia a second chance after she commits adultery. Do you think that you would be able to forgive someone after a betrayal like that? Why or why not? Do you agree with Alicia that she owes him for loving and trusting her again? Is their relationship healthy? If not, please explain why.

2. It's obvious that Melanie has issues with her body that come from a difficult relationship with her parents, specifically her mother. Have you ever felt unhappy with the way you look? How did friends and family affect this? How did you work to overcome these feelings?

3. Very early in the book, Alicia realizes that she will never love anyone as much as she loves Levi. Do you believe in soul mates? Do you think Alicia's only true love is Levi

or can you love more than one person? Should you be with someone you truly love even if it disappoints or hurts someone else?

4. Were you surprised that Alicia decided to go through with the wedding? Do you think Alicia and Phillip should have gotten married? Do you think Alicia was in denial about whether she could get past her feelings for Levi?

5. How does Melanie's father's illness change his relationship with his daughter? Have you reconciled with someone after a near-death experience? Why do you think that Melanie's mother doesn't change?

6. Should Brad have kept his child a secret from Melanie? Is there any way he could have handled the situation differently to make things better? Please give examples of what he might have done.

7. Were you surprised by how Phillip reacted to the news of Alicia's betrayal? Do you think there was a way that Alicia could have prevented what happened?

8. Are you happy that Alicia and Melanie

repaired their friendship? Do you think Melanie will stay healthy? Why or why not?

9. In terms of romance, what do you believe is still in store for Alicia and Melanie? Do you think Melanie will forgive Brad? Do you want Alicia to be with Levi?

10. Do you think there are other women, like Alicia, who feel they are married to a great man but not the right one? Could you remain in a marriage where you love your spouse but you're not *in* love with them?

ABOUT THE AUTHOR

Kimberla Lawson Roby is the *New York Times* bestselling author of the acclaimed Reverend Curtis Black Series. She lives with her husband in Rockford, Illinois. For more information, please visit www.kimroby.com.